Marilyn in Manhattan

BY THE SAME AUTHOR

Artahe
The Song of Montségur (with Sylvie Miller)

Marilyn in Manhattan

by
Philippe Ward

Translated by
Brian Stableford

A Black Coat Press Book

Visit our website at www.blackcoatpress.com

To my son Mickael,
to whom I owe the encounter with New York
full of marvelous moments.

ISBN 978-1-61227-767-7. First Printing. August 2018. Published by Black Coat Press, an imprint of Hollywood Comics.com, LLC, P.O. Box 17270, Encino, CA 91416. All rights reserved. Except for review purposes, no part of this book may be reproduced or transmitted in any form or by any means, electronic or mechanical, including photocopying, recording, or by any information storage and retrieval system, without permission in writing from the publisher. The stories and characters depicted in this novel are entirely fictional. Printed in the United States of America.

Author's Note

In order to write this novel I used the basic details of the life and death of Marilyn Monroe and various theses relating to the assassinations of John and Bobby Kennedy, but the book nevertheless remains a work of fiction, purely the product of my imagination.

Prologue

Manhattan, 19 May 1962.

Marilyn Monroe emerged tranquilly from the Carlyle, one of New York's greatest palaces. Although it was early, the sun was beginning to warm up the city. She raised her arm and a taxi immediately stopped in front of her.

"Four forty-four Fifty-Seventh Street," she said, in a soft and charming voice. It was the address of the thirteenth-floor apartment that she occupied when she stayed in the Big Apple.

The driver turned round and stared at her, unable to articulate the traditional greeting. She smiled at him and repeated the address. He stammered a vague acquiescence. His gaze returned to the street and he started the meter with a mechanical gesture.

The taxi pulled away along the avenue, which was practically deserted except for taxis and a single police car that overtook them with its siren howling.

Several times, the driver looked at her in the rear-view mirror in order to convince himself of the reality; he was carrying one of the greatest stars in Hollywood.

Curled up in the seat, Marilyn reconsidered the evening at Madison Square Garden and its prolongation in a suite at the Carlyle. In the first instance, she had participated in a social event intended to reimburse the expenses of the campaign that had seen John Fitzgerald Kennedy accede to the presidency of the United States of America. In the second she had slept with him—too bad for Jackie, the country's first lady! She was a free woman herself, having divorced Arthur Miller more than a year before.

Earlier, the benefit concert had brought together numerous stars who had generously come to sing or sign a check, among them Maria Callas, Ella Fitzgerald, Peggy Lee and

Henry Fonda. After having weighed up the pros and cons for some time, Marilyn had finally agreed to take part in it: her, the former mistress of the most powerful man on Earth, the discarded woman, cast aside like a used handkerchief and immediately replaced by someone else.

Two weeks before, John Kennedy's people had literally begged her to make the trip. According to them, John was insistent that she come. She was one of the greatest stars in America, if not the greatest, and her presence at the occasion constituted a plus for the President. Worse than that, if she did not put in an appearance, her absence would be noticed and everyone would wonder whether she had become unapproachable.

Marilyn had no doubt that her former lover had another idea in the back of his mind. She knew him well; he still desired her; and it was precisely that reason that had convinced her to go the ceremony. Then she had to persuade Fox to give her the evening off.

She was presently filming *Something's Got to Give* with Dean Martin and Cyd Charisse for the studio, which was threatening to cancel her contract if she quit the shoot one more time. After several refusals, Bobby Kennedy had personally telephoned Milton S. Gould, the company boss, in order to get him to give her the two days necessary to make the trip. The result had been another refusal.

The young woman was not particularly astonished; the filming was considerably delayed, and it was her fault. She did not like the film; the director, George Cukor, changed the dialogue as he pleased and she had only agreed to do it reluctantly. That was why, when she should be filming scenes, she sometimes felt ill and deserted the set.

She had decided to by-pass the refusal. Nothing and no one could have prevented her from being present on the stage at Madison Square Garden. That evening, she would be the queen, and everyone's eyes would be fixed on her, especially John's.

So, the previous evening, she had acquitted the responsibility of her participation; her pride had even made her sign a considerable, even indecent, check, bigger than those of other participants. She had chosen a provocative dress composed of thousands of sparkling stones, specially designed for her by the French couturier Jean-Louis, for twelve thousand dollars: a costume comprising twenty layers of silk that she alone could wear, with nothing underneath; eighteen people had worked on it full-time for a week.

Two hours before her entrance, a seamstress had sown it directly on to her bare flesh like a second skin, highlighting her perfect body, about which all men fantasized.

She had rehearsed her speech alone: a pathetic platitudinous homage written by Richard Alder, a Broadway star. She would have liked to write it herself, but met with a refusal. So, before a mirror, she strove to give her *Happy Birthday* the warmest and most erotic tone possible. She employed the full palette of her voice. When young she had taken singing lessons, and, in spite of a limited register, she knew how to get the most out of her voice by singing close to the mike, playing on intimacy and sensuality.

Such was her curse: she was known as an actress she would have preferred to be known as a singer.

In her dressing-room she had waited patiently; her performance would only last a few minutes, sufficient to render it unforgettable.

Finally, her turn arrived.

When Peter Lawford, who as introducing the guests, had announced her name at the mike she had made herself desired, remaining in the wings. She wanted Madison Square Garden to explode when she arrived. Massed on the steps, the President's fifteen thousand fans had waited in a quasi-religious silence, as had the millions of viewers behind their television screens.

Peter had told a joke before howling once again: "Ladies and Gentlemen Marilyn Monroe."

She had drunk a glass of champagne slowly to collect herself. Then, with an ermine coat on her shoulders, she had got up, aided by two bodyguards, who carried her to the stage.

Suddenly, seams had split. She had had to go back to the dressing-room, where seamstresses repaired the damage in a matter of seconds. She could not present herself naked before puritanical America.

The damage repaired, she had resumed her march, difficult in her folded dress. Proudly, she had advanced toward the spotlights. That evening, she entered smoothly into legend.

Finally, she appeared on the stage in the midst of the lights, more beautiful than ever, to thunderous applause. Behind her, Peter Lawford had uttered some quip that she had not picked up.

She saw herself again walk to the mike, sure of her beauty and her sex-appeal. She could sense the waves of human pleasure reaching her. Everyone only had eyes for her. With a delicate movement she had removed her cape, which had fallen at her feet. Immediately, the glare of the spotlights made the multitudinous pearls of her dress shine, to give her an unreal aura.

Silence had fallen in the Madison: a heavy silence, which she had enjoyed for a few brief seconds. Stopped in front of the mike, she had tapped it with her middle finger, as if to discover whether it was working: a simple, unnecessary gesture—technicians had been checking the apparatus all afternoon—but in the audience, all the spectators had held their breath.

She had understood that she held the audience under her spell. No one dared speak, or even murmur. She possessed absolute power over every participant. But only one was important: the Prez, as she had nicknamed him in the intimacy of their embrace.

She could not see him, but she knew that his eyes were upon her: John Fitzgerald Kennedy, the man America venerated, the man who directed America, the man she still loved, who had rejected her for someone else.

Nothing, and no one, could any longer come between them, especially not that she-devil of a woman who had decided to shun the ceremony when she had learned of her presence. That night, Marilyn had sworn to herself, he would be hers.

For one night only, for he knew that henceforth, she would not be part of his world. Her old dream of becoming the first lady was impossible. She had thought of it, before, when he had made it shine for her...but today, reality had resumed its rights.

She was a vulgar actress, and he was the master of the free world.

But not this evening. This evening was her evening, and she had no intention of letting her chance pass by. To arrive at her goal, she was not going to recite the speech imposed on her by the organizers. No, she was going to wish the Prez happy birthday *her* way.

She had leaned over the mike and had breathed:

"*Ha...ppy Birthday...toooo youuuuuu.*"

The classic phrase, repeated a thousand times over, had exploded in the immense hall. Her voice, more sensual than ever, had filled Madison Square Garden, which trembled with desire.

Marilyn had given herself entirely to her public:

"*Ha...ppy Birthday...toooo youuuuuu.*"

She always remained the actress who inflamed men, in the cinema as well as real life, she did not hide it. With those simple words, however, she obtained her revenge. Disappeared forever, the slightly plump little girl raised in an orphanage, the young woman who had worked in a factory before disembarking in Hollywood and become a symbol instead of a recognized actress.

She had moved her arms slowly and continued her song:

"Everybody sing with me, Happy Birthday."

At that precise moment, she had understood that the game was won. All the spectators had stood up to applaud and take up the song in chorus. She was the queen of the event, and no one could steal its stardom from her, not even the Prez.

She knew his penchant for sex. He would bitterly regret having abandoned her. This would be their last night, but she would hold him in her arms, between her legs, one last time, and he would never find as much pleasure in the arms of another woman.

That would be her vengeance.

"We've arrived, Ma'am."

The driver's voice extracted her from her thoughts. She opened her eyes and came back to reality.

Marilyn looked at the meter, rummaged in her handbag and brought out a fifty dollar bill when she held out through the glass.

"Keep it," she said, suavely.

The driver took the bill and stammered a thank you. She walked away from the taxi, feeling the weight of his gaze on her back. She knew her power over men, from a simple taxi driver to the President of the U.S.A. None could resist her.

Marilyn opened the door and went up to her apartment. She undressed and, faithful to her legend, got into bed naked, only dressed in her perfume, Chanel no. 5.

The memories of the evening immediately returned to her mind.

Her performance had only lasted a few minutes, but they remained in all memories. No one would forget her passage, the guests or the millions of spectators in front of their television sets. The other artistes, after her, had not existed, mere phantoms brining their obol to the President.

Everyone had come to her dressing-room to compliment her. She had remained modest, contenting herself with thanking them all, replying that all the merit belonged to the President.

As she had expected, he had joined her in the wings as soon as the spectacle was over, to congratulate her. He had not dared to ask her immediately to spend the rest of the night with him, but his eyes had betrayed his desire.

She had waited sagely, knowing that the moment would come; she knew him so well; he could not resist her. The evening had continued; he had returned to salute the other guests, and Marilyn had chatted with several people while drinking champagne.

An hour later he had come back, accompanied by his brother Bobby.

The gaze of the two brothers had demonstrated the magnitude of her power of attraction. Both desired her. Bobby had also been her lover, but he was not the Prez, just a simple minister of justice.

John had complimented her again and had then drawn her into a corner of the room in order to murmur in her ear that they should terminate the evening together.

She had hesitated, as a matter of principle, offering the pretext of having to accompany the father of her ex-husband, Arthur Miller, to his hotel. Immediately, John had ordered two secret service men to take care of it. Without giving her time to escape, he had taken her to the Carlyle.

In the room, Marilyn had bought out her big game, without stinting on the means. A legend ran around in her regard; her curriculum vitae indicated an expertise in fellatio. She had never sought to deny the rumor.

Several times, in the course of the night, John had asked for mercy, but she had only acceded to his request at first light, when he had collapsed, completely exhausted.

Then, no longer entirely conscious of where he was, or with whom, he had released *the* confidence: a revelation so surprising that Marilyn had looked at him, nonplussed, when he fell silent.

She had frowned, not knowing whether it was the truth or whether the President was boasting—which he did at times. But John had continued speaking for half an hour, as if he could not keep that revelation to himself. She had not dared to interrupt him. When he had finished his story, he had collapsed into a profound sleep.

Beside him, Marilyn had been anxious, not knowing what attitude to adopt.

That night, she had held the President of the United States in her arms, even obliging him to crawl before her. She smiled as she recalled the scene—a smile that was quickly transformed into a grimace when she understood the situation into which she had just been plunged.

She would never have imagined that he would confide such a secret to her.

She picked up the notebook in which she recorded all her exchanges with John or Bobby, not with the objective of keeping evidence of their discussions but to seek information afterwards about various subjects. That way, she did not appear to her various lovers to be a brainless actress, since, when they met again, she could participate in the conversation. She carefully consigned the President's confidence to it, and as she set out the revelation on paper, fear took possession of her.

Abruptly, she realized that her mere presence in the room put her in danger.

She dressed quickly, while her mind continued to reflect.

John was sleeping blissfully—but that would not last.

When he woke up, John Fitzgerald Kennedy would remember the pleasure they had obtained together, but also having confided a story to her that she should never have heard. He would surely curse himself for his carelessness, for having indulged in pillow talk, but Marilyn knew him well; his career came before everything. He would stifle his scruples rapidly. In a fraction of a second he would decide to get rid of her. After all, she was a negligible quantity, a mere actress that he could sacrifice in the name of the nation.

As he never got his hands dirty, he would confide the affair to his brother. Marilyn could easily imagine the sequence of events. Bobby Kennedy would speak to the director of the F.B.I., Hoover, who did not like Hollywood at all, much less her ex-husband Arthur Miller, whom he considered to be a communist.

Hoover would act without asking any questions: eliminate America's enemies, that was his credo. John Fitzgerald Kennedy would continue to direct the country and slake his thirst for fresh flesh; she would be inside the concrete of a building or at the bottom of the Pacific Ocean, devoured by the fish. Hollywood would mourn the star for a few days, and a new girl would take her place.

She had fled the room, saluted the secret service men who protected the President. They had watched her leave with eyes empty of any expression, insensible to her charm. She had left the hotel and hailed a taxi.

Now, in her own bed, she had to make a rapid decision. After the President's confidence, her life was only hanging by a thread. For a second, she was tempted to return to her home town—but wherever she went, the F.B.I. would find her sooner or later. No one would ever find her body, and her disappearance would be attributed to the Mafia or drugs. She had to match Hoover for speed, before he sent his killers.

To disappear was the only solution. She had money, enough to live, and men ready to do anything for her.

The idea came to her suddenly: she had to die, in order not to die. Like a cinema death.

Her former life ended on that day in May, and a new, different, one began. She had to draw a definitive line under her career, under her past. Except that she needed one last success: the final act that would mark her rebirth.

As a sole farewell gift, she had the secret that John had confided to her: a secret that she would never share; a secret so enormous that, in any case, no one would believe it.

At that thought, she could not help smiling: a wry smile.

Then she went to sleep.

PART ONE

Chapter 1

Manhattan, Times Square, 12 October

"We are the ninety-nine per cent."

That cry was rapidly drowned by the hubbub in Times Square, amid the noise of helicopters flying over the most famous avenue in New York, the sirens of police cars and the horns of taxis. Unlike her physique, which attracted the attention of tourists and policemen alike, the young woman's claim passed unnoticed.

Clad in black trousers and a denim jacket, Kristin Arroyo measured half an inch short of six feet, and possessed an athletic body, long hair and a bronzed face in which, just beneath the tight eye, a thin inch-long scar was designed. An incredible strength and grim determination emanated from her: the determination of a woman ready to do anything to carry her convictions to the end.

High above her head she was brandishing a placard on which the same slogan was inscribed that she had just uttered in a loud and determined voice, to overcome the sonorous ambient buzz.

"We are the ninety-nine per cent."

Her protest mingled with hundreds of others launched at the tourists surprised by the thousands of demonstrators of the Occupy Wall Street movement who, in the space of an evening, had come to take possession of Times Square, the mythical location of American capitalism.

Without any organization behind them, those men and women had quit Zuccotti Park, where their tents were installed, and had marched peacefully to Times Square, in spite of the presence of hundreds of policemen.

Never, even in the time of the Vietnam War, had the artery seen such an event. The demonstrators had immediately mingled with the thousands of tourists who no longer knew where to look, simultaneously solicited by the advertisements that glittered all round them, the ships opens until midnight, the sellers of *I Love New York* T-shirts and the agencies offering bus tours of the city.

The New York Police and the F.B.I. agents watched the Occupy Wall Street people, ready to intervene at the first sign of excess, but for the moment, the demonstration was unfolding calmly. The protesters did not manifest the slightest aggression; quite the contrary. The orders were clear: no provocation, no confrontation, all smiles and conviviality. Their aim was to disseminate their ideas to as many people as possible.

Times Square remained the ideal location.

So, exactly like Kristin Arroyo, hundreds of rebels, young and not so young, were walking through the crowd with their placards—simple pieces of cardboard or pizza boxes with a punch-line written in felt-tip—waving them above their heads when they saw cameras aimed at them.

The spontaneous Occupy Wall Street movement—which journalists now designated as OWS—had been born after the first gatherings of European indigenes, Greeks, Spaniards and Portuguese. The American had picked up the baton and had installed themselves in the heart of capitalist finance, adjacent to the enemy.

Her throat inflamed, Kristin Arroyo stopped shouting, her placard still above her head. She frayed a passage through the crowd, and took advantage of it to read the other slogans combined in the same conflict: *Democracy in America; Occupy the U.S.A.; Afghanistan—a war for the rich; Ready for the Revolution; Fair Taxation for the Rich.* All of them were pointing a finger at a world in the grip of a handful of privileged individuals, while the immense majority were suffering from the crisis or dying of hunger.

Kristin continued her protest march in Times Square, avoiding glancing sideways at the shops, still open at that belated hour, which were attempting to attract clients by means of all the artifices of communication and advertising. Those boutiques represented an adverse party.

Often the tourists smiled at her, or held up their thumbs to show their support. Some even deposited a bill in one of the cardboard boxes brandished by the demonstrators. Kristin thanked them with a warm smile.

At thirty-four, life had not spared her. The only child of a Mexican immigrant and a pure-bred New Yorker, she had cracked the whip hard to find a place in American society, initially in the streets of Brooklyn, where she had spent her youth. Out there, being a half-Hispanic girl was a hard cross to bear. She had suffered numerous gibes from young people of her own age, and her school attendance had felt the impact, with numerous brawls and multiple bandages.

Even so, having obtained a bursary by dint of sweat, she had quit her neighborhood for New York University, which she had frequented for two years without obtaining any diploma, sickened by the professors and the attitude of other, more fortunate, students who did not have to work in fast food joints the evenings for a pittance. For them, she was the token Hispanic; she had received financial aid not because of her intelligence but because of quotas.

Two years without making any friends, without the slightest flirtation, two years spent gritting her teeth and weathering the blows.

Then came the active life and the refusals. With the exception of a job as a waitress in one of the numerous restaurants of Manhattan, she strung together checks and months without salary. With rage in her belly, two months after the tragedy of nine-eleven, she had decided to enlist in the Armed Forces.

For her, the military appeared to be the only means of climbing the social ladder. Even though she knew that racism and sexism were ever-present there, she possessed the intimate conviction of being able to confront both.

For ten years she had traveled numerous theaters of operations where the American military was fighting for liberty—at least, she thought so then. She had soon reached the rank of lieutenant; and although the American army was very sexist—women still did not have the right to fight—and sometimes racist, she had known a certain camaraderie there nevertheless, in default of encountering amity or amour.

She returned to New York five times. The first time was for her parents' funeral, after their death in a car accident—there, in addition to the pain of losing two people dear to her, she had been obliged to take care of administrative formalities. During subsequent leaves, she had returned to her birthplace, but felt alone there, never having had any real friends there, men or women. Then she had stayed away from the U.S.A. and visited other countries: Spain, France and England were the stamping-grounds of her privileged leave. The military became her new family, solitude her daily bread.

She devoted herself to it fundamentally.

The use of weapons, and hand-to-hand combat, soon had no more secrets for her—nor killing people, even if nightmares sometimes haunted her. She was fighting for liberty, against barbarity and injustice, in a world in which she believed. Never, during ten years, had she asked herself the slightest question about the foreign policy of any American government.

The she learned Arabic—a bad idea. Her superiors made use of her as an interpreter during forceful interrogations in which human dignity no longer had any currency. And even if some prisoners were terrorists and had blood on their hands, she had increasing difficulty in supporting the torture.

At the beginning of 2014, something within her broke: too many deaths, too much suffering, too many unscarred wounds. She did not renew her contract and returned to New York.

The solitude, which had weighed upon her so much before, no longer bothered her. She had made her decision. She was no longer looking to find a twin soul or to have children; that life no longer interested her.

Nevertheless, her return was not devoid of ambushes; she no longer recognized her homeland, not longer finding herself in the America that she had quit so long ago.

She was, however, prepared for a psychological impact. In the military, soldiers often talked about returning to their homeland and the fashion in which civilians would greet them. They all retained the memory of the trauma of Vietnam veterans, abandoned, practically considered as a pestilence. Many had sunk into alcoholism or drug-addiction, or had ended up committing suicide. The welcome reserved for the wounded was often terrible, as if civilians, ashamed of seeing a hero on a street corner, having lost an arm or a leg—or both—in a war that they had supported, preferred to ignore them thereafter. Not to mention the difficulty they had of finding employment, however modest.

On returning to New York, Kristin had met that ostracism. There was no one to welcome or advise her, except for an officer who had thanked her for her years of service with a prepared speech, a final punctuation mark. For the rest, she had to struggle alone. Although Americans celebrated their heroes with parades, films or television broadcasts, no provision was made to reinsert them into real life.

Every man for himself had become the country's only motto.

She had also discovered an America sickening by virtue the economic crisis, an America divided into two irreconcilable camps. Far from home, she had believed in Barack Obama, and had voted for him twice, for his ideas and his "Yes we can." On her return she had understood that powerful lobbies weighed ever more surely upon society, to the extent of becoming even more important than the votes of American citizens.

She was frightened by the Tea Party movement, which had been practically non-existent when she left. She became fearful on seeing those men and women only thinking about themselves, huddled in their petty lives in their petty towns and rejecting everything that was poor or foreign, and frequently their fellows. Her Hispanic blood boiled when she watched them parading on Fox News, where commentators wanted to send hundreds of thousands of immigrants back home—even children born in the U.S.A.—or on seeing the new heroes, like regularly re-elected sheriffs whose sole aim was to imprison the maximum number of foreigners in degrading conditions.

She experienced as much anger confronted by those Americans, whose parents had also been immigrants, as by Iraqi or Afghan terrorists. Hatred had not quit her when she returned home; worse than that, it was still seething in her head, more alive than ever.

She also felt rancor toward all religions, the principal cause of the conflicts through which she had lived. Although her parents had raised her in the Catholic faith, she now considered herself to be an atheist—yet another difference from the American majority, who believed in God and guns, the two pillars of the Constitution.

After her return, she spent long hours at Ground Zero, the place where the twin towers had stood before the accursed day of nine-eleven. She had looked at the two new ones, almost finished, a new symbol of triumphant America.

As she went back along the file of protesters, Kristin went past a pseudo-country-singer clad only in a pair of Santiago boots, a cowboy hat and briefs. With his body-builder musculature, particularly appreciated by Asiatic tourists, the "naked cowboy" was an unavoidable icon of Times Square. She ignored him and addressed a nod of the head to Ralph Curtis, a twenty-year-old student with whom she had a certain sympathy. The latter was parading in front of one of the branches of the Chase Manhattan Bank, waving a red flag ornamented with the head of Che Guevara, in defiance of policemen who were striving to take the revolutionary standard away from him.

As she turned round in order to go back along Times Square toward Forty-second she bumped into a man who was taking a photograph of her. She apologized and continued on her way.

Chapter 2

Manhattan, Times Square, 12 October.

"Excuse me, Miss."

Kristin continued walking, without paying any attention to the request. A tourist, undoubtedly, desirous of having a souvenir of the evening. But as the appeal resounded a second time, she turned round, her features set firm, in order to discourage the importuner.

The man, about fifty years old, smiled at her. In his magnificent hands—artist's hands—he was holding a camera preciously, as if it were a musical instrument. The young woman's aggression was reduced by a notch, but she remained on her guard.

"May I take a photo of you?" he asked, in a soft voice.

"You don't need my permission," Kristin told him. "Look around—everyone's taking pictures without asking."

"I'm not a simple tourist," he said, "I'm a professional photographer. My name is Nathan Stewart." He held out a business card, which she took, mechanically. "I have a gallery in Hell's Kitchen."

"I'm not a model; I'm not here to pose, but to protest," Kristin snapped, hoping to get rid of the hindrance rapidly."

"I understand, and I share your point of view. I'd like to compile a series of photographs of your combat, here and in Zuccotti Park. It might help you to propagate your ideas. I don't want to make any money by exploiting you, that's why I want your permission."

Kristin hesitated before replying. Ordinarily, she would have put an end to the discussion, but something in the man's gaze, and in his smile, tempted her to give him a chance.

"What do you want from me? I don't know how to strike a pose. I'm an ex-soldier, who fought for her convictions and those of numerous Americans. I'm not very photogenic..."

She stopped, surprised. She rarely said as much to strangers. Stress, surely...

"Exactly—I find you just right as you are. March, protest, act as if I weren't here."

He tilted his head with an engaging smile, which ended up convincing her.

"You accept my proposal, then?"

Kristin bit her lip. The man inspired confidence in her, without her really knowing why. A calmness emanated from him, an aura, that softened her. Given his age, moreover—over fifty—he didn't seem to be trying to pick her up.

She sought other protesters with her eyes, in order to ask their advice, but they were drowned in the tourist tide, and she could find no aid.

"All right," she said, in a gasp.

She immediately regretted her decision. She did not like to be in the front line, but in that ultra-connected society, communication became primordial. Without the famous "buzz" it was increasingly difficult to put forward her ideas or make them understandable to the great majority. The more the media talked about the Movement, the more it reached people.

She had no choice.

She therefore got a violent grip on herself and resumed walking, trying to remain natural.

But she could not do it. Mechanically, her eyes sought the photographer in the crowd. For a moment, she imagined herself again back in the Afghan mountains, with the eyes of the Taliban riveted to her back.

She continued walking for a minute before stopping. Knowing that she was being watched like that, she could no longer demonstrate. Having reached a small square, she perceived a dozen unoccupied metal chairs. After having cast a glance around, she sat down in one of them and placed her placard across her knees.

She breathed in deeply. Around her, the crowd of demonstrators and tourists was moving without paying any attention to her. Further away, on Forty-second, police cars were cleaving a path through the traffic, sirens blaring. As at any hour of the day or night, in all weathers, Times Square was black with people.

Emerging from who knows where, Nathan Stewart approached her. The fellow had definitely melted into the landscape—doubtless a useful talent in his business.

"I'm sorry," she said, apologetically. "I've been walking all day and I'm tired—and I'm not really at ease knowing that someone is following me in order to take photographs of me."

"No problem—you've been very good. In any case, thanks for your help. It's not every day that someone agrees to be photographed. Since the outset, I've encountered more refusals than acceptances."

Kristin smiled at him. Concentrating on her own appearance, she had not noticed the dark rings around her interlocutor's eyes. He must be exhausted too if he had been covering the event for several days.

The man sat down alongside her. He rummaged in his bag and took out a sheet of paper and a pen.

"I'll need your signature to authorize me to use the photos in an exhibition I'm putting on in November."

"An exhibition?" Kristin exclaimed.

The young woman felt a sense of panic submerging her. When she had given her consent a few minutes earlier she had not imagined that he photographs would end up in an exhibition rather than a second-rate periodical or a blog. She did not like to go back on her word, however; even if nothing had been signed, her word remained sacred.

"Can I see them beforehand?" she stammered.

"Of course," Nathan replied. "I won't do anything without your consent. Even so, it would be better to show them to you on a large screen rather than on my camera. In the evening light, you wouldn't be able to see very much."

The photographer seemed to know his business. He looked her straight in the eye. "What name should I put on the contract?"

"Kristin Arroyo."

He asked for her address, filled in several blanks, and handed her the sheet of paper and the pen.

Kristin read the contract diagonally. It was almost as long as the one she had signed when she had joined up. Not being accustomed to such formalities, she added her signature without being certain of knowing exactly what it was she was agreeing to.

She returned the document to the man named Nathan.

"Thanks very much," he said, "putting it in his jacket pocket. Don't worry, I won't publish anything without your consent. You can trust me."

The young woman acquiesced, while promising herself that she would make enquiries about the photographer that evening.

"So, you're putting on an exhibition about the Occupy Wall Street movement?"

"Exactly. It's still a project, but I hope to be able to make it concrete soon. For a week I've been spending my time photographing the Movement from every angle, in the street or in the park. That's what I was doing again today when I stumbled across you. You're an ideal model. An undeniable strength and beauty emanates from you. You're a genuine *Pasionara*."

Kristin looked at him, nonplussed. It was the first time anyone had ever described her in those terms; she was someone who faded into the mass in order not to be noticed. She could not help bushing at the compliment.

"I'm only a simple citizen conscious of the fact that the world's sliding down a bad slope, who decided to do something instead of sitting at home."

Nathan placed a hand on hers. There was nothing sexual in his attitude—it was more of a paternal gesture—so she did not withdraw it.

"That's entirely to your honor," he told her. "In my opinion, the media don't pay enough attention to people like you. They prefer, for reasons I don't know, to interest themselves in artificial pseudo-stars...who aren't interesting."

Kristin saw passion illuminating Nathan's eyes, and envied him.

"Your Movement merits interest in itself," he continued, in the same tone. "For a week, I've been thinking of nothing else, only living for it...and you're going to make fun of me, but I've got to the point of forgetting to eat and sleep. I spent my days taking pictures and my nights sorting through them." He paused in order to catch his breath, and went on: "It's not the first exhibition I've organized, but it's the first that has gripped my heart—your movement has gripped my heart. It's high time the economic model was changed; and I'm trying, at my modest level, to participate in that evolution."

Mechanically, the young woman thought about her grandfather, who was also a professional photographer. She was momentarily tempted to talk about him, but she abandoned the idea. Although he had had some success fifty years ago, no one had heard of him today.

Nathan stopped abruptly. "I must be boring you. When I get started on the subject, I become a real wordmill."

"Not at all. It's very interesting. You've reassured me about the use that you're going to make of the photographs."

Nathan withdrew his hand and stood up.

"You're truly adorable," he breathed. "Thanks for everything."

Kristin thanked him in her turn, and he photographer drew away as rapidly as he had arrived. Alone again, the young woman quit her chair. Placard in hand, she rejoined the protesters.

As she slipped into the melee she noticed that the police presence had increased in the avenue and the adjacent streets. In the sky above the buildings of Manhattan, several police helicopters were now circling.

Sensing that the situation might degenerate rapidly, the protesters were going back on foot to their base camp in Zuccotti Park. The demonstration had achieved its objectives for today: no trouble, and images that must already be looping through all the communication channels of America and the whole world.

Proud of her day's work, Kristin held her placard up high and resumed shouting: "We are the ninety-nine per cent!"

Chapter 3

Manhattan, Chelsea, 13 October.

"*Latino tû, latino yo, La misma sangre y corazón.*"

Kristin turned up the sound on her smartphone and murmured the words without paying any heed to the gazes of the other subway users.

"*Eso es mi Latinoamérica, Hay que luchar, Latinoamérica.*"

She restrained herself from shouting the words of the song *Latinoamérica* by the Spanish group Mana. Since a sergeant, also Hispanic, had lent her a CD by the band after a battle in Kabul, she had become a veritable groupie. She had immediately bought all of their catalogue, a mixture of rock and calypso sung in Spanish—her paternal language, which she spoke fluently.

Although she had since discovered other hispanophone singers, Mana remained her preferred group. It would not be long before she could finally see them in concert, at Madison Square Garden in the coming December.

When Kristin emerged into the open air, she was greeted by an odor of grilled meat coming from a street-vendor, of which there are hundreds in Manhattan. It was still too early to eat, although in Manhattan, there was really no set time for that. She would doubtless get a hot dog on the way back.

The young woman was going to see the photographer who had invited her to come and check the prints for the exhibition. She looked round to get her bearings, which she did immediately.

New York had changed very little during the ten years she had spent away from the Big Apple. At any rate, it was easy to get around, thanks to the grid system of avenues numbered from north to south and streets from east to west: a simple and infallible system, even for tourists. Only the streets of south Manhattan had names.

When her parents had died she had sold their apartment in Brooklyn and transferred her effects to a loft in the heart of Chelsea that had belonged to her maternal grandfather, who she had never known. A photographer, who preferred traveling the world to occupying himself with his family, he had died of cancer in 1975, two years before she was born.

Her parents had kept two rooms for her. Nested in a four-story building at the intersection of Eighth Avenue and Fifteenth Street, it had a value that had never ceased increasing over the years while Chelsea had become the fashionable district of Manhattan. She had rented it out during her time in the military and had put the money aside to provide for her future. After the non-renewal of her military contract she had asked the tenant to move out because she wanted to live in it herself. She could not see herself living anywhere else than in New York. She thought that the city and its inhabitants would protect her against her own demons.

The savings accumulated during her years of service would permit her to live serenely for a number of years; she was a property-owner, with health insurance and no luxurious tastes.

As soon as she was installed she had spent her time zapping channels and following the news from the entire world. After two months, however, inactivity had begun to weigh upon her. She had sensed depression insidiously taking possession of her, and if she had not reacted she would have plunged straight into it. She had pulled herself together and started going out.

She had begun by going to the cinema, then going to see Broadway musicals praised by the critics and eating in chic restaurants.

One evening, when she was drinking a cocktail in a fashionable bar in Chelsea, a young man had accosted her.

In the army she had had several adventures, and one of them had nearly terminated in marriage, but she had been

31

transferred and the separation had been fatal to their relationship. Later, Kristin had realized that it had been bound to fail.

The young man at the bar was with friends, and he had darted several interested glances at her before daring to approach. Making an effort, she had accepted a drink. They had the spent more than an hour taking, and Kristin had recovered her smile. The thirty-one-year-old bachelor worked as an accountant for the Knicks, the New York basketball team. The encounter was going quite well, when he had asked her about her solvency. Kristin had looked at him uncomprehendingly.

He had politely explained that a financial statement was now an important pre-requisite—indispensable, even—for commencing a healthy amorous relationship, along with a negative HIV certificate. It was, in fact, a matter of a mathematical formula that took account of incomes, patrimony and debts. He concluded by confiding to her that he could not see himself embarking on a relationship with anyone whose credit rating was less than 600.

Kristin had observed that he was not joking. At first she had nearly flung hr cocktail in his face, but she had channeled her anger, and had replied politely that her credit rating must be very low. As a gentleman, the young man had insisted, even so, in paying for the drinks before leaving.

Kristin had gone home angrily, but her decision was made. She could no longer live wrapped up in herself. She was going to fight for her country—at least, the country in which she believed, a country that would not be in the hands of extremists or ultraliberals. She did not know yet by what means, but she would find a course of action.

The following day she had gone for a walk in Battery Park, at the southern tip of Manhattan, opposite the Statue of Liberty. She had sat on a bench to reflect; she thought about joining an NGO. It was while going back to her apartment that she had chanced to pass close to Zuccotti Park, where the incongruous presence of tents, policemen and journalists had intrigued her. In site of an unhealthy timidity, she had dared to approach the strange squatters and had debated with some of them as if she had known them for years.

They had talked to her about their war against Capital. Then she had confided her own story, telling them about Iraq rid of Saddam Hussein, where religious violence still remained present, and then Afghanistan, where the Taliban would return to power one day.

Kristin had not noticed the time passing. She had never talked as much—not to strangers at any rate. It was better than psychoanalysis; at last the people really listened, and above all, understood; she did not have the impression of talking in a vacuum. After hours of discussion, Kristin had decided to enlist in Occupy Wall Street. The movement pleased her, by virtue of its spontaneity, the absence of a leader, and the slightly crazy ideal of a new world. She had just found a reason to live.

Without the slightest hesitation, she had bought a tent, put a few clothes in a knapsack, locked up her apartment and returned to the park, where she had installed herself in the midst of the other indigenes. And that was where her life was today.

She put all that reflux of the past out of her mind. Nathan was waiting for her. Even so, she was in no hurry to see her photographic image; she would have to look herself in the face.

She walked rapidly along the sidewalk, finishing the coffee that she had bought from a street-vendor a few minutes earlier. Coffee was undoubtedly what she missed most about her time in the army. During her various sojourns in Europe she had developed a taste for good coffee, and what was found in New York was, at best, insipid.

She threw her cup into a refuse-bin, switched her large bag from one hand to the other, and then started humming the chorus of *El verdadera Amor Perdona*.

After her encounter with the photographer she had not gone back to the park and her companions in the struggle but to her apartment. She had switched on her computer, connected to the internet and had set about researching her maternal grandfather.

She knew almost nothing about him. Articles on Wikipedia and a couple of other sites told her that he had enjoyed a measure of success. Several of his photographs were on display in the New York Photographic Museum. On seeing them, she had remembered a trunk containing her souvenirs and her grandfather's. She had never really been interested in him, but the discussion with Nathan had impelled her to exhume his heritage, even though she did not know the reason as yet.

She had opened the trunk and bought out files of numerous photographs. They had seemed to her to be something. There were portraits of artistes and celebrities—Frank Sinatra, Dean Martin, Marilyn Monroe and others to whom she could not put a name—and pictures of soldiers in the Vietnamese jungle. Even those exhibited at the museum were there. After fifty or so, she had stopped and put them in the bag without paying any more attention to them.

So, when Nathan had called her an hour before, she had picked them up, with a nod of the head. Now she was advancing into Hell's Kitchen, whose inhabitants called it Clinton, not in homage to the former President but an old mayor, who had owned the land at one time.

Today, Hell's Kitchen no longer merited its name. The once disreputable neighborhood had been rehabilitated, and as now renowned for its restaurants and television studios.

Nathan Stewart's gallery was two blocks away. Kristin crossed Tenth Avenue and arrived outside the window,

She took off her earphones and put her smartphone back in her bag. She looked at the photos on display, all in black and white, representing men and women in everyday life. They seemed beautiful to her, but, photography never having interested her, she was no judge.

She opened the door to the gallery, unleashing the tinkle of a little bell placed above it.

Chapter 4

Manhattan, Chelsea, 13 October.

Nathan Stewart passed his head around the door situated at the back, and smiled on seeing her. He showed her the mobile phone stuck to his ear and addressed a little signal to her before disappeared into the shop's back room again. Kristin found herself alone in the gallery.

In the middle of the immense room was a modern fireplace whose aluminum flue rose up to the ceiling. A dozen chairs distributed in the corners, awaited visitors. The white walls were hung with photographs.

Kristin made a tour of the room.

All the photos depicted taxis on the New York streets. The city and its people were in black and white; only the yellow color of the cabs stood out. In the beginning, the young woman could not see where the art resided; several times, she made the reflection that she could have taken the pictures herself. After a few minutes spent examining them, however, she had to admit that the success of such photographs was undoubtedly not within the scope of just anyone. Each of them was suggestive of a kind of alchemy, between the city and the people.

After a long interval, Nathan emerged from his lair and advanced toward Kristin.

"Excuse my impoliteness; I was talking to a journalist who's going to cover my next exhibition—the one that concerns us. Thanks for coming so quickly, although I must say that I didn't expect you today."

"I'm eager to see the photos."

"No problem; I'll show them to you. Before that, though, put your bag and coat on that chair; you'll be more comfortable."

Kristin did so, with an ache in her abdomen; contradictory sentiments—impatience and fear—were knotting her stomach.

Nathan divined her unease. He did not give her time to increase her anxiety. He took her by the hand and drew her into the room situated behind the gallery where he had been on the phone when she arrived. The interior was cluttered with computers and screens. He invited her to sit down on an empty chair, and then pressed the button of a video-projector set up in a corner.

An image appeared on the blank wall.

Kristin could not help grimacing on seeing it. She did not like either her boyish figure or the scar striping her face, which she could not succeed in hiding with her long hair. On her return to civilian life she had even considered cosmetic surgery—the army was ready to pay part of the cost—but she had abandoned the idea. Whether she liked it or not, that mark was an integral part of her life, and she would keep it until she died.

"My God, how ugly I am!" she murmured, when a new photograph appeared. "You're not really going to exhibit them? I'd be too ashamed. I look like a veritable idiot. And that scar...you could remove it with a program."

"On the contrary," said Nathan, approaching the wall. "You're perfect! You're the symbol of a new America, a long way from the modish mannequins that parade during fashion week, and a long way from the Tea Party women. Frankly, don't run yourself down, you're fine. As for that scar, it doesn't disfigure you...I'll even say that it enhances your natural charm."

Kristin shook her head, scarcely reassured by the photographer's words. She did not find herself ugly in all the photos, but some seemed to have been taken in order to bring out her imperfections. She sighed. She knew, of course, that the photographer was right; she corresponded exactly to the Occupy Wall Street movement.

Nathan was a professional. He had located perfect angles, original lighting, backgrounds that were sometimes precise and sometimes blurred, as many elements that gave more weight to the Movement and its claims. She took account of the fact that he had begun to photograph her long before asking her for authorization, but she could not hold it against him, so much did his talent show in the prints.

"I want to work on some of them, though," he said, "without exaggeration or deceptive retouching—but on the whole. I'm satisfied with the result."

"You can be," Kristin replied, with a smile

She had to admit that in certain pictures, she really did look good; Nathan had succeeded in making the best of her. She had to stop denigrating herself and accept herself as she was—and she wasn't bad.

"I'll take some more, if you don't mind."

"Don't you have enough for your exhibition?"

"No, I'd like others—in the park, especially. My angle of attack is to show the Movement when it isn't filing through the streets, to show the men and women behind it. That's my project. I hope you'll be there, and in the foreground."

"I'm expecting that," she said, with a slight grimace. "I've given you my word."

It was the photographer's turn to smile. "Your confidence is touching. In return, I'll show you every photograph I've chosen—that's a promise. And I hope that you'll give me your opinion of each of them, and that we can make the choice together of which ones to keep.

"I'd like that...but I don't know anything. It's an art whose codes I haven't mastered. I wouldn't be any use to you."

"You'll learn. Every photograph has its own 'codes,' as you put it. The essential thing is what you feel when looking at the photos."

"When do you intend to organize the exhibition?"

"The end of November, if all goes well. Just time to take more photos, work them up to their best and prepare the advertising. One sector where I'm something of an expert," he added, with a smile.

Kristin redirected her gaze to the wall, where the photos were cycling.

"I ought to abandon you and go back to my companions in the struggle."

They left the room together. When they reached the chair on which her effects were lying, she remembered her grandfather's photographs. Bag in hand, she turned to Nathan.

"If the exhibition leaves you any free time, I'd like to show you some of my grandfather's photographs."

She paused; Nathan encouraged her to go on with a hand gesture.

"He was a photographer. Perhaps you've hard mention of him. He died more than forty years ago. His name was Edward Pyle."

Beside her, the photographer almost choked.

Chapter 5

Manhattan, Chelsea, 13 October.

"Edward Pyle? *The* Edward Pyle?"

Kristin's eyes widened. She had not expected her grand-father's name to engender such a reaction. Nathan's gaze was shining like a child's on Christmas morning.

"I don't know whether there were any others, but yes, that was his name. According to what I've read on the internet, he had some small renown."

"That's the least one can say. He's still considered, among certain aficionados, as one of the masters of portraits of personalities and war photography. He paused, and asked: "Have you brought the photos with you?"

"Yes, I thought they might interest you. As for me, I'd love to know a little more about him."

"I'm truly curious to see them."

Kristin opened her bag and took out a box-file.

"Over to you. Perhaps you can tell me whether they have any value."

"For that you'd need to get a specialist opinion." As he read the disappointment in her eyes he added: "But I can examine them and give you a preliminary opinion. Can your companions wait a few more minutes for you?"

Kristin acquiesced.

"There are also negatives in separate files. They're still at home. I'll bring them to you, if you're interested."

"Certainly. I've kept old apparatus for developing photographs. Although the digital has invaded everything, I still work the old-fashioned way from time to time.

Nathan picked up the first print delicately. It represented Steve McQueen in front of a Broadway theater. The following ones showed film stars, singers and even politicians, on the sidewalks of New York. Then came a few photographs of Vietnam.

Kristin watched Nathan go through the photographs, completely absorbed in his task. Sometimes, he examined a photograph with intense attention, sometimes he flicked rapidly from one to the next.

Suddenly, he uttered an oath.

"What's the matter?" asked Kristin anxiously.

"Excuse my rudeness, but I can't get over it!"

He held out a photo to her. She immediately recognized Marilyn Monroe. The young actress was posing over an air vent, her skirt elevated.

"I know that one. One finds it everywhere, on calendars or books about Marilyn. It's an image taken from a film, I believe," she said, handing the photo back to him. "I don't see what's so extraordinary about it as to merit an oath."

Nathan took back the print and stared at it again, frowning.

"No, this photo isn't taken from *The Seven Year Itch*. If you remember, in the film the shirt isn't raised so high, doubtless because of the censor, and the angle isn't the same. This photo comes from a special shoot organized in New York in 1954. Your grandfather must have been among the privileged party."

"It must be one of his early ones. He was born in 1931. He was twenty-three years old then."

"Amazing!" murmured Nathan, still plunged in his observation. "The angle is truly surprising. The other shots are very well-known, but not this one. With your consent, I'd like to show it to an admirer of Marilyn who might be able to give me some information about it, and whether the shot is archived."

The young woman acquiesced. Any advice was good to obtain. Afterwards, Nathan examined other photographs of the famous actress. He handed them to Kristin.

"That shoot has become mythical for every self-respecting photographer or fan of Marilyn Monroe," he said. "They'd pay a great deal to go back in time and witness it."

"Not much chance of that!" said Kristin, smiling at Nathan's fervor. "I only know the scene in the film, and to tell you the truth, I wouldn't be able to name the director or a single other actor."

"The film was directed by Billy Wilder, and its cast included Tom Ewell. But as I told you, this photo isn't taken from the film. The shoot was held at the corner of Lexington Avenue and Fifty-second Street. I don't know if you can visualize the place; it's changed a lot since."

Kristin put on semblance of being offended. "I'm a pure New Yorker...so yes, I can see where it is."

This time, it was the photographer's turn to smile.

"Oh, New Yorkers and their pride...I can say that, having been born here myself. To get back to the shoot, it was organized alongside the film by the producers. Only twenty photographers and journalists were invited to it. Legend recounts that the cold was particularly glacial that evening. Faithful to her habit, Marilyn arrived late, but her presence warmed the atmosphere in a matter of seconds.

Nathan Stewart stopped to admire a photograph, his gaze lost in the void, as if he had succeeded in going back through time and find himself in the midst of his colleagues. He shook his head and continued, in a slightly troubled voice: "Marilyn appeared in that skirt, staggering in her beauty and provocation. She struck the pose and suddenly, a gust of wind—a blower underneath, in fact—lifted up her skirt like a parachute. The cameras started clicking. And she...she laughed, laughed in bursts, as if all that was quite natural."

Nathan handed her another photograph.

"Look at that gaze. She's the tamer of the photographers, the wild beasts. She's holding them under her spell. She's the one leading the dance."

Kristin studied the actress more attentively. In her youth she had seen one or two of her films, but she no longer remembered then. She was part of the generation raised on *Star Wars* and *Titanic*. Her iconic actresses were the likes of Julia Roberts, Angelina Jolie and Nicole Kidman. Marilyn was only a star of the calendar, a prototypical blonde.

And yet, behind the face that was laughing in bursts at seeing the skirt rise up like that Kristin discovered a woman; not a great actress who was posing, but a simple woman in her plenitude.

She contemplated the other photographs. Nathan was right. Marilyn really was subjugating the journalists, conscious of the power that she was exerting over them. She was playing with them, by means of her smile or her poses.

Kristin held out the prints to Nathan, but he, plunged in the examination of another of her grandfather's works, did not even notice the gesture.

"Marilyn is truly beautiful," she murmured, to break the silence. "I would never have imagined that my grandfather had crossed paths with her. No one ever talked about him at home. My mother and my father must have known about this photo, though..."

"It's one of the mythic ones, and will remain engraved forever in the memory of the men present at the shoot. That evening, it's said that Marilyn's fans nearly unleashed a riot; they literally howled on seeing her white knickers. As the Fox press agent said in the days that followed: 'The Russians could have invaded Manhattan that day and no one would have noticed.' The session lasted more than five hours."

"Her dress looks as if it's being held up by invisible strings."

A malicious gleam traversed the photographer's eye. "But if you look carefully, the person occupying the best place can't be seen."

Kristin examined the print again and tried to work out what he meant. Finally, her face cleared. "The man who's projecting the air."

"Exactly—the blower. It wasn't the first time that photographers used such a means to life her skirt. In any case, that photo didn't bring much luck, for Marilyn at least, not senti-mentally. Her husband at the time, Joe Di Maggio, a former baseball player, had been told about the shoot by some well-intentioned person. Jealous, he wanted his wife to give up the cinema. When he saw that scene he left in a fury. According to some witnesses, the argument that night was violent. The next day, Marilyn's face bore the marks."

"The bastard!"

Nathan put that series of photos aside and plunged into anther, also devoted to Marilyn. Kristin waited patiently for him to finish. Seized by a suspicion, she checked her watch and realized that she was going to miss the first demonstration. She could still be there if she hurried, but the photographer was not giving her the opportunity.

"What's this…?"

Nathan left the rest of his sentence in suspense.

Chapter 6

The photographer's face contracted, his brow furrowing again. She would have liked to know what had occasioned the question, but her timidity regained the upper hand. She did not want to disturb him, so she waited for him to speak.

"These are truly strange. See for yourself."

He held out two photos to her.

In the first Marilyn was standing alone at the side of a road, soberly dressed—nothing comparable to the previous ones. Behind her, the desert was visible.

"Look at the background," said Nathan. "That's the most interesting thing."

In the background, to the left of the actress, she made out an enormous metallic structure: a rocket, she understood, squinting. Nevertheless, she could not succeed in identifying the base.

"Cape Canaveral?" she asked.

"Possibly. Marilyn died in August 1962. I'd need to find out where the first rockets were launched."

"Why do you say that the photo is strange? Marilyn at Cape Canaveral seems logical to me. If I remember my history lessons, 1962 was the time of the first space flights..."

"Yes, you're right. Nevertheless, I'm willing to bet that no one knows about these photos. Let's pass on to the second."

In the second, Marilyn was posing on the platform of a subway station, but she was not alone; behind her, a man was reading a magazine. Once again, the young actress was splashing the scene with all her beauty. Her grandfather had found the ideal angle, the perfect light that made the most of the young star's face.

"Still as beautiful," murmured Kristin. "My grandfather was truly lucky to have her as a model."

"If my memory isn't playing tricks on me," Nathan went on, "this was taken in the fifties...I can't remember the exact year..."

As if gripped by a revelation, he changed the subject. "Do you have any documents written by your grandfather? A notebook, for example, where he jotted things down? That might help us to identify and date the photographs."

Kristin reflected for a few seconds.

"No, nothing occurs to me. When my parents died I threw out a lot of stuff, especially old clothes. I only kept these photos...and the files of negatives I mentioned just now. When I got home I'll look to see whether I have other documents amid my clutter...but I don't think so."

Beside her, the photographer was pensive. "As I said to you a little while ago, I'd like, with your consent, to send these photos to a friend who works for the Marilyn Monroe Foundation, to see whether he can give us any information about them."

"No problem."

Nathan passed a hand through his hair. "I think you've discovered a treasure. I wonder..."

For the first time, the photographer seemed to be searching for words.

"...If we could work in association to mount an exhibition devoted to him? It's the anniversary of his death next year."

"But... what about your Occupy Wall Street project?" snapped Kristin, in a chagrined tone. "I thought that was your priority."

He stroked his chin, and a smile lit up his face. "Let's combine the two!"

As if seized by frenzy, he seized all the photos contained in the bag and headed for the back room.

"Follow me!"

Surprised, and so late for the demonstration that she was no longer thinking about joining it, the young woman obeyed. The gallery owner was already sorting through the photos that he had placed on his desk.

"Help me find the photos with Marilyn Monroe."

Kristin made a slight grimace. Compared with Marilyn, the Movement's weight was negligible, and she hoped that Nathan would not abandon the project. Perhaps it had been a mistake to bring the photos. Nevertheless, she gave the photographer the benefit of the doubt, and began to sort out the photos.

They spent a little while arranging them in categories. In the end, there were about fifty of the actress.

From the pile, Nathan carefully selected ten. Then he went to the blank wall on which he had previously projected the photographs of the Movement and hung up the prints of the young actress. Nine of them had New York as a background. On the tenth, the rocket appeared.

The photographer stepped back and looked at them silently. Kristin dared not speak, for fear of disturbing him. Then he restored to his desk and tapped the keyboard. The printer hummed. He took possession of the two sheets it had just ejected and fixed them to the display alongside the photos of Marilyn.

Kristin's eyes widened as she saw herself to the right and left of the Hollywood star. She scowled.

"You're not having any pity on me," she said, turning to Nathan, angrily. "No woman can compete with her. And then, me, with my scar and the rest…it's frightful. I don't want to look at that."

Nathan remained mute. He printed a few more photographs taken during the demonstration in Times Square and interleaved them with her grandfather's.

As the photographer still made no reply, the young woman's anger ebbed away. She tried to comprehend where Nathan was trying to take her. Why juxtapose one of the greatest stars of the cinema and her, a simple disfigured Latino? And why the presence of Marilyn in the demonstration?

"I understand," she said, coldly. "You're looking for the contrast: the beauty and the beast..."

"Not at all! You're completely scornful of yourself! Please stop denigrating yourself and let me present the argument. You possess two totally different personalities...but which are connected. I'll explain: you're two rebels battling the system, and also, two lovers of New York. We have a good idea there."

Kristin clenched her fists. She did not like that juxtaposition of the star and herself—not at all. The contrast between her face and Marilyn's was too flagrant; it really was the beauty and the beast. Deep down, however, she had to admit that he explanation held...but that approach did not charm her at all; she still could not see herself exhibited alongside a star...and what a star!

"I don't agree," she snapped. "I signed up for an exhibition on Occupy Wall Street, not on Marilyn Monroe and me."

"I don't like speaking on behalf of the dead," Nathan contained, taking another line of attack, "but if Marilyn were alive, she'd support your movement."

"What tells you that? Your idea has no solid foundation."

"I know a little about Marilyn's life, and behind the Hollywood façade, she was a rebel."

"They why not organize an exhibition uniquely concerned with Marilyn Monroe? You have time to think about that—you have until next year—and another on Occupy Wall Street. I can't see any interest in mingling the two...especially in comparing us."

"You don't understand. My idea isn't so much to produce two exhibitions as to find an original angle for both, in such a way that one elevates the other, and *vice versa*. Think about it: what better way is there to promote Occupy Wall Street than to attach a figure like Marilyn to it?"

The photographer was not wrong. Nowadays, to make an impact on minds, one had to sow audacity and originality, to create a *buzz*. And although the idea of being juxtaposed with Marilyn scarcely delighted her, that association might add value to the Movement.

Kristin unclenched her fists, and eventually said: "What do you want me to do?"

Nathan opened a drawer in his desk and brought out a small reflex camera, which he held out to her.

She hesitated before taking it, as if it might bite her.

"I'm giving it to you. Take photos—lots. Save them to your computer afterwards. Go to Wall Street, walk around New York, and take pictures of whatever you like, without worrying about the development."

"All right…but in order to do what?"

"Bring me your photos. I'll look at them and tell you what I think. If you grasp the game, I'll give you some advice. Try. If you don't like it, you can drop it. What do you have to lose? Nothing—absolutely nothing."

"Okay, I'll try. But you still haven't answered my question. What do you want to do with my photos?"

"Exhibit them," said Nathan, smiling.

The man definitely had a knack for bring out ideas, each one crazier than the last. The worst of it was that he had a steely belief in them. Kristin stood there open-mouthed for a few seconds, and then looked at the camera. She nearly burst out laughing, but suppressed it in the face of Nathan's seriousness.

She pressed the ON button and the screen immediately lit up as the objective lens extended. Unthinkingly, she took aim at Nathan Stewart and took a few pictures, which she inspected immediately afterwards. Nothing terrible, but the material was quality. Looking at a screen and pressing a button was insufficient to improvise a photographer.

But why not? she asked herself. So what if that manner of defending the Movement was not the one she had thought…and what if, hiding behind the crazy idea…? The camera might become a weapon to serve her combat better than a rifle, or a bomb. She began to imagine other scenarios, other exhibitions...why not books, websites? But before then, she had to learn to make use of it, and, as in the army, she needed an instructor. He was standing in front of her.

"You'll teach me?"

The photographer nodded his head.

"Agreed, then...but no privileges."

"That's not my habit."

"I'll begin by photographing our combat. Tomorrow."

"Take pictures. They always have an impact on public opinion. For my part, I'll contact my friend at the Marilyn Monroe Foundation; he'll advise us. I'll come to see you in the park after my meeting, to give you a summary."

The young woman had taken note of the utilization of "us."

"If I'm not in prison," Kristin said, smiling.

"I'll pay your bail," he replied, tit for tat. "After all, we're partners now."

Kristin held out her hand, which he shook as if to symbolize their accord. Then he leaned toward her and made the gesture of kissing her cheeks.

The young woman smiled. If her military experience had taught her anything, it was how to judge men. In this case, her instinct told her that she had been right to trust him.

Impatient to try out her new toy, Kristin saluted the photographer and left the gallery. When she arrived in the street she breathed out profoundly.

Her gaze wandered over the buildings that loomed over her with all their height. Mechanically, she took out her smartphone, placed the earphones over her ears and pressed the PLAY button. Then she picked up the camera that she had suspended around her neck and shot buildings passers-by and vehicles at random.

She turned on to Broadway and headed at a tranquil pace for the financial district. Nearby, taxis were going passed at top speed, as well as ambulances and police cars, the sound of their sirens reverberating between the buildings.

With a flick of a finger, Frank Sinatra replaced Mana in the speakers. Sinatra was singing solo; New York was a lover, not a mistress, and did not share with another woman, even Liza Minnelli.

She murmured the words of *New York, New York*.

"*Start spreading the news, I'm leaving today. I want to be a part of it, New York, New York.*"

For the first time in a long time, she felt good. Her life was taking on meaning; she was invested in a conflict in which she believed, and she had found a job—a slightly crazy job, of which she had never thought before, but a job.

She did not know that the future had in store for her, but it did not matter; better than that, it was exciting.

In spite of the distance she decided to go back to Zuccotti Park on foot: an opportunity to rediscover her city with a different gaze, a photographer's gaze.

PART TWO

Chapter 7

Manhattan, Chelsea, 16 November.

Kristin marched along the sidewalk, with a knot in her guts. Today, she had not donned her earphones. Nothing could dissipate the fear that dominated her mind. Even in the Afghan mountains or in Mosul, it had never been so violent. Several times, the young woman was tempted to go back to the park, to her friends.

But she had never turned her back on danger.

The month of October and the first fifteen days of November had gone past like a film in fast-forward. Between the fight with Occupy Wall Street and the preparations for the exhibition, she had been caught in a veritable whirlwind.

With her companions in the struggle the situation remained the same. They were still in Zuccotti Park, demonstrating every day. But the forces of order would soon intervene, they knew; it was a matter of days now, if not hours. The authorities, municipal as well as governmental, would not tolerate the occupation much longer. The signs of police intervention were intensifying.

After their publicity coup in Times Square, media interest had fallen away like a punctured balloon. The battle to bring about change would be long and difficult: a consciousness that rendered the coming event even more important.

In less than a month Nathan had succeeded in making his initial idea for the exhibition concrete; it was now entitled *Two*

Rebel Women in New York. Not without a heartfelt pang, Kristin had accepted the idea of being associated with the star. Nathan had vanquished her reticence by closing his gallery for a whole day and preparing a fictitious exhibition in order to help him to plan it. That evening, Kristin had been able to admire the photographer's talent. He had been able to take full advantage of her physique, her features and her gaze—even her scar.

She had taken account of the fact that, even if she could not hold a candle to the star, she radiated a strength that pleased her. In addition, the photos gave full value to the Movement, faithfully describing the daily life of the demonstrators and their non-violent actions.

Kristin had congratulated the photographer on his work.

Afterwards, Nathan had kept her up to date with the procedure, associated her with all the decisions. He always had an adorable word to dispel her fears or doubts. Kristin had appreciated enormously collaborating with a man she now considered as a friend. Simultaneously professional and complicit, he listened to her and took account of her observations. She was grateful to him for that, even if she had not yet found the right words to tell him.

Without overmuch difficulty, the photographer had obtained the consent of the Marilyn Monroe Foundation for the use of her grandfather's photographs. As a cherry on the cake, the Foundation had even acquired some of them for a considerable sum. Kristin had not hesitated for long; she needed the money—or, rather, the Movement needed it.

Kristin hoped that the media coverage of the exhibition might also rebound on the Movement. Nathan had a mastery of communication; newspapers and magazines had featured the exhibition in advance and he had responded to several interview requests that Kristin had refused. She preferred to wait a while.

In fact, after having raised the subject with several of her friends in the Movement, they all supported her step, convinced that all means were good to add visibility to their action. Some of them had even promised to come and see the exhibition.

And this evening was the big occasion.

After having left the park, she had gone home to take a shower and change. She had hesitated over the choice of garments before opting for a blouse, skirt and jacket: something simple and natural. Then she had put on make-up.

On arrival at the gallery she took a deep breath before opening the door. The inside was noisy with the conversations of guests crowded round the buffet or the pictures. She darted a circular glance around. She did not know any of the participants, of course. Nathan was not in the room.

Not knowing what to do, she zigzagged between the guests and headed for the buffet, where she poured herself a glass of fruit juice—not champagne; she wanted to keep a clear head.

Glass in hand, she seemed strangely invisible to present gazes, even though her face was displayed on all the walls. Although she had not expected to receive a standing ovation when she arrived, that lack of reaction surprised her and, she had to admit, offended her slightly. Collecting herself, the young woman suppressed yet again the desire to leave in all haste, and forced herself to stroll through the heart of that exotic fauna emerged from favored environments, with a defiant smile on her lips.

As she passed by, some turned their heads, others ignored her superbly. Then a well-dressed couple in their thirties approached her.

"Our compliments, Miss," said the man. "It's an honor to meet you in the flesh. The photos are magnificent, but they don't do you justice. I..."

"We sympathize with your struggle against finance," his wife cut in. "What sacrifices it must require to live in the park!"

Kristin stammered vague thanks, uncertain of what attitude to adopt.

The day before, Nathan had advised her to remain natural, simply to be herself, and that everything would be fine. But that was not the case. She felt like an elephant in a china shop. Whatever she said or did would render her ridiculous. She had only one desire: to get back to Occupy Wall Street as quickly as possible...

But she could not; Nathan was counting on her.

She thanked the couple warmly and carried out a strategic retreat to a less crowded zone of the gallery. She found herself facing a photo that she knew well. It represented her friend Thomas Goodman playing the guitar at the foot of the statue of Washington outside the Federal Hall National Memorial, a few yards from Wall Street. Her name appeared immediately beneath the frame.

From among the hundreds of photographs she had kept, Nathan had picked that one. She had not dared to refuse at the time, and had even been glad, since the result now made her proud.

She shook her head. What would the guests take her for, looking at her own work like that? She therefore frayed a passage toward the centerpiece of the spectacle, the two photographs that Nathan had put in pride of place: Marilyn and herself in the same subway station and the same position, with the sign *Uptown Local—Grand Central* above their head: Marilyn the blonde and Kristin the brunette, holding a placard on which was written: *We are the 99%.*

Underneath it was inscribed, like a graffito: *Sin mujeres no hay revolucion.* She had seen the tag on a wall in Brooklyn and asked Nathan to reproduce it here, since it fit in perfectly with the image that the exhibition projected.

Three people were standing in front of it. Kristin dared not disturb them and stayed in retreat, motionless. According to Nathan, newspapers of newspapers would probably acquire the photographs in which she appeared. It was even possible that she would make page one.

The consequences of that foregrounding frightened her a little. Was she not risking becoming a symbol in spite of herself? What would her companions in the struggle think? If they no longer wanted her beside them, what would become of her?

She trembled at that idea before putting it out of her head. She had chosen, in her soul and conscience, an alternative that she believed to be the right one. Too bad if it offended the opinion or ego of some!

"Kristin!"

Lost in thought, she shuddered, turned round, and found herself face to face with Nathan.

The photographer smiled at her. By his side was a man of about thirty with a boyish face; only a few nascent wrinkles in the corners of his eyes betrayed his age.

"Kristin, I'd like to introduce you to Michael Pear."

Chapter 8

Manhattan, Chelsea, 16 November.

The man had been extending his hand to her for a few seconds, it seemed. Surprised, Kristin hastened to return the polite gesture.

"Thank you for coming," Nathan said to her, embracing her. "For a moment, I thought you might not dare." He held her in his arms for a few seconds.

"I thought about it," she replied, "but I chose to pass over my unhealthy timidity when I heard there was a buffet."

"Like most of the people here," he whispered, confidentially.

The young woman smiled.

"And then, I couldn't abandon you."

"Thanks," said Nathan, moving aside. "The attention is touching. Kristin, let me introduce Michael Pear; he's the friend who works at the Marilyn Monroe Foundation, whom I've often mentioned to you."

"I'm delighted to be able to meet the star of the evening," declared the man, brightly.

"Thank you, but it's Nathan that it's necessary to congratulate. He organized the project and directed it from beginning to end. I'm only one of two models."

"Nathan has just told me that the other model is unfortunately not free this evening," the newcomer continued, in the same conspiratorial tone that Nathan had earlier adopted, "so I won't have the opportunity to speak to her in person. Nevertheless, don't tell her, but I think you're much prettier."

"There again, all the merit belongs to Nathan," said Kristin, turning her head to hide her blush. Even if Michel Pear seemed to be a smooth talker, she was not accustomed to receiving such a compliment from such a seductive man.

"Michael wants to talk to you about your grandfather's photographs," Nathan confided to her, putting a hand on her shoulder. "I'll leave you with him. I'll go…I have to do a few interviews."

A silence accompanied the photographer's departure. Kristin watched him draw away, grimacing. It would not have taken much to make her think that Nathan was playing matchmaker and trying to fix her up. As she searched for words with which to recommence the discussion, Michael got in ahead of her.

"I wanted to give you the check for the Foundation's acquisition of the photos of Marilyn personally."

He took an envelope out of the inside pocket of his Armani jacket and held it out to Kristin. She hesitated before taking it.

"It's me who ought to thank you. This check will permit the Movement to face up to the next few months more serenely."

"Furthermore, as you stipulated in the negotiations, I reaffirm our promise and desire to promote this exhibition in our advertising. I'll also make it a duty to relaunch your grandfather's name in photographic milieux. He was a great photographer.

Kristin could not help grimacing. It was all too much, and arriving too suddenly.

"Nathan has told me vaguely what you do," she said, "but I'd like to know more about the Marilyn Monroe Foundation, especially if we're going to be working together one day."

"We're neither more or less than the executors of Marilyn Monroe's estate. I won't tell you the details of her will— they're confidential—or give you an account of the people who administer her fortune; it would be tedious and take too long. To put it simply, we manage all he rights derived from the Monroe myth: mugs, postcards, T-shirts, etc."

"That must bring you a tidy sum of money. Marilyn is still very popular."

"Yes, the profits are considerable. Marilyn is in the top ten highest-earning dead celebrities. On the other hand, the Foundation is entirely benevolent; we redistribute all the profits to charitable associations."

"But…what about the check or Occupy Wall Street?"

"Association or political movement—it makes no difference to us. It's also one of the aims of the Monroe Foundation to support such initiatives."

Kristin shook her head. What her interlocutor was not admitting was that the Foundation would support a capitalist organization if it were in its interest. Nevertheless, with such a fine check she could not put on a sour face.

"Have you carried out research on my grandfather?"

During the past month, she had visited the Museum of Photography, where several of her grandfather's pictures were on display. She had been able to take account there of the fact that Edward Pyle was a recognized photographer, whose renown was still vibrant in knowledgeable circles. She had learned, in particular, that he had lived in Vietnam for a few years before returning to New York and specializing in photos of celebrities.

She returned to the present while her interlocutor replied to her.

"I sought information after discovering the existence of the photos via Nathan. Unfortunately for us, he seems to have fallen into forgetfulness, and all we know about him is what the Museum could tell us—which is to say, not much more than what is posted there. In that regard, I have to confess that we're somewhat adrift in a fog."

"I really don't know any more either. He wasn't much appreciated in my family and no one ever talked about him. For some unknown reason, his name was banished from all discussions."

"I understand perfectly. My family has a few black sheep too."

Kristin took advantage of that personal allusion to rebound.

"You said just now that the Marilyn Foundation is benevolent. Forgive me if I'm being indiscreet, but what do you do for a living?"

"That risks taking us on to discordant terrain. I fear that you won't like my reply. I'm one of the famous one per cent against whom you're protesting."

The young woman had not expected so much frankness on her interlocutor's part.

"That's not your fault," she stammered, before taking account of the absurdity of what she was saying.

Michael uttered a loud burst of laughter, which disconcerted her. "On the contrary! I don't come from a rich family. I always dreamed of being part of the famous one per cent, and I achieved it. Even so, I propose a truce for this evening, if you don't mind. The battle can continue tomorrow."

"The battle never stops," snapped Kristin, in a tone more cutting than she might have wished—but she continued more gently: "However, I accept your offer and won't go into the economic and democratic inequalities between the elites and the rest of the population with you."

As she smiled in saying that, her interlocutor imitated her.

"Why don't we discuss the subject around a table one evening? And before you ask, yes it's an invitation in good and due form."

Kristin could not help scowling, but her eyes were still sparkling.

"A meal offered by Big Capital? That would go against all my principles."

She smiled, but she had not replied to his invitation.

The millionaire changed the subject and turned to the photo of Marilyn.

"To get back to our discussion regarding your grandfather, we've carried out research in our own archives. We haven't found any mention of his encounter with Marilyn—which isn't at all unusual, of course; it happens frequently. For example, there's the series by Ed Feingersh or the one found six months ago in Poland. Others will emerge one day or another.

"What do you do with these photos?"

"In the first place, they obviously have an artistic value, but they're also interesting from a historic viewpoint. Your grandfather's, for example, show us a Marilyn we didn't know. For the moment, we've left everything to Nathan."

He stopped, frowning, before resuming in a passionate tone: "According to a specialist at the Foundation, they must have been taken in May 1962, in the last months of the star's life, somewhere between her return to Los Angeles and her suicide. Before your discovery, we possessed very few photographs taken in that period, so you'll understand their value for us—as demonstrated by the check in your pocket," he added, with a smile. "Nevertheless, I won't hide it from you that one of them is more precious than the others."

"Which one?" asked Kristin, intrigued.

"It's not on display here. It's the one in which Marilyn is posing in the desert with a rocket behind her."

"Yes, I remember. Nathan mentioned it to me. On the other hand, if it's so precious, why not exhibit it?"

"It's precisely for that reason that Nathan decided not to exhibit it. As I told you, that photo is more valuable than all the others put together. Wait for me for a moment—I'll go fetch it..."

Chapter 9

Manhattan, Chelsea, 16 November.

The millionaire disappeared into the back room that served as Nathan's office and came back with a photo that he placed before her eyes.

"It's true that it appears ordinary at first glance, but where it differs from your grandfather's other photos is the place and the date. Where and when? One of our informants has been able to give us a partial answer to the second question. By magnifying the image of the rocket and analyzing it, he's concluded that it was taken at the end of May 1962—but before the twenty-fourth, the date when Scott Carpenter lifted off into space aboard a Mercury capsule."

"That's the rocket that carried the Mercury in the background, then?"

"Exactly."

Behind the cool and arrogant golden boy, a passionate historian was concealed. Ice and fire—a mixture that pleased Kristin, even though she dared not admit it.

"I still don't see what's so exceptional about it," she retorted, lending herself to the game.

"No one has ever mentioned a visit by Marilyn to Cape Canaveral at that time," Michael continued. "According to our archives, she was in Los Angeles."

"You said just now that your archives don't constitute an exact science."

"You're right. If we don't possess any indication that confirms her presence at that moment, we don't possess any that denies it either. In fact, we don't understand what reason Marilyn might have had for going to the rocket base in the company of your grandfather. We're a long way from the glamour shoots to which we're accustomed. We don't possess any evidence of that side of Marilyn—that's why I was interrogating you just now about your grandfather."

"Unfortunately, I can't help you. As I told you before, no one in my family ever talked about him. Nathan asked me whether he kept a diary or left any notes, but having searched through his effects, I don't believe he did. At any rate, there's nothing in what was bequeathed to me. All that I know about him I learned from visiting the New York Photography Museum."

Michael could not hide his disappointment, but he did not have time to respond. A man approached them and pointed at the photograph.

"Can I see that?" he asked, without bothering with any formula of politeness.

The man was about a five-four, rather plump, with black hair and a nondescript physique He looked at the photo attentively before Michael plastered it against his body.

"No," he said, harshly. "Do you think everything's permissible? This photo isn't part of the exhibition."

The man did not have to be told twice, and he quit the gallery under the angry gaze of the millionaire.

"What an asshole!" said Kristin. "Some people really have no inhibitions."

"It's nothing serious, Kristin," he said. "I can call you that, can't I?"

Unthinkingly, Kristin nodded her head. Strangely, the millionaire attracted her. She ought to have detested him for his physique, his self-confidence and his money, but she couldn't manage it. He awoke a certain emotion in her...

She pulled herself together. Doubtless the millionaire collected conquests; numerous women must fall under his spell, or that of his bank account.

At that moment, Nathan came toward them, a smile brightening his face.

"The exhibition is a real success! Everyone's congratulating us. I hope you've come to a satisfactory arrangement?"

"Yes," Michael relied. "The Foundation has acquired the photographs and the negatives, in exchange for a check made out to Occupy Wall Street."

"Perfect!" Nathan concluded. "I'll send you the negatives after the exhibition, if that isn't inconvenient."

"Not at all. And as I was saying to Kristin, you can count on the Foundation to give all possible publicity to the exhibition." Michael turned to Kristin. "To the exhibition and the Movement, of course." He smiled. "Occupy Wall Street bought by Big Capital—that's amusing, no?"

The remark did not have the intended effect. Kristin looked him straight in the eyes. "It's the photos that you're buying, not the Movement," she replied. "We don't need your money, or your publicity."

"That's not what I meant," Michael continued, "as you know very well. I meant that the Foundation's money will be very useful to the Movement, for its existence."

As he finished the sentence he bit his lower lip, conscious of having committed a gaffe.

"Its existence?" said the young woman. "You really think that without your money, our battle couldn't continue?"

"That's not what I meant," he repeated, sensing that the situating was slipping away from him.

"But you said it. Behind your appearance of a millionaire philanthropist, you're just like all the rest. You think that the world only exists because of you and for you."

"I won't permit you to talk to me like that," replied the golden boy. "You don't know me."

Nathan interposed himself between them and tried to restore calm. "This isn't the place for launching a political debate."

"Why not?" Kristin interjected. "Are their special places for debating politics, then?" She paused and pointed at the photographs. "This exhibition is dedicated to rebels. Or do you prefer them mute, in photographs?"

Kristin looked at the assembly. All the conversations around them had fallen silent. She had become the attraction of the evening.

"You can say what you like," Michael murmured, unaccustomed to scenes, "but I think that the best thing is to end the conversation there. There's no point in it."

Kristin uttered a brief laugh. She had hit a sore spot. Under pressure, the golden boy showed his true colors.

"For you, it's just a matter of a gesture to a charitable association or a world-changing movement, a matter of passing for a saint. One poses with an activist, one gives her a check, and afterwards one hides under the carpet."

"I don't want to get rid of you. You're attributing intentions to me that aren't mine. I'll be frank: I like your movement but I don't think it has any future. You have no leader and no concrete economic program, just a few threadbare slogans."

Kristin was jubilant. In Zuccotti Park she debated with people who shared her convictions, but tonight, in front of her, was a true contradictor, one of those against whom she had been fighting for months.

"Are you going to tell me that you have nothing to do with the present crisis, that of the millions of unemployed the country has, the millions of poor people obliged to leave homes seized by the banks, the millions of immigrants who live in hiding, working for you, but whom you send home penniless...?"

"It's more complicated than that..."

"Do you take me for an idiot who doesn't understand anything?" Kristin cut in. "You make us doubt our own democracy. So yes, we have no leader, and no political program, properly speaking, but we have ideas. In the park we come together to approve all decisions democratically, not by a majority vote but by a large consensus-far from your political system dominated by lobbies and the media."

"Your system isn't democracy, it's anarchy," Michael countered, his face red. "With a system like, that the United States would be in chaos, and an unprecedented crisis."

"That's already the case. Perhaps you don't look at the news, but we're living in an unprecedented crisis. Your compatriots detest you, the world detests you but you're still convinced that you're right."

"I give up," snapped Michael. "You're reciting slogans. Try to think for yourselves and you'd soon see that you're following a false path."

"You're right. I'm an idiot and I have nothing to do here—so I'll leave you in good company and go to join my companions in the park."

Angrily, she brought out the check that he had given her a few minutes earlier.

"Know that I only have one thing to say. My grandfather's photos are yours; it's a gift."

She tore up the check and threw the pieces in the air before the bewildered audience. Then, without another word, she left the gallery.

A few timid plaudits accompanied her.

Chapter 10

Manhattan, Chelsea, 17 November.

Nathan locked the door of the gallery, the last visitors having just left. He brought down the metal curtain and then went back to his office. The excitement and stress of the evening had chased away fatigue. He would not be able to sleep tonight.

That was not the worst of it. It was absolutely necessary to wrap up the work on the exhibition. He should have finished it before the opening, but all his time had been devoured.

He sat down in his armchair, and his gaze fell upon a photo of Kristin pinned to the wall opposite. He smiled. As he had thought, the young woman had been the star of the private view—but not quite in the manner that he had expected.

The exhibition had been a success. His idea of associating such different women had worked marvelously; the contrast between them, the alchemy he had succeeded n creating, had bluffed the critics present. Even the photo taken by Kristin had made an impression. He hoped that she would continue; she possessed a certain talent and a revue photographer's gaze. If he was not mistaken, he would harvest good coverage in the specialist press, but also in major magazines like the *New Yorker*.

The argument between Kristin and Michael had been the climax of the evening. Even if the virulence of the young woman's speech had not intimidated him slightly to begin with, he would not have intervened. Michael was a big boy and could defend himself on his own. Accustomed to board meetings, however, the millionaire had seemed paralyzed by that hurricane of wrath.

And to cap it all, there had been Kristin's theatrical departure. After having torn up the check, she had passed through the audience without a glance, proudly. When the timid applause had rung out, the photographer had felt an impulse to go after her, but as the evening's master of ceremonies he was obliged to remain neutral and not offend an eminent member of the Monroe Foundation.

Michael Pear had been understanding. He had stayed for another half hour, talking to various people, minimizing the incident and its importance, even adding that the young woman had a determined character and that America would need people like her to get out of the crisis. Then, after congratulating him one last time, he had departed.

Yes, the evening had been a success: a slight scandal, positive critics and promises of purchases—some of those present had ordered copies of the prints, and the receipts surpassed his expectations. They would certainly get his accounts out of the red...

He had not dared confess it to Kristin, but for him, the exhibition represented a last chance. His financial situation was very poor. The magazines were buying fewer and fewer photographs, collectors preferred paintings and he had had a few setbacks. But after what he had seen this evening, he was reassured; he would be able to pay the rent for his gallery for a few more months.

He switched on his computer, which displayed the photo of Marilyn in the subway taken by Edward Pyle. Michael had given his consent for him to work on it before handing it over to the Monroe Foundation. The Foundation had allowed him to hang on to the negatives in order to study them and pass them on later.

Why not now? In the recovered silence of the gallery, the photographer smiled. He could accord himself that small pleasure. Too bad for the books; they would have to wait one more day.

For a start, he needed to date the scene. The best means consisted of enlarging the photo, hoping that the cover of the periodical that the man in the background as reading might be sufficient legible to get something from it. There were two ways of doing that: the technical and the artisanal. Based on experience, the photographer had more confidence in the old methods than programs for retouching images. He therefore decided to fall back on primary technique and operate manually on the negatives, which he was keeping in a locked drawer as precious relics.

Nathan got up and went into a small room devoid of windows, where he had installed his laboratory and all the equipment necessary for the development process that he continued to use, like an old dinosaur.

Meticulously, he opened the file in which the negatives were arranged and numbered, and took out a strip, which he inserted in an apparatus. The image was displayed directly on the table. He prepared several trays of chemicals, took out sheets of special paper and replaced the white light with red.

He began the most delicate part of the work, first enlarging the individual and then concentrating on the newspaper. He deposited a white sheet in the first bath, where the photo gradually appeared; then he plunged it into a second, filled with water, and then a third. It was the work of a true artist, which had disappeared with the advent of digitalization.

He repeated the operation several times, using other negatives; although Edward Pyle had only developed one photograph as a print, he had taken several shots. Every time, he toyed with the angle or the enlargement.

That night, Nathan was not trying to find the most perfect photo, merely the one that provided the best glimpse of the periodical. After half an hour, he left the room in order to aerate his mind and empty his lungs of chemical vapors.

He decided to tidy the gallery and clear away the buffet. When he had finished he took down the photos, now dry, and placed them on the work-table. He picked up a magnifying-glass, lit a desk-lamp, and examined them.

He frowned. He rubbed his eyes; fatigue and the chemical products were troubling his vision. He remained motionless for a few moments, reflecting. He was uncertain of what he saw. His imagination...or his exhaustion...was playing tricks on him.

He went back to his office, not knowing whether it was preferable to continue working or to go back to his apartment, situated directly above, and try to sleep.

In the end, temptation was stronger; he could not sleep without knowing.

He sat down in front of his computer and started an internet search. He printed the illustration on the screen and placed it beside him. He looked at the image several times, and then enlarged the photo, and then the image, again.

Suddenly, he exclaimed aloud: "Good God! It's not possible!"

And yet, it was before his eyes; there was no mistake.

The first thought that went through the mind was that Edward Pyle had faked the photograph, but he swept it away immediately. He could not see any means by which the photographer could have modified the negative in that fashion. And in that case, why not make use of it? Or perhaps he had wanted, like so many other photographers before him, to fake an image just for the pleasure of it, an image that he would never destroy.

Nathan shook his head; that hypothesis did not hold water. Edward Pyle was a professional photographer, he would never have permitted himself to patch up an unpublished photograph.

Second hypothesis: he had photographed a double of Marilyn. But there again, for what reason? Why photograph a double when one knew the original? And then, the Foundation had been definite about that: it really was Marilyn in the photograph.

The last solution was completely crazy: the photo was genuine. If that could be confirmed, Nathan had before his eyes the scoop of the year, not to say the decade.

But the idea was absurd, fantastic, impossible.

But...

What if...?

He ought not to act precipitately. He was tired, his nerves highly strung. He needed to know more...

Kristin! He had to call her. Before picking up the phone he passed the relevant photos in review and noted their number on a loose sheet of paper. Then he took out his smartphone and tapped out the young woman's number, in order to reveal his discovery to her.

It went directly to voicemail. He hesitated over hanging up, but decided to leave a message.

"Kristin, it's Nathan. I wanted to tell you not to worry about this evening; you were perfect. I..." He searched word words. "I've discovered something strange about your grandfather's photos. It's a matter of the subway series, DSC00126, 138 and 144. I'd like to talk to you about them as soon as possible. If you can come by any time tomorrow, that would be fine. I can't tell you anything without more inf..."

He heard a beep and was unable to conclude the message. He cut the connection and looked at the photo through the magnifying glass again.

No, he wasn't mistaken. And yet...

He needed to go to bed, to rest and relieve the stress that had been governing his life for days. Sleep would doubtless flee him, but he could not get any further forward tonight, so he might as well get a little rest. Perhaps the night would bring counsel...

The door of the back room grated...

He raised his head and perceived two men. He did not have time to be frightened, or to ask them why they were there. One of the visitors aimed a pistol at his head and pulled the trigger. A detonation rang out.

The bullet went through the photographer's forehead, smashing his skull. He did not suffer, and died instantly.

Methodically, the gunman pressed the trigger a second time. This time, he aimed at the heart, to finish the job.

"Good," said the second man., looking at the corpse at his feet. "The way's clear. Go tell the others, and tell them to take everything. *Everything*, you understand!"

As the other obeyed, he advanced to the desk, and picked up the mobile phone placed on the table. He displayed the history of recent calls.

Kristin Arroyo. The second name on the contract.

"Good," he repeated, to himself. "Tomorrow, we go to the park. We really need to get a little air."

Chapter 11

Manhattan, Zuccotti Park, 17 November.

Solely accompanied by the chords of the guitar, the refrain of Bob Dylan's *The Times They Are A-Changin'* rose up in the park, but neither the words nor the music could chase away the electric tension that reigned between the demonstrators and the forces of order. In the wan morning light, the two camps watched one another like china dogs, ready to leap at one another.

The day before, on the pretext of sanitary reasons, the authorities had demanded that the Movement quit the location—a departure refused unanimously by Occupy Wall Street. Henceforth, it was only a question of hours before the police made their move and dislodged the demonstrators. Before the day's end, Kristin and her fellows would have to abandon Zuccotti Park, but they would find other places and other means to continue the struggle.

Kristin thought again about the evening. She would have liked to go and apologize to Nathan, but it was impossible to leave her comrades for the moment; it would have resembled a desertion. Too bad—she would see the photographer later.

Sitting on a low wall, the young woman listened to Thomas Goodman. The young Canadian was singing the Bob Dylan classic in a soft voice, while his fingers strummed the guitar. Like the other protesters, he was using passive strength to signify his opposition.

Kristin was in no doubt regarding the sequence of events. They were not in any position to resist, and had no wish, above all, to resort to violence. Nevertheless, they did not intend to depart without an honorable fight. The media, knowing that full well, were awaiting the impending confrontation impatiently. On the edge of the park, the journalists were equipped, mikes in hand and cameras shouldered, ready to interview the actors in both camps.

They would have value for their money...

Kristin was ready for the confrontation. She had brought a bottle of water to moisten her handkerchief when the tear gas fell on them.

"Kristin!" called a voice.

The young woman turned round and saw James Lovett, a retired teacher, coming toward her, his expression anxious.

"Two men are looking for you," he said, when he reached her.

"My photographer friend?" Nathan Stewart was now a familiar face among the demonstrators.

"No, two men in loud clothes, thirtyish, arrogant, sure of themselves. Not jokers, in my opinion. They had a package to give you."

Two men with a package...who could they be? She thought, strangely, about Michael Pear, but she could not imagine a businessman taking unconsidered risks and coming to find her in the park on the day when the police were going to evacuate it—unless he had sent two hirelings to apologize on his behalf, with a gift.

An offer to put you in films, old girl, she thought.

"Police?" Kristin suggested, frowning.

The professor burst out laughing. "I don't think so...although they're just as sympathetic. I sent them in the other direction and came to warn you, just in case. In view of the park's dimensions, though, they won't take long to come this way..."

"You're right," said Kristin. "Thanks for your help."

"Those fellows come from little Italy," the professor went on. "They have the local accent."

"Italians?"

"To judge by their gold chains, their accent and their insolence, one would say yes—perhaps the Mafia wants to support our conflict," said James, laughing.

"I can't imagine associating the Mafia with us," she retorted, seriously.

Her interlocutor raised his arms in a gesture of appeasement. "I was joking. At any rate, the fellows might be all right. Perhaps I've just been watching too much *Sopranos*."

Kristin smiled, thinking about the TV series. But her smile vanished quickly when a voice became audible, amplified by a megaphone. A policeman. She pricked up her ears, and succeeded in making out a few words and fragmentary phrases: *leave...reasonable...no violence...*

An ultimatum.

Faithful to their habit, the police were taking the side of the law and the powerful in order to justify the use of violence, although they were obeying orders, quite simply, as they had done for years, without asking questions. For a moment, she was tempted to go and talk to them, but it would serve no purpose; they would not listen.

Anyway, it was no longer a time for talk, but for resistance, and the equation was simple: on one side, the police, on the other, the demonstrators, as in the time of the Vietnam War or the battle or civil rights. Nothing had changed, whatever Dylan's song said.

In response to the police presence, cries of protest and insults rose up throughout the park. Nearby, the professor had taken advantage of the opportunity to disappear. The young woman let herself down from the wall. Things were about to get serious. She put the two men who were looking for her out of her mind and turned to the singer.

"Hide your guitar, Thomas," she said, "or it'll end up in pieces. You can pick it up later."

"My guitar will be my weapon," he replied. "As Woody Guthrie said, 'This machine kills fascists.'"

Kristin smiled. The young Canadian lit too many fuses for his own good. Nevertheless, she could not help sympathizing with him. The policemen were massed, ready to strike. Fortunately for the demonstrators, they had to bear in mind the presence of the TV cameras. The New York Police might not survive another scandal.

On the far side of the park, three dull sounds were heard, and immediately, gray smoke rose up in the pathways, emitting the characteristic odor of tear gas.

Kristin took the kerchief that she was wearing around her neck and soaked it with the contents of the water bottle she had placed on the wall. Then, anticipating the situation to come, she plastered it over her face. On her advice, the singer did likewise.

The police were trying to asphyxiate them in order to constrain them to leave the place rapidly, thus avoiding a hand-to-hand struggle and the bad publicity that would come with it.

On impulse, Kristin headed toward the upper section of the park, where the confrontation had commenced, and where she could employ her know-how. Around her, screams, insults and universal coughing responded to the exploding grenades.

Compared to Central Park, Manhattan's veritable lung, Zuccotti Park was minuscule. Its evacuation would not take long.

Obedient to orders, the police invested the park. In a military manner, they quartered the place, destroying the tents, pushing over the caddies—a derisory barricade before the concert of deployed force.

The first arrests were effected by force, protected from the cameras by the smoke. Following a few well-placed baton-thrusts, militants were thrown to the ground—on the grass or the gravel, it did not matter—and then handcuffed and hustled away militarily to the cars provided for that purpose.

Kristin could not do anything for them.

Suddenly, a policeman appeared in front of her, like some monster surging from the fog. He raised his baton.

The young woman stepped sideways, too rapidly for the policeman. She grabbed his arm and twisted it, just enough to avoid breaking it and to oblige him to drop his weapon, which she sent flying with a kick. Then, with an adroit trip, she threw the man to the ground.

She turned round and evaded the attack of another policeman, who had come to lend his colleague a hand. This time, she did not try to disarm him. Well-trained, the man was expecting the maneuver, and she would no longer benefit from the effect of surprise.

She dropped back a few yards, in order to gain time.

Her heel collided with a metal tube—the foot of a chair. She picked it up and hurled it into her adversary's face; then she took advantage of the distraction and the smoke to flee.

All around her, the chaos was general. With her improvised gas mask over her nose, she knew that she could not hold out for long. The fumes, or a policeman, would reckon with her. Nevertheless, she continued: an honorable gesture, for form's sake.

She progressed through the fog, avoiding a group of policemen dragging demonstrators unceremoniously toward the vehicles stationed on the edge of the park. She would join them soon enough. She was heading for the center of the park, which had become a veritable Alamo for Occupy Wall Street, when she found two men in front of her: the ones the teacher had warned her about a few minutes earlier. She recognized them easily; they had to be the only men in the park wearing suits and ties. Holding handkerchiefs over their mouths they were looking in all directions.

Each of them was holding a pistol in his hand.

Chapter 12

Manhattan, Zuccotti Park, 17 November.

Kristin did not react for a second or two.

For the moment, the men had not seen her. Not yet...

What could two armed civilians want with her in the midst of that chaos of smoke, noise and violence? Above all, who were they? Agents provocateurs paid by Wall Street bankers or instruments of Big Capital? The history of the U.S.A, was replete with men of that kind, who had broken strikes or murdered inconvenient individuals for money.

Another explanation crossed her mind: perhaps they had bought out their weapons to protect themselves from the chaos around them—but she dispelled that idea immediately. They had asked to see her. Why? Why not one of the Movement's thinkers?

She retreated, shielded by the smoke, trying not to be noticed.

Why her? The question occupied her entire mind. She hid behind a tree. It was absolutely necessary for her to know what she was dealing with. The exhibition! She could not see any other reason. In being put forward in that fashion, she would become a symbol. Her future celebrity had been to the taste of some people, and they were taking steps in consequence.

But the hypothesis did not hold water. Members of the secret service would never have intervened, clad in suits and ties, in the heart of a demonstration filmed by dozens of cameras, as plain as the nose on a face.

She could not stay there. She darted a glance around the tree. The two men were marching in her direction, and would discover her in a matter of seconds.

An end to reflection; she had to act, and escape.

Without any abrupt movement, she frayed a passage through the smoke. She went around a second group of policemen occupied in taking away a few demonstrators. The air was increasingly unbreathable. She hid behind another tree and waited for everyone to draw away.

She was ready to move when an appeal went up to her left.

"Kristin, help!"

She raised her head and vaguely made out Thomas at grips with two policemen. They had not held back; the guitarist's face was already showing several bruises.

Even in this situation, with killers on her heels, she could not abandon him. She headed toward the trio.

Suddenly, she heard a gunshot. Close at hand, the tree-trunk exploded, at the very place where she had been standing a second before.

"There she is!"

She turned around. The two men in beige raced toward her, heads down and weapons raised. From their position, they could not see the policemen—or did not care about them.

In the general din, the shot had passed unperceived. She turned round again and saw the two policemen carrying her friend way toward the edge of the park. He was complicating their task by writhing in all directions.

Kristin reacted instantly. Her military reflexes took over. As a second shot rang out she dived behind a low wall, knowing that it would not protect her for long. She hoped that the policemen might notice the two armed men and react in consequence.

But the situation got worse. One of the policemen retaining her friend observed her presence. He judged, visibly, that she represented a threat to them—in which he was not mistaken—and threw a tear gas grenade in her direction.

The young woman gauged the trajectory of the projectile and, contrary to what her instinct told her, headed toward its point of impact. It fell a yard away from her, already releasing a plume of smoke. Kristin picked it up and threw it, without delay, at the foot of the tree behind which she had been standing a few moments earlier...at the very moment when the two killer emerged.

Taken by surprise, they protected their eyes with their arms—a futile gesture—coughing as if to rip their throats, but not letting go of their weapons for so little.

She had to find a solution, and quickly. Without a gun, she could not confront them. She had to get away. But how? She would never get through the net of the forces of order. Police trucks were circling the park, not to mention the dozens of TV cameras. Even a former soldier could not become invisible.

But that might be her means of salvation.

She made her decision.

She ran toward the policeman who had just thrown a grenade in her direction, howling with all her might. She crashed into him full tilt without him having time to react. They both fell into a heap of dead leaves. Although she could have got the upper hand she no longer defended herself, and allowed her adversary to pin her to the ground.

In less than ten seconds, the two policemen lifted her up brutally, dragging her by the hair. There again she did not react. They grabbed hold of her and handcuffed her. Then they carried her away, along with the unconscious guitarist, to one of the cars stoned on the edge of her park.

She swallowed her anger and her shame—her plan had worked marvelously—and looked back at the bench where she had hidden a few moments before.

The two men in beige were looking at her impotently.

Chapter 13

Manhattan, 18 November.

The next morning, the authorities released the demonstrators in small groups; only the Movement's ringleaders were held.

That was why, after a night hidden from view, Kristin found herself on the steps of the police station, in the company of five other demonstrators, with a formal instruction from the chief of police not to set foot in Zuccotti Park again. Ironic smiles and a salute from Thomas Goodman replied to him. Somewhat debilitated, the young Canadian had lost his guitar the day before, a policeman having smashed it against a tree.

They all had drawn features, fatigued by their night in the holding cells and what had followed. The policemen had taken them one at a time into a small room where they had collected their names, their fingerprints and their statements, not without reading them their rights beforehand.

In order to reinvigorate themselves, the young people bought a coffee, which they drank on the move. They went to Washington Square, where other Occupy Wall Street members were already waiting for them. A few had bought the daily papers, where they appeared on page one. No one could ignore them now.

On TV screens, images of their confrontation were on a loop, drawing a wave of sympathy in their regard. The Movement's Facebook page was registering tens of thousands of "likes," coming from all over the world. The demonstrators could be proud; they had succeeded in turning the abandonment of the park into a media victory.

In the midst of the excited discussions, Kristin remained mute, holding back slightly, the events of the day before still going through her mind. She glanced rapidly at the pictures in the newspapers that were being passed from hand to hand, but saw no trace of the two men who had tried to kill her.

"What do you think?" Thomas asked.

Lost in her preoccupations, the young woman had not listened to a single word of the conversation, so she contented herself with a frown, giving herself time to find an appropriate response.

"I'm all at sea," she confided, regretfully. "I think I need rest and a good shower before making any decision." She looked around. "I don't think I'm alone in that..."

Several smiles told her that she was not wrong.

"I'm for a sauna too," Thomas replied. "I haven't slept all night and my throat is dry because of the tear gas. I'm dreaming of a nice little siesta."

"That's all very well," protested a young woman Kristin did not know. "But where are we going to meet up again? We no longer have an HQ."

"I'll post something on the Movement's Facebook page after my siesta," Thomas replied, more motivated than ever. "I'll find a place, however temporary, where we can gather."

No one had any objection to raise; some of them were almost asleep on their feet.

"Okay," Kristin concluded. "Until then!"

At the entrance to the subway, the young woman hesitated. On her guard, she decided to return home on foot. Her apartment was not very far away and she would feel safer in the crowded streets of New York than the poorly lit underground tunnels.

Throughout the journey she remained vigilant, walking in the middle of the sidewalk, looking in all directions, with the same question ever-present in her mind: why would the two men want to kill her? She was unaware of any enemy and could not see that anyone could have anything against her sufficient to try to kill her. It might be an error of some kind, but according to the professor, the two killers had asked for her by name.

She reviewed all hypotheses, even the most absurd. She even considered the trail of her former life in the military and the possibility that an Iraqi or an Afghan wanted revenge. But that hypothesis like all the rest, did not hold water. Who would seek to kill a simple soldier, at the bottom of the military hierarchy, or very nearly?

The young woman was losing her mind.

Having arrived outside her building, she greeted one of her neighbors coming out, and opened the entrance door. She ran up the steps, savoring in advance the refreshing caress of the shower on her body. She went into her apartment.

She swore.

Inside, everything was devastated; the shelves were hanging off the walls, the coffee-table had been smashed and the refrigerator door, ajar, appeared to have vomited forth all the food that it had been trying to keep fresh. In one corner, three paintings inherited from a distant cousin, of no great value apart from the sentimental, were lying on the floor, lacerated by a blade. The camera that Nathan had given her had disappeared.

The further the young woman went into the room the more her rage increased. She opened the rear door and revealed her bedroom, habitually tidy, as she had learned to do in the army, transformed into a veritable rubbish-top. The mattress had been disemboweled, the cupboards emptied, her clothes maltreated. She trembled with wrath, and thumped the wall. She wished that she could get her hands on the two men in beige, there and then—she was sure that they were behind the trashing of her apartment—in order to tell them what she thought.

Chagrined, she punched the wall a second time, and suddenly understood that there are certain wishes that one really ought not to want to see granted.

Angry, she had let down her guard. She went to the window and moved the curtain aside with one finger. Opposite the building, a man was using his phone, his eyes riveted in her direction.

Chapter 14

Manhattan, Little Italy, 18 November.

Joseph Carneglia attacked his plate of lasagna, prepared by the best cook in the neighborhood, voraciously. With three thrusts of the fork, he emptied half his plate. One again, Gino had worked wonders. As usual, the owner of the place had reserved him a room on the first floor, apart from the tourists who filled the ground floor—a favor for services rendered long ago.

Eating helped him to channel his wrath. The day before, his men had failed to carry out a simple mission: to kill a woman in the middle of a demonstration—ideal conditions; everyone would have thought it a police blunder.

He finished his plate and ordered another. He swilled his glass of Chianti without tasting it. Then he plunged his fork into the new helping of lasagna.

The first part of the mission that his father had confided to him had gone like clockwork. During the private view, one of his men had overheard a conversation that had confirmed that all the documents were still in the gallery. They had eliminated the photographer the same evening. His men had opened the grille, and then recovered all the material at a stroke and delivered it to the client—professional work. The next day, before going to the park, a crew had gone to the Hispanic woman's apartment in order to make sure that she had not hidden anything at home.

Then the mission had gone bad.

In the park, his men had given proof of a disappointing incompetence. For that, Joseph had to admit his part in the responsibility for the failure. He had acted in haste and chosen inexperienced men for the mission. In addition, he had revealed the identity of the two targets to them without having obtained preliminary information, and had thus committed a gross error that his father would not hesitate to throw in his face at the first opportunity.

When the men had returned to inform him of their failure, he had made a few inquiries. Who was the woman who had triumphed over his killers? How astonished he had been! The demonstrator was a former soldier, experienced in the best combat techniques.

The men had not been able to take advantage of the element of surprise, and he had no doubt that the young woman would arm herself once she was released by the police. And there was no question of terminating the work in a police station. The time was over when the members of Little Italy ruled the New York Police and were permitted to settle an account in the cells.

The Mafioso was seething with chagrin. He picked up the napkin from his lap, wiped his mouth and threw himself upon the tiramisu that had been mocking him since the start of the meal.

And to think that he was rendering this service gratuitously. When his father had come to see him to charge him with the mission, he had been strangely evasive, which was not like him. According to him, the honor of the Carneglia family was at stake. Those two people had to die, that was all...

After having hammered him with questions, Joe had succeeded in extracting a few details. It was a matter of an ancient debt that his father had contracted with regard to a woman. On the other hand, the old man had not wanted to reveal either the identity of the woman in question or the nature of the debt. It was impossible to unclench his teeth on that matter. He had thought then that it was only a postponement, that he would find out once the mission was accomplished...

And now the woman was still breathing, on the alert and doubtless with some desire for vengeance.

He finished his dessert and then extended his hand toward the bottle of red wine, but he changed his mind in favor of an Italian beer—a Moretti, ideal for the digestion.

Suddenly, his mobile buzzed on the table. After glancing at the number, he answered it. He listened attentively, and then replied in a curt tone:

"Don't move, understand? Don't try anything. I'll send a crew to join you right away. No initiative, or you'll have problems. *Capice*?"

He shut the lid of his phone and addressed a hand-signal to the waiter and the man who was waiting with him in a corner. He ordered an espresso—a real one, not American dishwater.

Then the mafioso leaned toward Charles Tobias, his faithful lieutenant.

"Go to the girl's domicile—she's there. Take Peter with you. Tony's waiting for you on the spot. I'm counting on you to finish the mission.

Chapter 15

Manhattan, Chelsea, 18 November.

Kristin swore. She had just walked straight into a trap. A former soldier should have known that her enemy would place a sentinel in case she were stupid enough to return home. A beginner's error. Now the man had called for reinforcements.

She had ten minutes before her, at the most.

She took her phone out of her bag in order to call the police, but changed her mind at the last moment. What could she tell the receptionist? "Someone's trying to kill me, but I don't have any proof I can give you." They surely wouldn't take disturb themselves. At the most, they'd send an ambulance. No, she could only count on herself.

And for the moment, the wisest decision was to decamp as quickly as possible.

She put the phone back in her bag. She opened the ventilation grid in the kitchen where her revolver as hidden: a souvenir of the army, which she had brought back on the quiet during a leave.

She uttered an oath. Naturally, her gun had disappeared.

Before leaving she ought to change—the killers in the park knew the color of her clothing. Returning to her bedroom, she opted for a gray hooded top and track-suit bottoms. Then she went into the kitchen and picked up a kitchen knife—a derisory weapon, but better than nothing.

She looked at her apartment one last time before leaving. The young woman went up the two flights of stairs that led to the roof at top speed and opened the door with a sharp kick. On the terrace she immediately headed for the external stairway at the rear of the building. She had never thought that she would have to make use of it one day, and yet...

She thanked her paranoia for having taken note of the emergency exit.

She ran down the old iron staircase in a metallic cacophony. Down below, a few pedestrians looked up and then continued on their way, not without shrugging their shoulders. After all, New York also harbored a few lunatics.

Having reached the last stairway, which ended a yard above the ground Kristin let herself drop in front of a man walking his dog.

She smiled at him and said: "Good day."

"Same to you," he relied, imperturbably.

Instead of leaving the neighborhood, Kristin chose to go around the building. Flight is not a good solution when you have no idea who is attacking you and why. If the young woman wanted to identify her mysterious enemy and understand his motives, she would not get a better chance.

At the corner of the building she leaned out toward the entrance, just sufficiently to see the man she had spotted earlier. He was not wearing a beige suit like the killers in the park, but he had same inexpressive features—a minor player in a Mafia movie. How had she not noticed him before? She was going soft...

The man seemed to be waiting for something or someone: reinforcements, for sure.

The young woman had to strike quickly, and hard.

She put her hood up and then headed toward her target. As in the park, the soldier in her took command again. She approached the man at an even pace, not rapid enough to alarm him.

A few meters from the entrance, she took out her keys as if she were about to go in.

The man did not see the attack coming. She struck him a curt blow just above the nose. The man collapsed, stunned.

Kristin leaned over him, grabbed him by the collar and lifted him up brutally. She pinned him against the wall and looked him straight in the eyes.

"Why do you want to kill me?" she demanded, in a harsh one—the same one she adopted for interrogating terrorists.

The man coughed; a trickle of blood ran from his nose.

"Why?" she repeated, more aggressively.

As the man opened his mouth, a vehicle drew up in front of the entrance. In the interior of the vehicle, she caught a rapid glimpse of two faces, one of which she knew. It was not one of the killers in the park, though. No, she had seen him before all that madness...

But she did not have the time to think any more about that detail.

Chapter 16

She kneed her prisoner violently in the testicles; he collapsed, mouth open, incapable of crying out; then she ran, heading downtown, in the direction contrary to the traffic.

She crossed Eighth Avenue, obliging a taxi to brake brutally. The driver sounded his horn and cursed her, but she paid no attention to him. Nothing else counted any longer for her except getting away, running, putting as much distance as possible between herself and her pursuers, and then finding an escape route.

Several people got out of her way. She ran, and darted a quick glance behind in order to analyze the situation. Her pursuer was also weaving between the pedestrians and the vehicles. He was running.

The young woman looked further back, at the foot of the building in which she lived. The car had disappeared. It was doubtless going around the block in order to come at her from the other direction.

The chase was on.

The former soldier accelerated her pace all the way to Twelfth Street without getting out of breath, and congratulated herself internally for having maintained her fitness since her resignation from the army. Rare individuals turned round as she passed, but the immense majority paid no attention to her, taking her for an imprudent jogger.

Her idea was to string out her pursuers by means of her physical resistance, changing street and avenue as often as possible.

Suddenly, as she had feared, the car turned the corner of the street and plunged toward her to try to run her down. It would pass for a simple traffic accident,

Kristin reacted immediately. She turned right into a street with two causeways separated by a row of trees planted on a raised meridian. Behind her, her pursuer swerved at the last movement and found himself—fortunately for her—on the other side

She did not profit from that advantage for long. No vehicle was coming in the opposite direction—a stroke of luck for her pursuer, who accelerated to draw level with her. As he slowed down Kristin saw the driver pass his weapon through the window and take aim at her. She heard a detonation, but the bullet missed her by a long way; driving and shooting simultaneously requires a great deal of training; few soldiers are capable of it.

In order to complicate her adversary's task further, Kristin zigzagged along the streets, as if between invisible plots. For a moment she thought of doubling back, but she did not know the location of the second man, the one on foot.

A second detonation rang out. A fragment of a tree exploded, scarcely two yards away. That was not far enough. His aim was getting dangerously closer.

She accelerated.

In front of her, fifty yards away, the row of trees came to an end, like a punch in the nose from destiny. Her adversary had also taken account of it. He braked and adjusted his speed in such a way as to be able to change lane and come out directly behind her.

Kristin felt the trap closing.

She had to react: counter-attack and take her enemy by surprise. Her mind was working at top speed.

The young woman stopped dead and picked up a small metal rubbish-bin abandoned on the sidewalk. She hurled it with all her might between two trees toward the vehicle, which was slowing down, the driver surely fearing that she was turning back.

The missile took the driver by surprise. Under the weight of the bin, the windshield shattered. The driver lost control of the vehicle, which crashed into a tree at low speed. It would not take long for the killer to pull himself together.

Hands on her knees, Kristin breathed deeply for a few seconds. She hesitated to head for the vehicle in order to neutralize the driver, but the latter was already getting out.

She turned round, in a military reflex. A hundred yards away, the second killer was running in her direction.

Kristin raised her head. Ten meters above the street was the High Line—an immense urban park of two square kilometers, prohibited to vehicles and accommodated on the tracks of the old elevated railway. That was why the trees stopped.

The young woman plunged toward the metallic staircase and ran up the steps four by four. Behind her, she heard the killer from the vehicle launching himself after her. In spite of a nascent stitch, she did not slow down.

When she reached the High Line she ran between the trees and flower-beds toward the crowd of tourists strolling in the haven of peace and greenery. That presence worked to her advantage. As she had seen in the park, the killers would hesitate to shoot her in front of witnesses, doubtless under orders from their superior, whoever he was.

A surge of anger rose within her as she thought again about how close she had come to learning for sure the identity of the killers and their motivation—a matter of seconds...

While running, Kristin looked back. The two men were a long way off, clearly visible in their beige garments. Both seemed to be having difficulty maintaining their speed. If she continued at this speed, she would string them out—but she did not do it.

On the contrary, she headed for a group of tourists.

She had decided to change strategy. Running away would serve no purpose. She has to find out who wanted her dead and why.

Thus camouflaged, she took out her knife and looked round in search of a place to set her trap. Finally, she plunged into a thicket.

Less than thirty seconds later, she perceived her pursuers. The first was pale, clutching his belly; the other, the driver of the car, was gasping like a grampus, scarcely in any better shape. They had both put away their weapons in order not to attract notice or start a panic. They were walking rather than running now. They exchanged a few words, which Kristin could not understand, and headed toward the exit—toward her position.

Still hidden, the young woman tensed her muscles. When the two men came alongside, she sprang out of the thicket like a jack-in-the-box.

As her sergeant had taught her in hand-to-hand fighting lessons, she stuck the first killer at the level of the thoracic cage, at the place where the last two ribs join in a V. Sunned, her adversary collapsed.

The second did not have time to react before she stuck her knife under his throat.

"Why are you trying to kill me?" she said, applying the knife to the carotid.

The man looked her in the eyes. Then he smiled.

"Help!" he howled. "Help!"

Chapter 17

Manhattan, Chelsea, 18 November.

Kristin was momentarily nonplussed. The killer had just turned the situation against her. Now, in the eyes of the passers-by, she was the one who represented the danger—the world upside down.

Sensing heroic virtues, an employee of the green spaces who was working a few yards away turned round and directed his jet of water in her direction, before fleeing when she raked him with her gaze.

Further away, a woman had already taken out her mobile phone and was tapping out a number, doubtless that of the police. The young man by her side—her son?—was filming the scene with his latest-generation smartphone

The former soldier swore loudly. She hit the killer above the nose and when he crumbled, she stole his wallet. Then, with her hood over her head, she resumed her course toward the exit stairway. She went down the steps at top speed.

Having reached the street she paused to look round. Nothing seemed suspect to her: no policemen, no men in beige.

She melted into the crowd and went up Ninth Avenue, her head full of questions, still without any answers. Nevertheless, one question surfaced above all the rest: what to do?

At first sight, alerting the police seemed the evident solution, especially as they would not take long to start looking for her for assault on the public highway. In a matter of minutes the police dispatched to the location would see the video the boy had filmed, where her face was clearly visible. From there, they would rapidly discover her identity—she was on file in military records—and her address. In a few hours, at the most, they would visit her ravaged apartment.

In the meantime, if she tried to explain, she would need to have evidence.

She took out her attacker's wallet and found inside a driving license and bank card in the name of Charles Tobias, thirty-six years old, born in New York, domiciled in Grand Street, in the vicinity of Little Italy. Then she thought of the flash of recognition she had experienced earlier, outside her building. She had seen that man before. But where?

It was not in the park; she could recall the faces of the first two killers distinctly, and neither was his.

No, it was before then...before the demonstration...

Suddenly, it clicked.

During the exhibition!

It was the visitor who had interrupted her argument with Michael Pear during the private view and had looked at the photo of Marilyn posing in front of the rocket. When the millionaire had abused him, the man had gone away without a word of apology, like a thief.

She threw the wallet into a rubbish bin; the name and address were imprinted in her memory.

First, she had to go see Nathan, to ask him whether he knew the man, and only then would she go to the police. She therefore headed for the gallery, while continuing to survey the surroundings.

She stopped in front of a street-vendor selling tourist items and bought a Yankees cap, which she pulled well down on her head. Perhaps it was an unnecessary precaution; by the time the police discovered her identity and started searching for her, she would be facing them...but one never knew...

Her heartbeat resumed its normal rhythm. He brain continued to work at top speed. For her, the hardest thug to bear was not knowing why the men wanted to kill her.

Twice she had escaped them, but luck would not always save her, and her attackers would surely not make the same mistakes again. The next time, they would come in larger numbers and better armed.

During the journey she racked her brains trying to figure out who might have something against her, but in vain.

Finally, she reached Hell's Kitchen. In front of the gallery, she stepped back. No luck! The shutter was lowered, an indication that the photographer was out. She was turning round, grumbling, when she noticed that the grille was slightly open. Strange...

She knelt down and perceived that the gallery door behind it was also unlocked,

Kristin had a sudden presentiment. The photographer never forgot to close his gallery. She raised the grille without difficulty and went inside.

The room was empty. There were no longer any photos on the walls; the entire exhibition had disappeared.

For several seconds, the young woman remained motionless, wondering what could have happened. Then she went to the back room, and stopped on the threshold.

Stretched out face down at the foot of his armchair, Nathan Stewart was lying in his own blood, dead.

Chapter 18

Manhattan, Chelsea, 18 November.

Kristin closed her eyes. She felt empty. Mechanically, like a robot, she went through the motions as she had been taught. She knelt down and gripped the wrist of the man on the floor. Nothing. Then she turned the body over and identified two bullet wounds: on in the heart, the other in the head. He killers had not given the victim any chance. The victim...

Nathan, the man she had been hanging out with for months, had become a true friend, one of the only ones she had, in fact, in the city. And the man had been executed.

The young woman wiped away a tear. In the army, she had become used to seeing people she liked die. But they had known the risks; they had had the means to defend themselves.

At that moment, Kristin realized that she had got mixed up in a dirty business—a deadly business. In her mind, Nathan's murder and the events of recent hours were linked, even if she did not know how.

Once again, time was against her. She had to make a decision, and quickly. She could not stay in the gallery. She had no doubt that this whole story was connected with the exhibition, but she would think about that later.

There was no sense now in alerting the police. They would not believe her; they might accuse her of having killed Nathan. They would have no difficulty finding a motive—sex or money, there was no lack of them, not to mention their altercation. Furthermore, she had just attacked a man in front of numerous witnesses. Nor would her military past work in her favor; she knew how to handle firearms. She could easily imagine the consequences; they would send her to a women's prison, Rikers Island or elsewhere...

For a moment, she was tempted to wait for the killers in order to put an end to it once and for all. The death would be easier.

Kristin rejected that idea, unworthy of her, unworthy of a soldier. She would fight.

She went through the gallery and cast a glance outside the partly-open door. The street was calm. Before leaving, though, she thought about the traces she might have left. Apart from Nathan's body she had not touched anything. In any case, there was nothing to touch; the killers had taken everything with them. Fingerprints didn't matter; she had the alibi of her private view.

With regard to the gallery's video cameras, Nathan had never connected them up, counting on their deterrent effect. As for others in the street or elsewhere, she had her hood and cap to hide her face.

She left without anyone paying any attention to her and headed in the direction of the Hudson. It was necessary to find shelter, somewhere that neither the police nor the killers would think of coming to look for her. That meant keeping clear of all the places she had frequented—they were not very numerous.

She walked instinctively, without any precise goal, in order to clear her head, in order not to think of her friend's corpse lying on the floor.

On the way, the stopped at an ATM and took out some money. She needed to take advantage while she could, while the police were not yet searching for her.

Further along, she bought a coffee and a hot dog from a street-vendor. She needed to restore her strength in order to think, and her stomach had been grumbling for some time. She let her steps take her to a park to where she had not gone for a long time.

Disappearing would pose no problem for her; she no longer had any family, no friends, no one to care about her. If she wanted, she could even leave the city and change her life. But it would be necessary to live while always looking over her shoulder. The killers were determined; they would not let go of her.

Kristin had to vanish. The dark corners of New York could accommodate her or a few days; time to take account of the course of events.

She arrived in front of the silhouette of the USS *Intrepid*, moored there for years. The aircraft carrier had served during the Second World War before becoming the masterpiece of the Intrepid Museum, which sheltered numerous aircraft, including a Concorde and a submarine.

She sat down on a bench and put her bag and her food down beside her. The odor of the ocean reached her. She breathed in deeply, and then burst into sobs. The young woman did not attempt to hold back her tears, and abandoned herself entirely to the grief of the loss of her friend. When her chagrin dried up, she started eating.

Before disappearing, there was one last thing to do. She took her smartphone out of her bag in order to destroy it, but as a thought occurred to her, she switched it on. It charged for a few seconds and then posted a familiar logo.

One message.

Her heart skipped a beat.

Nathan.

Chapter 19

"Kristin, it's Nathan. I wanted to tell you not to worry about this evening; you were perfect. I..." A pause. "I've discovered something strange about your grandfather's photos. It's a matter of the subway series, DSC00126, 138 and 144. I'd like to talk to you about them as soon as possible. If you can come by any time tomorrow, that would be fine. I can't tell you anything without more inf..."

The responder had cut him off before the end.

Kristin listened to the message twice before putting the telephone down. She rummaged in her bag and found the USB key that Nathan had confided to her. What had Nathan discovered, then, that justified him phoning her at two o'clock in the morning? Had that discovery any connection with the killers?

The affair was getting worse. Never, even in her craziest hypotheses, had she imagined that the killers had their eyes on the photographs—especially the ones that belonged henceforth to the Foundation.

Michael's face floated into her mind. For a moment she was tempted to call him, but she renounced the idea. One person involved in the affair was already dead; there was no point in extending the list.

Without thinking about it, she finished the hot dog and the coffee, both cold. She had to undertake the investigation alone. But first, she had to create a void around her.

To begin with, she seized her smartphone, and after removing the SIM card, threw it into a rubbish-bin with the hot dog wrapper. Then she headed for Forty-second Street. She went in search of a free access computer, where she could analyze the contents of the photos tranquilly. She found two of them in a small fast food outlet.

She bought a bottle of Coca Cola and a pretzel and installed herself in front of one of the two machines. She inserted the USB key cautiously. The computer, in its second or third youth, windmilled for a few seconds. Then she clicked on the file list, and searched for the first document identified by the photographer in his audio message and opened it.

It was the photograph of Marilyn posing in the subway. She studied it from all angles, but she could not find anything significant—nothing, at least, that could justify a murder. Behind the young actress, a man was reading a magazine, the lower half of his face hidden by the cover. It would not have taken much for Kristin to think that he was smiling, and mocking her.

She examined the other two photographs with no more success, apart from two or three details, they were similar, and doubtless belonged to the same sequence.

She loaded the first photograph again. What had Nathan seen there? Her instinct whispered to her that the answer was there, before her eyes...

The young woman swore in frustration. She would find out later. For the moment, she had to run.

She finished her cola and asked the owner if she could print the photographs. He replied that he did not have a printer but that a shop a little further along the street had the requisite equipment.

After a visit to the toilets, Kristin went to the shop indicated by the restaurateur, from which she emerged a few minutes later, her mission accomplished.

He marched at a rapid pace as far as the Port Authority Terminal. Situated alongside Times Square, the great New York bus station saw dozens of buses coming and going every day to all the neighboring cities and some even further away. In the seventies the neighborhood had sheltered everything the city possessed of drugs and prostitutes, but the municipality had undertaken several clearance operations to expel that inconvenient fauna and replace it with hordes of tourists eager to stay in the vicinity of Times Square and he Broadway theaters.

Finally, she reached her destination: the headquarters of the *New York Times*. Three hundred and nineteen meters high, it possessed fifty-two floors and could be reckoned one of the largest buildings in the city. In front of the entrance was a long queue of yellow axis, and not many clients.

The man she was looking for could not be far away.

She examined the foot of the immense edifice. Then she perceived him, faithful to his post.

He was stretched out n a blanket on the bitumen, a novel in his hands, scornful of the crowd strolling by without a glance, a smile or a coin. Set beside him a piece of cardboard proclaimed: *I'm an old soldier with no right leg, no roof and no money.*

Kristin approached the man and slid a five dollar bill into the plastic cup provided for that purpose. Then man raised his head and smiled at her on perceiving her.

"You're not obliged," he told her. "You've already given me a lot of help."

At twenty-eight, Ian Fountain appeared at least twenty years older.

Kristin had appreciated having him under her orders in Afghanistan. Unlike some, he obeyed a woman as he would a man and had proved to be an excellent companion in arms. Following an accident, however—a mine—he had returned home two years before her, with one leg fewer. Afterwards, they had lost sight of one another.

Kristin had found him again entirely by chance, when she disembarked at Port Authority after having not renewed her contract. The old soldier had pretended not to recognize her at first, wounded in his pride—to beg in front of strangers is already difficult, while before someone whom you respect...

Then he had started talking, and had told her his story. On his return, the loss of his leg had made him bad-tempered. He had quarreled with everyone around him; his family first, then the administration, which did not pay him any salary, and finally with the veterans' associations. Since then, he had lived with a piece of cardboard for his sole company. Worse, he refused all aid, when she gave him a five-dollar bill.

The young woman sat down beside him, as she did from time to time. Several times, she had invited him to drink a beer or eat something at a corner restaurant, but he had never accepted. The detritus of misplaced pride.

They chatted about the situation of former brothers-in-arms before Kristin decided to get to the heart of the matter.

"I'm in the shit."

"Why are you giving me a bill then? Take it back."

"It's not a question of money. People are trying to kill me and I don't know why."

Ian put his book on the ground and looked at her. "And the police can't do anything for you?" he said, sarcastically.

"You've understood completely."

"And you really have no idea what they have against you?"

She grimaced. "I've got the shadow of an idea, but nothing more."

"In concrete terms, what do you need?"

"A place to hide in New York for a few days. I need to think, and clear this matter up."

Ian Fountain picked up his cane and got to his feet. Kristine imitated him.

"Will you help me?" she asked, in a voice that was more tremulous than she would have wished. Her nerves were giving way.

"Of course. Follow me—I know somewhere you'll be safe, a place where no one will look for you."

PART THREE

Chapter 20

Manhattan, Financial District, 19 November.

Michael watched the policemen leave his office, accompanied by his lawyer. He uttered a sigh of relief. The two men had bombarded him with questions, without the slightest smile, without letting him breathe. The millionaire did not like finding himself under the fire of insinuations, or having to justify the use of his time.

And it wasn't over. Now he had to reassure his employees, and explain to them that the policemen's visit did not concern the business, that it was purely a private matter in which the police wanted to consult him as a witness. Even then, the gossip would spread rapidly, very rapidly. In a matter of hours, all Manhattan would be talking about nothing else.

The day before, he had returned to Nathan's gallery. He wanted to see the photographer in order to get Kristin's telephone number out of him. The argument during the private view was still stuck in his throat and he wanted to see the young woman to discuss it face to face. What a surprise to find the police there!

But worse was to come; he had learned about the death of his old friend: a murder.

At first, under the shock, the millionaire had wanted to know the details of the affair right way, but the police had contented themselves with taking his name, address and telephone number, assuring him that they would call in at his office the following day to ask him a few questions. Prudently, Michael had asked his lawyer, John Wingfield, to be present.

And they had come. They had interrogated him regarding the nature of his relationship with Nathan, and also about the photographer's private life. As a precaution, he had mentioned that his chauffeur could give them the exact time at which he had left the gallery, and that his concierge could confirm that he had not budged all night. Michael had replied honestly; he hoped that the investigators would be able to put their hands on the guilty party.

Then they had interrogated him about Kristin. Did he know her? For how long? In his opinion, had she any quarrel with the photographer?

The questions had been asked in a detached one, but the millionaire had sensed the importance that the two policemen attached to them. For an unknown reason, they were searching for the young woman.

On the advice of his lawyer, Michel had not hidden anything from them. He suspected that he police were already informed of the altercation that he had had with the pretty activist, so he did not pass over it in silence. In speaking, he had the impression of betraying the young woman, of displeasing her a second time.

When he had finished, he asked the policemen without any great hope of obtaining a response, why they were interested in the militant. They replied that the surveillance camera of a shop situated a few yards from the galley had filmed the young woman leaving the scene of the crime on the same morning that the body had been discovered.

Before leaving, the two officers demanded that he inform them if Kristin Arroyo tried to make contact with him. The millionaire smiled and assured them of his intention to cooperate. And they had left.

Michael let himself fall into his armchair, his mind in turmoil. It was the first time that he had been confronted by a murder.

His life had always been perfectly measured. Having emerged from a prestigious university, he had begun his career in a large American bank where he had brought a great deal of money to the shareholders, and he had profited from that himself. Afterwards, he had decided to work for himself. He had handed in his resignation and set up his own company: a venture capital fund. He provided young enterprises with the money, connections and experience necessary for success.

For two years his company had flourished and launched a dozen enterprises, of which at least four had proved highly profitable. Clients were queuing at his door; files were piling up on his desk, awaiting a positive or negative response. He scarcely had to set foot in the office anymore; the youngsters he had hired were hungry for success and could keep the earnings flowing as well as he could, to the point that he only had to appear at the occasional conference or board meeting.

Professionally, everything had smiled upon him: not the slightest hitch or check. He could, if he wanted to, go and take advantage of the sun on some paradisal island and simply pocket the daily profits.

The millionaire possessed everything for which people hoped, and even more...but he was bored.

Certainly, his activity at the Monroe Foundation maintained his eternal passion and broke the daily monotony, but important discoveries like the unpublished photos by Kristin's grandfather were rare, and most of the time he had to content himself with tedious financial or administrative labor.

Michael thought about Kristin again. She was in the sights of the police, the prime suspect. Although he had only met her once, the millionaire could not imagine that she was capable of killing the photographer. When Nathan had introduced him to her, he could not help noticing the amity that linked them, like father and daughter.

The intercom emitted a little beep. He pressed a button and his secretary's voice resounded in the office. "Two people from the F.B.I. would like to talk to you."

"Shit!" Michael swore. "Send them in."

Chapter 21

Manhattan, Financial District, 19 November.

Michael struck the desk with his fist, a gesture untypical of him. Then he took a deep breath and got up to greet the F.B.I. agents, interrogating himself internally as to the possible reason for their visit. Receiving the F.B.I. and the New York police one after another would not help his reputation. For a moment, he was tempted to recall his lawyer, but did not do it. He was a big boy and could sort it out himself.

After a firm handshake the two men came into the office, their faces firm. They took out their badges.

"Special Agent Norman Dyers, and this is Special Agent Paul Beato."

They sprawled in the chairs he indicated to them. He took his place behind his desk, and took advantage of it to study the newcomers. Norman Dyers was tall and thin, the exact opposite of the other, who was short, bald and tubby.

"What can I do for you?" Michael asked, in a voice that he hoped was firm.

"You were at the *Two Rebels in New York* exhibition the night before last?" snapped Norman Dyers, looking him straight in the eye.

"Indeed," said Michel, without lowering his gaze. "I gave that information the two policemen who came to question me ten minutes ago. You can ask them for my statement. That will be quicker for everyone."

"Don't worry, we will," said Norman Dyers, dryly. "According to our files, you're also a member of the board of administration of the Marilyn Monroe Foundation."

It was not a question.

"That's true—for three years—but what has that to do with the case?"

The two F.B.I. agents exchanged a conspiratorial glance. Then Norman Dyers went on: "I can assume, then, that you know a great deal about Marilyn's life?"

Michael smiled, without warmth. Again, he could not see how his passion for the young woman was linked to Nathan's murder. The ways of the F.B.I., like those of the Lord, were impenetrable.

"You suppose correctly. Like all the members of the Foundation, I collect all the works—books, films, interview, photos—that concern the actress. But why ask that question?"

The F.B.I. agent replied, but not in the fashion he had hoped. "In your view, are the photos recently acquired by the Foundation, presently exhibited in the gallery, exceptional?"

Michael swallowed his saliva. Once again, he could not see where the agents were coming from. He had made an error in not requesting the presence of his lawyer, Nevertheless, for the moment, he would not have been of any utility. If the interrogation took a more personal turn, he could always turn to Wingfield then.

"All unpublished photos of Marilyn are. Now, as I told your colleagues..."

"They're not our colleagues," the other agent, the one named Paul Beato, interjected. "They're conducting their investigation and we're conducting ours. Act as if you hadn't met them."

Evidently, the F.B.I. and the New York Police were engaged in their habitual small war.

"All unpublished photographs take on an exceptional character. They permit us, little by little, to fill in the gaps in Marilyn's biography, or to mount exhibitions like the one taking place at this moment. I can only recommend that you go and see it..."

The two agents did not seem to care for the recommendation.

"Know that we're on your side," the agent went on. "We want to discover the murderer. If you don't want to cooperate, we can just as easily continue this conversation in our offices," Dyers relied, dryly. "Without a lawyer—the Patriot Act. Does that mean anything to you?"

Michael preferred to calm things down.

"Please excuse me. The victim was my friend; my nerves are on edge. What do you want to know?"

"Among the photos that you acquired, would you say that me were…let's see…remarkable?"

"What do you mean, *remarkable*?" asked Michael, frowning.

The two agents seemed to be beating around the bush, without daring to pose the question that was really important to them.

"That's what it's for you to tell us—you're the specialist," the other replied, dryly. "A detail. Something that intrigued you?"

Michael reflected for a few moments. Marilyn had been dead for fifty years. Although the actress had frequented the upper strata of American society and had unleashed a few scandals, nothing in her life necessitated two government agents taking action half a century afterwards…nothing, at last, that he knew about.

"You man compromising photographs?" Michael asked, emphasizing his words.

The agent put his elbows on the desk, as if to add gravity to his reply. "Of that genre, yes."

Michael paused before replying. He did not want his interlocutors to think that he was taking their enquiries lightly, and did not answer immediately.

"Frankly, I'd say no. Those photographs have a real interest to collectors, but it's a matter, for the most part, of posing in light clothing, as was Marilyn's habit. No known political individuals appears in the prints."

"May we see these photos, Mr. Pear?"

"Of course—but I'm astonished that you don't already have them in your possession. They're almost all displayed in the gallery…"

The two agents looked at one another, surprised.

Paul Beato broke the silence. "We thought the police had told you. All the photographs of Marilyn have been stolen, as well as all Nathan Stewart's equipment. That's why we're here."

This time, Michael was speechless. The photos had been stolen...

Now, he understood the reason for all the questions.

But the two agents did not give him time to assimilate the revelation. They had already resumed.

"Just now, Mr. Pear, you said that *almost* all the photos were displayed in the gallery. Should I conclude that the Foundation possesses others?"

"Yes, of course. Some photos taken at the same session would have been duplicated in the exhibition. If the Foundation gives me its consent, I can send them to you if you wish."

For the first time since the beginning of the interrogation, Agent Dyers smiled. "That's very kind of you, Mr. Pear. I have no doubt that the Foundation will make the right decision in that matter. Collaborating with us will make the agents of the I.R.S. less curious."

Michael definitely preferred it when the man was not smiling.

The two agents stood up and shook his hand. Dyers did not let go immediately.

"Don't forget, Mr. Pear, that we expect to receive all the photographs in your possession. The contrary would upset us deeply."

Then they left the office.

Trembling, Michael waited for a minute before doing likewise.

Chapter 22

Manhattan, Financial district, 19 November.

Michael left the building, after having explained the presence of the police and the F.B.I. to his employees. He had asked them to co-operate unreservedly with the two organizations. His company had nothing for which to reproach itself. His speech had convinced them and appeased them—at least, he hoped so.

Outside, he could not help looking to the right and left, to sure himself that no one as following him. His chauffeur, who was waiting for him, opened the door of his limousine. Michal told him to go to Grand Central Terminal, the New York railway station where he was due to met his brother in one of the best restaurants in New York, for their weekly meeting.

During the journey Michael stared through the vehicle's tinted windows without seeing anything. He wondered where the young woman with whom he had argued two days ago might have gone to ground. He thought about her more than he ought to have done.

The limousine pulled up in front of the station's imposing entrance, at the drop-off point.

"Come and fetch me in two hours," he told the driver.

"Yes sir," the other replied, impassively.

Michael got out of the car and slipped into the crowd penetrating into the immense building. He traversed the magnificently decorated corridors and emerged into a gigantic hall where a sonorous hubbub reigned. The millionaire did not linger there and descended to the basements, heading for the restaurant. A maître-d'hôtel greeted him and took him to a table, where his brother Daniel was already waiting. The two men embraced before sitting down.

"How are you?" his elder brother asked.

"Tough morning."

"Dow Jones down?" Daniel smiled, mockingly.

His brother had temporarily renounced his habit for civilian dress. Five years his elder, Daniel had embraced the Catholic faith at eighteen, and was now one of the directors of Fordham University, New York's Jesuit College. Unknown to Daniel, Michael made anonymous donations to the prestigious school every year and had even helped two of its students to start up businesses.

Entirely orientated toward others, Daniel had never judged his choice of a more egotistical career, and he was grateful for it.

Michael recounted his misadventures, from the discovery of the corpse the day before to the visit from the two F.B.I. gorillas. Faithful to his habit, Daniel let him talk, and he was only interrupted by a waitress who took their order.

"I didn't know that Marilyn still interested the authorities," said Daniel, pouring himself a glass of mineral water. He had selected white wine himself.

"Me neither. Although I can understand the police visit, the F.B.I.'s took me completely by surprise. Especially as the murder hardly seemed to interest them. They asked me questions about the photos, as if Nathan's death was obviously not their priority."

"Perhaps that's the case. You ought to find out more, quickly."

Michael shrugged his shoulders. He was not sure he understood what the affair was about. As he did not continue the discussion, his brother went on: "Just now, when you were talking about the interrogation to which the police subjected you, you said that they have a suspect?"

"Yes, a woman."

Michael told him about the exhibition mounted by his friend, and the episode at the private view. He concluded his monologue by evoking the altercation with Kristin, now the prime suspect in the photographer's murder.

"The police told you that she was seen at the scene of the crime?" his brother asked.

"Yes. According to them, they have a video that shows Kristin leaving the gallery after the murder."

"Kristin?" his brother queried, smiling.

As usual, his brother could read him like an open book. He didn't give him the pleasure of playing his game.

"According to them, she's disappeared. Apparently, they don't know where she is."

The waitress brought them their plates.

"What are you going to do now?" his brother asked, beginning to eat.

"Nothing. If I took my own advice, I'd leave for a spell in Europe. I need a vacation."

Daniel burst out laughing. "I don't think so—I know you too well. You're not going to let it drop so easily."

The remark at least had the merit of clearing his expression.

"With the police and the F.B.I. in the vicinity, I have everything to lose by getting involved."

"Well, well—my little brother, afraid? Would it be more terrible than confronting the sharks of Wall Street?"

Daniel was far too good at repartee for a priest. Michael did not reply, and tucked into his bloody steak. The restaurant was reputed for its fish and seafood, but the millionaire remained faithful to red meat, which he preferred to anything else.

Internally, his decision was irrevocable; he would contact Kristin, one way or another. She must also be affected by Nathan's death. The photographer had confided to him that he felt considerable amity for the young woman, and from what he had seen, it was mutual. He did not know yet how he would do it, but he would find a way.

They ate in silence for a few minutes before his brother spoke again. "Is this Kristin very pretty?"

The millionaire blushed. He felt sorry for the devotees who risked lying to his brother in the confessional.

Michael preferred to change the subject. "I've only been talking about myself since the start of the meal. What's new on your part?" he asked.

"I'm leaving next week for the Basque country," his brother replied, not duped by the maneuver. "I'm on the track of an unknown work that might have belonged to Ignatius Loyola."

"A lost manuscript? Go on, tell me about it!"

Chapter 23

Manhattan, Downtown, 20 November.

Kaplan set down the report that Norman Dyers had sent him on the walnut desk. As always the F.B.I. agent gave proof of clarity and conciseness—two qualities that he appreciated in men in his employ. Everything was reported meticulously, without flourishes.

Kaplan rubbed his eyes and directed them at the immense bay widow that occupied an entire section of the wall. From his office, situated on the fortieth floor of a Downtown building, he had an incomparable view over the Hudson and Brooklyn. The United Nations building rose up to his right. The man smiled as he imagined all those petty diplomats, thinking that they could pull the world's reins. If they knew...

A former general in the American army, Clyde Kaplan had commanded G.I.s in all the world's zones for thirty years. Then nine-eleven had come along. On that accursed day in 2001 the United States had entered into a war without end—and worse, without victory. Terrorism struck no matter whom, no matter where, including American soil, without warning. The former soldier had understood that the rules had changed; that war could not be won on the ground, with men, but with weapons of a new kind.

Clyde Kaplan had therefore taken retirement and had become an adviser to American firms that were hand-in-glove with the Pentagon. Day after day, his lobbying work had borne fruit, and his influence had grown incessantly, to the point that one day, his associates had appointed him to a senior position in the Iron Triangle.

Those who knew that name were not numerous. It was, in fact, a matter of a secret pressure group composed of military men, senior government officials and directors of multinationals linked to armaments and influential negotiators in the Senate of the House of Representatives. Their sole objective was to secure the grandeur of the United States, by all possible means: a grandeur increasingly compromised by emergent power like China and India—not to mention the old adversary Russia, which was donning the wolf-skin again and no longer hesitating to start a new Cold War to counteract the U.S.A.'s plans on the world stage, especially in the Middle East.

But the enemy was not only beyond the frontier.

During the Bush years, the power of the Iron Triangle had reached its apogee. It dictated politics, imposed its vision of the world. But since the end of his second mandate and the arrival of Obama, the leftists had taken over, marking the veritable decline of the American Empire at every level: economic, diplomatic and military.

To counter the Afro-American President, Clyde had devised the Tea Party movement, based on a return to true values: nationalism, economic liberalism, political and religious hatred. The Tea Party was his baby; he was the one who pulled its strings in the shadows, securing its finances, directing its electoral campaigns and launching new faces into the political arena.

But the electors, the Blacks and the Hispanics, had decided otherwise, and the Republican Party had been swept away in the last elections.

Clyde had not changed his strategy, however. It was often easier to be in opposition than in government. The midterm elections, in which the Republicans had been victorious, had proved him right.

Kaplan smiled. The Iron Triangle would not take long to get the upper hand again.

Nevertheless, there was something more urgent to attend to today. The report he had just read concerned a problem that went way back in time—a problem that he had thought settled long ago.

To think that it was a Hollywood actress—a whore!—who had thwarted their plans in the early sixties. With the death of Marilyn Monroe and the Kennedy brothers, the Iron Triangle thought it had closed the file. And now an old photograph, unearthed who knows where, might start everything up again. In that uncertainty, he had asked Dyers to take change of the affair, even though, with the theft of the photographs and the murder of the photographer, it might eventually be resolved of its own accord. Even in the contrary case, he might be able to derive some advantage from the situation, if he could just figure out how.

Clyde picked up the tablet from the desk and began to read an email. Behind his employers' back, Norman Dyers was presently following all the trails and closing them, one after another. Kaplan hoped that the agent would be discreet; the high-ups in the F.B.I., above all, had to be kept in the dark.

For the moment, three people seemed to be implicated.

The first was the millionaire Michael Pear. In his report, the agent told him that the rich businessman did not appear to know anything about the disorder that concerned them. How surprised he had been on opening a file on him. Unlike his fellows, the man did not seem to be dragging any murky secrets behind him: no problem with drugs, alcohol or women, not even a diversion of funds or an initiate's misdemeanors; nothing. His only known passion was his love for Marilyn, which had driven him to direct the Monroe Foundation. The ideal son-in-law.

Secondly, the murdered photographer. The police report concerning him was succinct: break-in, two bullets in the body, instant death. The policemen wrote that Nathan had been arrested several times for drunk and disorderly conduct or fiscal fraud, banalities with no connection with the subject. But the man had debts—his bank records indicated that he was in a delicate situation—and in order to mount his exhibition, he had been obliged to take out a loan—which he would never be able to repay...

Finally, there was Kristin Arroyo, the central person in the story, the one thanks to whom everything had happened, when she had put her hand on the photos bequeathed to her by her grandfather, an old photographer.

Kaplan opened the file. That was the kind of soldier he liked. Arroyo had honored her fatherland and had not hesitated to get her hands dirty, faithful to her superiors and to the flag. But the young woman had resigned—doubtless her Hispanic side. That was not the worst of it; she had betrayed all her engagements by joining the degenerates of Occupy Wall Street. If it had been up to him, he would have sent the army to clear them out and the problem would have been settled in a day.

The last forty-eight hours had shown that Arroyo had not lost her bite. After having survived an attack in the heart of the city she had completely disappeared from circulation.

After having got rid of the photographer, someone was now attempting to kill the young woman. Who was that mysterious group? That was what Dyers had to discover, as a matter of priority, and for that, he had to track down Arroyo—a good means of testing his capabilities.

Thus far, the F.B.I. agent had never let him down.

Chapter 24

Manhattan, The Subway, 21 November.

Kristin jumped as the train went by. The New York sub-way functioned seven days a week and twenty-four hours a day, except in exceptionally bad weather—hurricanes or floods. Useful for its customers, less so for those who found refuge in abandoned subterranean tunnels.

The young woman, although she had been able to sleep under bombardments in Iraq, had slept poorly for three nights. The infernal racket of the trains, as well as the questions that were whirling incessantly in her head, had prevented her from finding reparative slumber.

The only advantage was that she was safe. Given the screeching brakes of the subway trains, the suffocating heat reigning in the tunnels and the presence of rats, no one would come to look for her here.

After their encounter at the bus station, Ian Fountain had brought her to this ancient subway station, abandoned at the end of the Second World War because of safety problems, where he lived in company with other homeless individuals. It was situated at the end of line 6, near the Brooklyn Bridge terminus. From there, it was necessary to go along the tracks corroded by rust and urine, paying attention to trains heading in the opposite direction, in order to reach it.

Only the agents of the subway company were aware that the place still existed, and of the presence of the men and women who had taken refuge there. For the moment, they left them undisturbed, but in Ian's opinion, that would not last. The hunt for the homeless was one of the priorities of the new mayor, who wanted a city fit for its inhabitants and voters.

When Ian had introduced her to the regulars who lodged there, he had emphasized her former rank of lieutenant. The consequence surprised her; several of the homeless, who sported military tattoos, had taken her in their arms; she had even recognized two former soldiers who had been under her orders. Under tension, the young woman had held back the tears that only wanted to flow.

"Welcome to the realm of the mole-people of New York," said one of them, standing to attention before her.

"The mole-people?" she repeated

"That's what the media call us," Ian replied. "In the eighties, a thousand people were living in the subterranean networks underneath the city. I detest the name."

"Like this one."

"Even lower down, underneath the subway stations. The craziest rumor ran around about them. People said that they were cannibals."

"And now?"

"Now we mostly eat vegetables," the old soldier replied, smiling. "We're less numerous because of the hardening of the law, but we're still here."

"Are you all former soldiers?"

"No, we come from all horizons. Poverty unites us."

After two days spent in the place, Kristin was beginning to find the time hanging heavy. The appeal of clean air, and above all, that of action, became more and more pressing. Inactivity weighed upon her, but she bore her trouble patiently, conscious of the efforts that the one-legged man made to render her sojourn as agreeable as possible. Every evening, her friend brought her provisions bought with money she had given him—she had been forced to insist to get him to accept it. He had also procured her a new phone with a prepaid card

In addition, the young man did not take long to come back with the information that she had asked him to obtain.

Huddled in a corner with an old blanket, for want of being able to sleep, Kristin had spent the last two days thinking about the situation into which she had been plunged to the neck. Armed with a torch, the young woman had examined all the elements in her possession: the photos she had printed and the documents the former soldier had brought down to her along with food. She had confided the name and address of the mafioso who had attacked her on the High Line. Ian had affirmed that he would get on to it immediately. In spite of the good will of which he gave proof, however, the information reached her in droplets, and the research was advancing too slowly for her liking.

And while the impression of marking time had taken increasing possession of her, one of the homeless had given her a copy of the New York *Daily News*: the previous day's edition, which included a series of articles about Nathan's murder, including a tribute by Michel Pear: a long interview in which the millionaire insisted as much on the talent and passion that animated the photographer as on the kindness and good will of the man. The young woman finished reading the article with tears in her eyes. The businessman mentioned the exhibition devoted to Marilyn, of course—according to him, one of the best ever mounted, with its original angle. Finally— which surprised her—he expressed his desire to renew the dialogue with the members of Occupy Wall Street. He concluded the interview with an enigmatic remark in which he confided to the newspaper the difficulties he was experiencing in doing that, not being free in his movements, nor entirely certain of the best way of obtaining forgiveness.

After reading it three times, the young woman had a few suspicions; after eight, she was certain that the millionaire was addressing himself to her. He was seeking to make contact. For what motive? To "obtain forgiveness," as he put it, or for some more obscure reason? And why affirm that he was "not free in his movements?" Was he too being followed or threatened?

The young woman shook her head. The answers would not be long in coming. Earlier that day, she had asked Ian to learn more about Michael Pear and his routine. The homeless man had retorted that he could hardly see himself getting close to and keeping watch on the millionaire, alone and dressed as he was. However, it was feasible. He had kept in contact with a few former soldiers, and found one or two ready to assist in his task in return for a few bills.

Ian Fountain rejoined her in the early evening, later than usual. The young woman, who was anxious for him, was just about to set off in search of him. Not in the least stressed, the homeless man had sat down beside her and handed her a sandwich and a bottle of water.

"Good day?"

"It's not Bagdad," she replied, attacking her turkey sandwich, striped with two lettuce leaves. Do you have news of Pear?"

"Your millionaire buddy isn't just anyone."

"He's not my buddy, but go on."

"Nor have you chosen the ugliest…"

"The report, soldier!" snapped Kristin, with a smile that tempered her words.

"At your orders, Lieutenant," Ian replied. "The target runs an investment company, whose offices are in the financial district. He lives in a fancy duplex on the top floor with a concierge and a view of Central Park, nor far from the Plaza Hotel."

"Good. And?"

"Every morning he goes for a jog in Central Park. A limousine comes to pick him up at the park exit. No bodyguards, just a driver."

"When he's jogging does he run on his own?"

"Yes, but this morning he seemed preoccupied—on his guard."

"What does that mean?"

"He often looked round, as if he was expecting to be attacked. In my opinion, he's a little paranoid; we didn't notice anyone…except for his driver, who picked him up at the exit from the park."

"Which doesn't mean that he isn't being watched. The men looking for me are professionals."

"Perhaps you're right. This morning, as we didn't know his habits, we were concentrating on him, in order not to lose sight of him." He paused before continuing: "If you want, we can continue the surveillance for a few days, to verify it."

Kristin reflected for a few seconds. "No, time's not on my side."

"What are you going to do?"

"I'm going to talk to him in the park while he's running, by matching strides with him."

"It's too risky," said the amputee. "As you said, we don't know whether he's being followed. Furthermore, are you sure that he's in your camp—that he won't turn you in, the first chance he gets?"

She grimaced. This time, it was her former subordinate who had a point. On reading the article, she had sensed that the millionaire was trying to contact her, but she might be mistaken—or it might be on behalf of someone else, those who wanted her dead. She cogitated at top speed.

"The ideal thing would be to kidnap him and bring him here—or take him somewhere else," she added, seeing her friend's scowl, "in order to talk to him in complete security."

Ian Fountain emitted a soft whistle. "Kidnapping a millionaire—you don't hold back. I'll remind you that we're no longer in the army."

"That's true, but it's feasible even so, if we plan it well. Consider this...Michael Pear goes jogging, as he does every morning. Except, this time, his driver isn't waiting for him at the park exit, being ill, or late—I don't know yet how we'll do it. For our part, we hire a vehicle and..."

Chapter 25

Manhattan, Central Park, 22 November.

Michael overtook two women of about thirty, who made no secret of eyeing him from head to toe. In order not to encourage them, the millionaire lengthened his stride and accelerated. He heard laughter behind him.

New York was a city of unmarried women and Manhattan was their favorite hunting-ground. When younger, during his days as a hectic trader, he had gone on a regular basis to the local pick-up spots—bars, night-clubs, fashionable hang-outs—accumulating conquests of a night or a week. Afterwards, the company had taken up all is time. Then he had had recourse to call-girls; he had the means and it was the simple solution. A little more than a year ago he had ended up realizing that all the pleasure was artificial, and that he wanted a more profound relationship based on respect and confidence. For some months, he had been seeking a twin soul. Perhaps it was one of the two joggers?

Michael sighed. Today, he was not looking to pick anyone up.

Neither the police nor the F.B.I. had given him any news, and he had not tried to call them. Everything he knew about the investigation he learned from the press. The police were still looking for Kristin—officially, in order to question her—but she had vanished completely from the radar. Since the discussion with his brother, the murderer was unable to prevent himself thinking that she might have been subjected to the same fate as the photographer. Deep down, however, he wanted to believe that she was alive. He realized that, in spite of the ideological difference that had opposed them, he wanted to help her. So, the millionaire made the decision to find her and cast light on the affair—he owed Nathan that.

He had thrown several bottles into the sea to try to reach Kristin. He hoped that she would read his interviews in various newspapers, in print or on the web. Then, knowing that the police and the F.B.I. were on is back, he had conducted a few discreet enquiries. He had asked a member of the Foundation, on the pretext of researching the young woman's grandfather, to widen the investigation to the whole family. He had learned that her parents were dead and that she had no close relatives. Like him, she appeared to be a solitary individual.

He had then reflected, trying to put himself in her place. She was being sought by the police. She could leave New York, but that solution would not satisfy her. A soldier did not run away, she confronted the danger. But in what manner?

He looked at his watch—this was not a morning when he would equal his record—and headed for the exit from the park where his driver was waiting, at the intersection of the Avenue of the Americas and Central Park South.

This morning he was due to see three young entrepreneurs who wanted his financial support in order to launch themselves. For two of them he already knew that his response would be negative; they were not rigorous enough. For the third, he was still hesitating and would make his decision at the end of the meeting.

He slowed down to a tranquil walk and got his breath back. Lost in his thoughts, he paid no attention to the taxi that stopped two yards in front of him; he only noticed that the man who got out of it was missing a leg.

In order not to jostle him, he veered slightly to his left, toward the railings of the park.

He was still thinking about his schedule for the day when two arms grabbed him and pinned him to the railings. One of the bars bit into his cheek.

He felt panic rising within him.

He tried to turn round but the arms held him like a vice. He jabbed with his elbows and kicked, trying to free himself, but to no avail. Worse, another pair of hands grabbed him and pulled him toward the taxi.

He tried to cry out, to call for help, but he had thought of it too late. He found himself pinned down on the seat of the vehicle, which pulled away with its wheels screeching.

Suddenly, the pressure on his arms relaxed. Beside him, his assailant was breathing heavily.

Curious, the millionaire looked up. He shivered.

Kristin.

In spite of the situation, he was glad to see her again. Had she read his message?

He was about to speak when she placed a hand over his mouth and placed a finger over her own, to tell him to keep quiet.

Chapter 26

Manhattan, Central Park, 22 November.

Kristin darted a glance at the rear-view mirror. Outside, everything seemed calm.

Installed in the death seat, Ian checked the surroundings and guided the driver—a former soldier he had hired—toward a temporary hiding-place. Before anything else, it was necessary to make sure which camp Michael Pear was in.

Earlier, before going into action, Ian had been categorical: no one was watching the millionaire during his jog, except for the two young women who, in his words, "had eyed him with appetite." Even through her ear-flaps, Kirstin had perceived the homeless man's smile, trying to make her jealous. She had not given him the satisfaction of reacting.

Afterwards, everything had gone like clockwork. The abduction had taken less than ten seconds and had had to eye-witnesses. The first part of the plan was concluded, but the hardest part was still to come.

The young woman abandoned her surveillance, therefore, and leaned toward her victim, who was looking at her with eyes full of questions. She removed the hand from his mouth, and then lifted up his pullover and his shirt. Surprised at first, Michael let her do it, even though she was off-target.

Finally, she looked at him, satisfied. No wire, no mike.

"You can sit up quietly on the seat," Kristin said, helping him up.

The golden boy straightened up slowly, with no abrupt movements. For his part, the young woman installed herself more comfortably beside him.

"I don't have any mikes," he affirmed. "You have my word. I'm glad to see you."

"I suspected that you wanted to see me when I read your interview," she said, in a level tone. "Now tell me why you wanted to catch up with me."

"It might take a while," Michel replied. "The meter's ticking."

The young woman smiled.

"Go on—I have all the time in the world."

He told her about his frustrations of the last few days. He too had had a few misadventures, even if no one was trying to kill him. He told her about the visit of the New York Police, and then that of the F.B.I. Occasionally, Kristin interrupted him to demand greater precision on some point. So far as she could tell, her interlocutor seemed to be telling the truth.

"Did the F.B.I. ask questions about me?" she asked him.

"No, and I confess that that surprised me. Don't take it wrongly, but you're the prime suspect in this affair, but they didn't mention you at all. Bizarre, no? They only seemed to be interested in your grandfather's photographs."

"Right. And what did they want to know about them?"

When Michael told her that the F.B.I. had asked him whether the photographs seemed "remarkable" to him, the young woman was as surprised as he was. On the other hand, when he told her that he had handed them over to the feds, the news did not delight her, even though she understood that the millionaire had had no choice.

Nevertheless, his story corroborated what she had already discovered: many people were interested in her grandfather's photographs.

"Why did you want to contact me, then?" she asked. "All the evidence is against me?"

"I don't believe that for a moment. I can't see you killing Nathan, your friend. That's not you."

Kristin could not mask her surprise; that the millionaire had a cast-iron belief in her innocence touched her, genuinely. In order not to show her disturbance, she immediately resumed speaking, and told him her version of the facts: the two murder attempts, the discovery of Nathan's body and, finally, her decision to go into hiding.

"Do you have any idea who might want to kill you?"

"I have no idea why, but the only clue in my possession goes back to the Mafia killers. For the moment, I don't know any more..."

"Don't look any further," Ian Fountain put in. "Judging by what I've just heard, the F.B.I. seem to be behind it all. In any case, it's very much their kind of thing.

"Do you really believe that it was them who killed Nathan and tried to liquidate me?" said Kristin, frowning.

"I don't say that they're definitely behind it—to tell the truth, I don't know anything...just that it wouldn't astonish me. It wouldn't be the first time that the F.B.I. was implicated in some dirty business. Then again, they've confided the affair to the Mafia..."

"For my part, I think that, just like us, the F.B.I. stumbled upon the affair," Michael confessed, cautiously, not wanting to get the amputee's back up. "If not, the two agents wouldn't have come fishing for information. No, they're in the dark too. On the other hand, I can't think of an explanation for the presence of the Mafia in the affair."

"By the same token, what could a millionaire like you know?" countered the former soldier.

Michael darted a glance at the young woman, in quest of support. It was wasted effort; she was plunged in thought. For a minute, silence reigned in the vehicle.

"All this must have to do with the three photos," Kristin said, finally.

"What photos?" Michael asked, intrigued.

"The ones of Marilyn posing in the subway."

"I don't understand. Those photos aren't worth killing for."

"Actually," said the young woman, "I'm not so sure about that. Shortly before dying, Nathan left me a message about those photos, in which he said he wanted to see me as quickly as possible. He seemed excited..."

Kristin fell silent.

For his part, the driver continued moving through the avenues and streets of New York. It was now Michael's turn to lose himself in his thoughts.

"Do you have a copy of those photos?"

The young woman nodded.

"Can you give me copies? I can carry out research."

"How?"

"Once again, don't take it wrongly, but while you're in hiding, you're devoid of resources. For my part, I have access to all the equipment I need. I can make the photos talk quicker than you can. I'll keep you informed of anything I find, of course."

Kristin interrogated Ian with her gaze. The latter shrugged his shoulders to signify that it was her decision.

"Before giving you my consent," said Kristin, "I have a question. Why? I mean, why are you helping me?"

Michel sat up in his seat. "I knew Nathan for years. I liked him a lot. I too want to know who killed him and why."

Kristin suspected that the millionaire was not saying everything, but the response was sufficient, for the moment.

"All right," she said, taking the USB key that Nathan had given her out of her pocket. "I trust you. You'll find the three photos identified by Nathan on this."

Michael took the key and put it in his wallet.

"If you want to meet me, go to Manhattan and mention my name to one of the former soldiers who are begging there. They're numerous, and easy to identify. They'll all be wearing similar tattoos: military emblems."

As her interlocutor nodded his head to show that he understood, she went on: "After that, it's me who'll make contact with you."

The car stopped two streets away from the millionaire's apartment. Surprised not to have seen it coming, Michael got out of the vehicle. Kristin darted one last glance at him.

"Look after yourself."

Then the taxi pulled away, rapidly.

Ian turned to her. "Do you think you can trust him?"

"I don't have any choice. He's the only one who can help me."

"Do you want him watched. You're taking a big risk giving him that USB key."

"It's a copy. The original is still in my pocket."

The one-legged man smiled. "I see that amour hasn't caused you to lose your head. Do you want him followed?"

The young woman reflected for a few seconds.

"Not worth the trouble. I need you for another kidnapping."

PART FOUR

Chapter 27

Brooklyn, 23 November.

While heading at a rapid stride for the residence of his friend Tyler Hoffman, Michael turned up the collar of his trench-coat. It was drizzling, and the icy November wind was penetrating everywhere. He had told his chauffeur to drop him a hundred yards in order to think. The day before, his discussion with Kristin had reinforced his determination to get to the bottom of the affair—for Nathan, of course, but also for the young woman. She attracted him. Having previously always sought out superficial women, he was now involved in covert dealings with a rebel who did not care about his money or his position. In the taxi, she had impressed him with her personality and her courage. He had quit her with regret, but resolute.

After their encounter he had one to see his old university acquaintance Tyler Hoffman, a real geek who only lived for IT. The two men had known one another since college and knew that they could count on one another.

At the beginning of his career, when Michael had been working for the bank, he had asked his old friend to make several important files secure. Several promising careers had sunk because of simple piracy. Tyler had responded to all his requests and had helped him climb the ladder by protecting his back. The day before, when Kristin had given him the USB key, he had thought of him immediately. He had taken his friend into his confidence and had asked him to analyze the three photos taken in the subway. Michael had gone to him rather than the information service at the Foundation in case the F.B.I. came to seize material from the building. Tyler had promised him to be exceptionally prudent before going out to begin his research.

Twelve hours later the millionaire arrived at his friend's domicile. After announcing himself via intercom, he was admitted into the building, where Tyler had not been living for long, and called the elevator. His friend welcomed him when the door opened, clad in old jeans and a ragged T-shirt. It was not his apartment—a real lumber-room in which a multitude of screen competed for space with piles of take-away cartons—that permitted a struggle against the geek cliché.

On a giant screen enlargements of the photos that he had confided to him were displayed. The computer expert looked at them, excitedly, got up and paced back and forth.

"I need two dates," he said, sitting down in his armchair. First, that of Marilyn's death."

Michael stared at him, surprised. With Google as his friend, the computer man obviously knew the answer to the question and was simply trying to raise the tension—his tension. Nevertheless, he lent himself to the game.

"August fifth, 1962. The fiftieth anniversary of her death will be next year. She was thirty-six. But you don't need me to tell you all that, do you?"

"Good," replied the computer man, ignoring him superbly. "I also need the date of the first Moon landing, if you please?"

"July twenty-first, 1969."

"Almost seven years, to the day, after Marilyn's death?"

"You don't need a calculator for that."

Tyler Hoffman tapped the keyboard. The screen displayed the cover of *Life* magazine. It announced that men had walked on the Moon.

"The cover of a familiar magazine. So what? I don't see where you're going."

The computer man played with the mouse. The zoom focused on the face of the man reading the magazine, and then the woman posing in front of him, Marilyn.

The millionaire remained mute. It seemed to him that the Earth had opened up beneath his feet and that he was falling into a bottomless pit.

He shook his head several times.

"A trick," he murmured. "You're putting me on."

"I'd like to be, but no. As for the possibility that the photo has been doctored…you can imagine that I've checked that. I've put the photo through several programs I have. They're definite—the photo is authentic.

Michel was submerged by a flood of contradictory thoughts. His entire body was trembling. He strove to master the quiver.

What the computer man had revealed to him was impossible—and yet, he knew that it was true.

Suddenly, the events of recent days made sense: the questions of the two F.B.I. agents; Nathan's murder; the killers pursuing Kristin.

History had not unfurled as the textbooks affirmed.

At that thought, the millionaire felt his legs grow weak beneath him. He sat down on the floor. Next to him, Tyler got up, plucked a bottle of Jack Daniels out of his drinks cabinet and poured him a glass. Michel emptied it in a single gulp.

"Impossible, it's impossible. She died in August 1962."

He held his glass out to his friend, who filled it again.

"You're the specialist. I've done my bit." The computer man fell silent and began to drink in small sips. On the part of the millionaire the tremors ceased after a few minutes. Michael wiped way the sweat that was running over his brow, and then took several deep breaths. Another hypothesis had just taken form in his head.

"A double?"

"Possibly. It would need an expert to determine it."

Before signing the check, the Foundation had already authenticated the photos, but perhaps in haste, Human error was always possible.

Michael had to go back there, in order to be sure.

"You don't say anything to anyone—and I mean anyone."

Tyler could not help laughing. "You really think that anyone sane would believe me, except for magazines that publish the testimony of fools who've seen Elvis with their own eyes?"

The millionaire did not laugh. Because he had had the misfortune to discover this, Nathan was dead.

"Tyler, listen to me carefully. People are looking for these photos. They're ready to do anything. They've already killed one person. So do as I say. Destroy all the files, all the impressions you've taken. Nothing must remain, not the slightest trace on your hard disks or in your brain. You've never seen these photos. Understood?"

The computer man nodded. "You have my word."

For a moment, the millionaire thought about offering him money for his silence, but he knew that his friend might take it the wrong way.

"All right."

Then Michael left.

Chapter 38

Manhattan, Little Italy, 23 November.

It was really him. Alone at his table, Charles Tobias was eating a piece of tart with unfeigned pleasure. The day before, Kristin had given his address to two mole-men, who had followed him all day, from his domicile to a restaurant on Mulberry Street. According to their report, the man had spent his time going in and out of local shops accompanied by two gorillas.

Now, he was finally alone.

Kristin did not spend any more time pretending to look at the menu, for fear that her target might end up noticing her. Clad in an enormous jacket that hid her face, she turned her back on the window and crossed the street in the direction of her homeless friend and he two ex-soldiers recruited as reinforcements. The young woman looked around.

On the sidewalks, the rare pedestrians were hurrying home. The glacial wind discouraged the tourists from going out, to such an extent that the usual restaurant touts were conspicuous by their absence. Nor was there any policeman in sight.

She had to decide quickly. Ian was right; abducting someone in the heart of Manhattan was risky. But such an opportunity—few witnesses, favorable terrain—might not recur soon.

She decided to attempt the coup. Her plan was simple: to take the man by surprise, knock him out and shove him into the taxi—the same one that had embarked Michael—all in less than a minute. If all went well, with the wind, the snow and the darkness, no one would notice.

"It's go."

"At your orders," the one-legged man replied, before turning to the two waiting men. "Tom, warm up the taxi. Jack, you come with me. We'll each take one side of the restaurant."

Without a word, the man named Tom went back up the street to the parking lot where he had left the taxi.

"Let's hope that we won't have to wait too long," said Kristin, blowing on her hands to arm then, "or we'll freeze."

While the two men took up their positions to either side of the building, Kristin installed herself on the street corner, behind a bicycle stand, from which she could see the entrance to the restaurant but not the target. In order not to get cold she moved back and forth, jumping on the spot..

She waited five, ten, twenty minutes...

Still nothing. Perhaps the man had opted for a drink after his dessert. Or perhaps he was simply chatting to the owner.

In the street, the taxi went past twice, and then a third time.

The mafioso still did not emerge.

Did he suspect something? By stealing his wallet, had she given him reason to believe that she was preparing a counter-attack? If that was the case, nothing in the mafioso's attitude had given any sign that he was setting a trap for her.

The young woman was beginning to have serious doubts that their plan would succeed when Charles Tobias finally appeared on the threshold. Kristin froze.

The mafioso lit a cigarette before stepping on to the causeway. Without delay, she followed him. Further along the street, the headlights of a vehicle were shining.

The man was walking slowly, without haste. The former lieutenant followed him ten yards behind. In the darkness, she could only distinguish the man by the red glow of his cigarette.

On the other sidewalk, Jack saluted her discreetly with a hand gesture when she arrived level with him. Behind her, the click of a car door told her that Ian had returned to the warmth of the taxi. For the moment, everything was going as planned.

Thirty yards further on, after a succession of restaurants, the bulbs of two street-lamps had been broken earlier in the evening. She had to act now.

She made a sign to the taxi that was following her, and then accelerated and approached the Mafioso silently. The complicit snow covered the sound of her movements. As she drew level with him and prepared to strike the man at the base of the neck a couple emerged, laughing, from a Chinese restaurant and bumped into her.

Knocked off balance, Kristin only just succeeded in not falling over.

In front of her, Charles Tobias turned round, curiously.

He recognized her immediately, and slid his hand into his jacket.

Chapter 29

Grand Central Station, 23 November.

Michael pushed the door of the restaurant and looked in the direction of the table that he reserved every week for their "fraternal meal," as they called it. Daniel had not arrived yet. He decided to go into the toilet.

A waiter quit the place as he arrived. He installed himself in front of a free urinal. When he had finished he washed his hands. Two men appeared at that moment: the agents Paul Beato and Norman Dyers. They smiled. The former wedged the door to the toilets with his foot while the other planted himself in front of him.

Michael sighed. He had expected to see them again, but not here.

"I don't suppose you've come to relieve a pressing desire."

"Game over," snapped Dyers.

The millionaire tried to reply, but the F.B.I. agent did not give him the opportunity. He punched him in the stomach. Folded in two, Michael fell to his knees, and tried to get his breath back. No time: another punch, full in the face this time, sent him sprawling against a wall.

The golden boy uttered a moan like a wounded animal. Pain propagated throughout his body. Lying on the cold tiles, he touched his face. Blood.

Dyers leaned over him.

"We're in the very heart of New York; there are thousands of cops around us, and yet I could beat you up without the slightest problem. You can scream, but no one will come. All I have to do is show my F.B.I. card for us not to be disturbed. You're at my mercy.

Michel spat on the ground.

"Go to..."

He did not complete the phrase. A violent kick in the face made him see stars. Stunned, the millionaire tried to get up, but his head was spinning and he did not succeed.

Dyers seized him by the hair and forced in into a sitting position, with his back to the wall.

"Yesterday, two people dragged you into a taxi at Central Park and took you for a little ride. My question is simple: who was inside it?"

Michael did not reply immediately. His mouth was full. He had bitten his tongue. Nevertheless, he knew that remaining mute would not help him.

"How's that? You're satellites didn't tell you?"

He tensed himself, prepared to endure a further attack. In vain.

Dyers laughed briefly. "You want to play the hero? You can try, but I warn you—you'll talk."

The F.B.I. agent took out a mobile phone, which he placed before his eyes. "That's your brother, no?"

A sentiment of impotence swept over the millionaire. He knew what was coming next: a film scenario that he had already seen several times.

"Bastards!"

"Come on, didn't your parents teach you anything? Your brother, it seems, is in the process of sending a text. He's wondering why you're late. What he doesn't know—look carefully—is that the man next to him is holding a pistol under the table. You'll never guess who the barrel is aimed at..."

"Shitheaps!"

"You definitely don't seem to like me—that's a pity. I was going to give you ten seconds to say goodbye to your brother. If you don't answer my question correctly, he dies—is that clear? I won't repeat myself."

Michel was not up to it. He nurtured sentiments for Kristin Arroyo; he knew that, even if he had never formulated it clearly, but he could not let his brother die. Not like this.

"Kristin Arroyo."

The response appeared to surprise the F.B.I. agent, who looked him straight in the eye, as if to determine whether he was lying, even though his brother's life was at stake. For that thought, the millionaire detested his torturer even more.

"That Hispanic woman definitely has resources. What did she want?" Dyers asked.

"She wanted information about Nathan's death." The millionaire remained deliberately vague.

"You talked to her about our visit?" Dyers asked him, putting his foot on his hand.

Michael did not try to lie. "Yes, but she already knew about it." But he did not tell the truth either.

The two gents looked at one another.

"Where is she hiding?"

"I don't know. She has to contact me."

"Don't lie to me!" Dyers spat. "If you don't tell me, your brother dies."

Michael looked at his torturer. He was about to play with fire.

"I swear to you that I don't know. Kristin Arroyo is suspicious. She didn't tell me anything. She thought I'd killed the photographer. She abducted me in order to question me, but when I showed her that I had an alibi, she believed me. She thinks you're behind it all."

Dyers smiled malevolently. "And I suppose you didn't try to put her right?"

The millionaire shook his head. "No, I was too scared that she might kill me. I wanted her to leave me alone."

That story seemed to satisfy Dyers. "It's not Arroyo you ought to be scared of. For the moment, I'll spare you, and your brother. But you're going to do us a small favor. If Arroyo ever contacts you again, you warn us immediately."

Dyers took a card from the inside pocket of his jacket, which he threw in his face. "And don't forget, you're being watched, and we wouldn't like to have a third discussion with you, understood?"

Michael nodded his head. Dyers kicked him in the ribs again. "One last point. It's not worth the trouble of making a complaint or going to the cops. They can't do anything for you."

Dyers rejoined his companion, who was waiting tranquilly by the door.

"Give my regards to your brother," he said, with a smile, before leaving him alone.

Michael got up, awkwardly, pain radiating through his body. He staggered to the sink, opened the cold tap and plunged his head underneath it. The cold water made his wounds smart, and he gritted his teeth.

He had emerged from the conversation damaged, but alive—and even more important, so had Daniel. In choosing to get to the bottom of the affair, he had known that he was taking risks, but he had not imagined that his brother might suffer the consequences.

For a moment, he thought about letting it drop, but he recalled the pleasure the two agents had experienced in humiliating him. Gradually, anger replaced pain in his mind—a cold anger.

He had to contact Kristin as quickly as possible and tell her about that conversation, and also the discovery he had made earlier. Thinking about it, Dyers had not interrogated him about Tyler and the research he had asked him to carry out. If they had known about the photos, they would have demanded that he hand them over immediately.

The F.B.I. did not know everything, but that did not reassure hum much.

Michel plunged his head under the water again before drying himself off. The room was still spinning.

He staggered toward the door of the toilets, which he opened, with difficulty, and then headed for the table he had reserved, but collapsed before he got there.

Chapter 30

Manhattan, Little Italy, 24 November.

Kristin had not had time to react when Jack threw himself upon Charles Tobias, knife in hand. The two men fell to the ground.

At that moment, the taxi stopped level with them, with a screech of tires, Frightened, the couple—tourists—went back into the Chinese restaurant precipitately, shouting. It was necessary to work quickly; curious people would not take long to surge forth.

Kristin collected herself. She delivered a kick to the mafioso's hand, the one holding the weapon, then bent down and grabbed her adversary by the jacket. Aided by Jack, she lifted him up and threw him into the taxi. Ian had just opened the door.

She got into the vehicle in her turn, which Jack got into the front. The taxi immediately pulled away.

"Shit!" exclaimed Ian, after lying Tobias down next to him.

He showed his bloody hand to Kristin. She opened Tobias' jacket to examine the wound. She grimaced. A large red stain was extending over the shirt. White-faced, the mafioso seemed to be experiencing great difficulty breathing. The blade had gone in near the heart.

Without rapid treatment, Tobias would not last very long.

"We need to drop him outside a hospital," her friend said.

"Not before he's talked," she snapped, determined.

For his part, Ian tapped Jack on the shoulder.

"Are you all right?"

"Nothing wrong with me," replied the former soldier. "I didn't want to hurt him."

"I know, said the one-legged man. "It was him or Kristin. You did well."

Kristin followed the conversation with one ear. She did not like what she was about to do, but she had no choice. She took the mafioso's face between her hands. The latter was declining visibly. She had to act fast.

"Who are you working for?"

The man uttered a groan, but did not reply.

"I know that you understand me. Someone hired you to kill me and I want to know his name. If you answer my question, we'll drop you off at the first hospital. If not, believe me, the pain you feel now will be nothing compared to what I'll do to you."

To support her words, she pressed on the wound. The mafioso screamed.

"Stop," said Ian. "You'll kill him."

The young woman paid no attention to him. She was thinking about Nathan, and the fashion in which he had been executed, without giving him the slightest chance. His executioners did not deserve any compassion. She pressed on the wound again. The man howled and writhed.

"The quicker you answer me, the quicker you'll be dropped at the hospital. For you, the choice is simple. Live or die."

With a trickle of drool on his chin, the man finally murmured something.

"Louder; I can't hear."

"I work for the Carneglia family."

Kristin frowned. She was not mistaken; the Mafia really was after her. But why?

"Why do the Carneglias want to kill me?"

"I don't know. I just follow orders."

His breathing was becoming increasingly hoarse. He coughed, and bloody bubbles appeared at the corners of his mouth. He wiped them away, mechanically.

"You don't seem to me be a simple hired hand. Don't lie to me, you doubtless have some idea of their motives."

"If I tell you, they'll kill me."

"If you don't tell me, it's me who'll kill you," Kristin insisted, moving her face closer to his.

The mafioso would not last much longer. She had to scare him, and quickly.

"Pass me your knife, Jack." As the former soldier hesitated, his gaze seeking Ian's approval, she repeated: "Pass. Me. Your. Knife."

The homeless man obeyed, and handed her the blade. She seized it and placed the blade under the mafioso's testicles.

"But before dying, you'll lose what you treasure the most," she threatened, raising her voice.

The mafioso looked into her eyes, to judge whether she was bluffing. What he saw seemed to convince him of the contrary.

"I've heard vague mention of an old debt, a debt that old Carneglia contracted a long time ago, before I even joined the family." He coughed and spat blood. "I heard a discussion between Joe and Vito. Joe wanted to know why he had to kill you, if it wasn't for money. The old man didn't want to answer, he got angry."

The mafioso was having difficulty breathing but she didn't hurry him.

"The old man said he didn't have to explain to his son, that he was till the boss, but as Joe wouldn't let go, he old man mentioned a debt. He was vague, but he talked about a debt to a woman. He didn't say her name, I swear."

It was Kristin's turn to look the mafioso straight in the eyes. He was not lying. She was about to ask him one last question when a further coughing fit took possession of him. He hacked as if to cough up his lungs. Then his head slumped on to his chest.

Dead.

For a few minutes, no one spoke.

"You got what you wanted," Ian said to her, a reproach in his voice.

"I had to know," Kristin replied, letting herself fall against the seat, her eyes moist.

Chapter 31

Michael went down the hospital steps on his brother's arm. A cold wind was blowing through Manhattan, and the millionaire breathed in deeply, glad to find clean air again.

The physicians had not diagnosed any fracture or lesion, only a few hematomas. He was walking with a limp and talking with a slight burr, but on the whole, he had come out of it quite well. It was his pride that had taken the worst blow.

"You ought to make a complaint," said his brother.

"To get beaten up again—no way. The police can't do anything against the F.B.I. The complaint would be filed away with no consequences. It's a waste of time."

Michael had told him about the beating.

"You're sure that he's really an F.B.I. agent?"

"He had a badge, a dark suit, a dirty mouth and thought anything was permissible. No, for me there's no doubt."

"You ought to make a complaint anyway," his brother insisted. "If you do nothing, they'll do it again."

"I can't," said Michel, evasively.

This time, he could not confide in his brother. The stakes were too high, the penalty for failure too great.

A limousine pulled up in front of the two men. The driver got out and opened the door for them. Michael whimpered when his head touched the back of the seat.

"You're certain that you don't want to stay with me tonight?" asked Daniel Pear, when the vehicle pulled away. "One never knows what might happen."

"Thanks, but I'm not risking anything in my apartment."

"I suppose you're still not going to tell me the reason that got you worked over?"

The millionaire sketched a hand gesture, preferring to ignore the question—but his brother persisted

"I suspect that all this has to do with the murder of your photographer friend, and the disappearance of this Kristin." His brother paused, a hypothesis doubtless surging forth in his mind. "Tell me that you're not involved in financial double dealing?"

Michael sighed. "You know that's not my thing. I can't tell you anything for the simple reason that I don't want to drag you into it with me. I've done nothing wrong, believe me…I just need to clear the matter up. For myself, but also for Nathan."

His elder brother seemed to settle for that. "All right—but if ever this matter, as you put it, takes on alarming proportions, promise me you'll let it drop."

Michael acquiesced for form's sake. The rest of the journey passed in silence. When the long vehicle pulled up in front of his building, his brother returned to the attack.

"You really don't want me to come up with me? I know a very good nurse."

Michael raised his eyes to the heavens. "I don't doubt it, but no. This evening, it's a shower and bed. Benjamin will take you home."

Before getting out, Michael turned to his brother. "When are you leaving for the Basque country?"

"In a week or so."

"Listen to me. I can't tell you why, but can you leave New York tomorrow?"

Daniel, of course, did not let himself be drawn so easily. "Why?"

"Do it. I'll tell you everything as soon as I can."

Daniel breathed out heavily, to make him understand that he was accepting the deal reluctantly. "Agreed—but I'll call you every day to demand a report."

"It's a deal. And especially, don't say anything to the parents; I don't want them to be worried."

Without waiting for a reply, Michael closed the door and tapped the top of the car with the palm of his hand. The driver released the brake and the limousine drew away.

He was not proud of himself. For the first time in a long time, he had hidden elements of his life from his brother; worse than that, he had lied about his plans for the evening.

He looked around. The streets were empty—the fault of the cold wind that was blowing through the region. The millionaire tightened his coat and headed for Manhattan. A nocturnal stroll would do him good. He thought with satisfaction that if the F.B.I. agents were still keeping close watch on him, they would not be going to sleep immediately.

He only hoped that Kristin had told the truth and that homeless men with military tattoos would not be difficult to find.

Chapter 32

Joseph Carneglia put down the phone with a curt gesture.

His father had given him a lecture, of the kind that only fathers are able to give, underlining his failures and making him sense the disappointment that he constituted for him. The old man had not spared him. The failed elimination of Kristin Arroyo had made the people who had ordered the hit angry. Who were they? Joe would really have liked to know. They had demanded explanations from his father.

But there was worse. The body of Charles Tobias had been found on waste ground: dumped; dead. No need to be a genius to understand that the Hispanic woman wanted answers, and was following the trail. By now, she doubtless knew who they were. At least there would be no more need to flush her out; she would come to them.

But his father did not see things that way. His father had been sufficiently clear on the subject; from now on they had to watch Michel Pear day and night. The famous millionaire was, it seemed, hand-in-glove with Arroyo. How? Joe did not have the slightest idea. His father remained fugitive, regarding his sources. On the other hand, he had repeated to him several times that he would not tolerate another failure.

Joseph had taken the scolding without saying anything. His time would come. For the moment, it was a matter of reacting, and rising to the top of the Carneglia family.

He got up and began pacing back and forth in the room.

The mafioso picked up the phone. He had several instructions to pass on. After the High Line disaster, he would leave nothing to chance, and would place an infallible surveillance around the millionaire.

This time, he would take care of everything personally.

Chapter 33

Manhattan, Washington Square, 24 November.

Michael replaced his mobile phone in the inside pocket of his jacket. As he had expected, his brother had called him to obtain news and try to get something out of him—without success. Daniel had also told him that he could not leave the country today. An urgent matter. The millionaire could not quite see what might qualify as an urgent matter among the Jesuits, but he did not say so aloud, in order not to vex his elder brother; the last thing he wanted to do was make him dig his heels in. So he repeated how important it was for him to know that his brother was safe, and hung up with the promise that the latter would leave as soon as his imperative business was settled.

Michael resisted the temptation to look around. If the F.B.I. men were watching him closely, he would not see them. He resumed walking, his leg trailing, his face bruised and rings around his eyes.

The day before, making contact had not been complicated. With the temperature so low, the majority of the homeless had sought the warmth of fires deployed by associations throughout the city. Alone, or nearly, in the streets of New York, he had wandered for ten minutes before perceiving a homeless man crammed under the stairway of a fast food joint. He had drawn closer. Huddled under a duvet covered with stains, he man was not exposing half an inch of skin—understandable in view of the weather. It was impossible, in consequence, to determine whether he was sporting a tattoo. The man had opened an eye. He reeked of alcohol. Michel had taken a five dollar bill out of his wallet and slipped out into the wicker basket placed on the ground.

"Thank y'sir."

The man had not added anything, his eyes closed again. Michel had cursed silently, thinking that he was mistaken. He was about to turn on his heel when he heard a voice whisper to him: "Rendezvous tomorrow. Ten o'clock Washington Square."

He smiled, suspecting that Kristin had circulated his photo among the homeless community in order to facilitate making contact—or, he thought, avoiding someone else passing themselves off as him.

Ten o'clock would chime in fifteen minutes, and he arrived in Washington Park. He breathed in deeply and went under the triumphal arch constructed in 1892 to celebrate the hundredth anniversary of George Washington's investiture with the Presidency of the United States. Michael rarely walked there; he preferred Central Park.

The park had now become the meeting-place of cliquey New Yorkers, chess-players, street artists and simple students, a society that did not resemble him.

As the indication for the meeting was vague, Michael wandered at random along the various pathways. The more he walked, the more he felt anxiety rising—not so much the fear of dying, he realized when he thought about it, but the dread of leading the F.B.I. to Kristin. He hoped that the young woman was paying attention.

When his legs began to make him suffer, he decided to sit down on a bench and let himself lean against the back. Facing him, a jazz trio was playing—two black men and one white; a sax, a keyboard and a drum set—who were performing for themselves.

Michael listened to them for a few minutes, until a squirrel passing close by recalled him to reality. The animal looked at him, seriously, and the millionaire smiled, thinking that F.B.I. surveillance techniques had certainly evolved. When the squirrel understood that the human on the bench had no intention of giving it breadcrumbs, it went away to pursue its quest for nourishment in the vicinity of a number of newly-arrived tourists.

Michael followed it with his eyes until he perceived a strange individual coming in his direction. The man—about fifty, white hair and beard—was clad in dirty and ragged jeans and a T-shirt that might have been white in the last century. But the most surprising thing was the dozen pigeons that were perched on his head and shoulders, cooing without budging.

The man, visible an eccentric, sat down on the bench directly beside her. He did not even look at him. He seemed to have eyes only for his birds. The strange individual took a handful of breadcrumbs from the bag slung round his shoulder, which he threw in the ground in front of him. Immediately, more birds came to alight before him.

Confronted by such a spectacle, Michael could not help smiling—but not for long, when the man whispered:

"You're being followed."

Chapter 34

Manhattan, Washington Square, 24 November.

Michel refrained from turning his head toward the man with the pigeons.

"In two minutes," his neighbor continued, "Someone will come to sit down beside me and give my pigeons something to eat. We'll talk a little. When he goes, count up to twenty and follow him."

Michael did not reply. He stared at the jazz trio and contented himself with nodding his head to the rhythm of the music to show that he had understood.

Two minutes later, a man did indeed appear, two pigeons perched on top of his head—decidedly, Kristin as appealing to some funny people. Michael looked straight ahead and saw nothing of his face except his black hair. The newcomer sat at the other end of the bench, near the other eccentric, with whom he exchanged a few words in low voices. The millionaire did not understand anything of what they said, and to tell the truth, he did not really care. An invisible hand was pulling the strings. In a few moments, he would gamble his life and Kristin's. The F.B.I. was here, somewhere, waiting for the slightest false step on his part. He did not have the right to make a mistake.

Suddenly, he noticed that the second man had got up and dusted off his trousers, full of breadcrumbs. He addressed a slight hand gesture to his companion and went back along the path by which he had come.

Michael counted to twenty before following him. In front of the jazz musicians he placed a bill in their hat, negligently. He forced himself to remain impassive, gazing at the passers-by, a simple Sunday stroller. Internally, however, he was seething. His entire body was tense, expecting at any moment to perceive an F.B.I. agent, to find himself pinned to the ground.

Thirty meters apart, the two men walked for nearly a quarter of an hour. The individual paused several times to speak to musicians or chess players. Visibly, he was not unknown in the neighborhood.

Michael followed him, taking care not to stop at the same time. He was beginning to get impatient when the man stopped near the triumphal arch, where he bought a hot dog from a vendor. Then he left the park.

The serious business was starting.

When the man stopped in front of a pedestrian crossing. Michael wondered what he ought to do—wait or join him? He chose the latter option. Having arrived level with him, he stared at the traffic light.

"Don't move," murmured the man. "Your taxi will be here shortly."

Michael watched for taxis. Several passed by without stopping. Finally, one of them pulled up before him, a door opened, and he plunged inside without further thought. The driver did not wait for the door to be fully closed to set off again.

Kristin was sitting on the back seat. He had an impulse to take her in his arms, but retained himself at the last moment.

"I'm being followed."

"I know. At least three people. And the strangest thing about that is that there are two distinct teams."

"Michael could not conceal his surprise. "Two? But..."

"Yes," she cut in. "The F.B.I and another crew, as yet undetermined. But don't worry about it; we won't have to deal with them. For the moment, switch off your phone and take the SIM card out."

She grabbed his chin. "I assume you didn't fall downstairs?" she said, examining the bruises on his face. Her eyes were burning with anger.

"A souvenir of Agent Dyers," Michael replied, in a light tone. "Disappointed at not having his imprint on Hollywood Boulevard, he decided to leave it on my face."

Kristin smiled. She was about to reply when the driver bellowed something that Michael did not understand. The young woman turned toward him.

"When I tell you to get out, open the door and get out, don't hesitate."

The millionaire acquiesced. Ten seconds later, the taxi braked brutally.

"Now," Kristin howled.

Michael obeyed. He landed on the pavement in front of a hot dog stand, whose vendor looked at him, eyes wide. Michael got up and looked around. If he was not mistaken, the taxi had gone around the park and he was now on the other side of Washington Square, in a street whose name he did not know.

Without a word, Kristin took his hand.

They crossed the artery in the midst of a concert of horns. Once on the other sidewalk, the young woman let go of his hand in order to hail a taxi.

"Same again" she said to him, when a new vehicle pulled up next to them. with a screech of tires.

Chapter 35

Manhattan, 24 November.

Michael lost track of time. They repeated the maneuver several times; they emerged from the vehicle, at rest this time, before taking another taxi a few meters further on. They plowed the length and breadth of the city, without any apparent logic except that of confusing their enemies. After an indeterminate number of journeys, Kristin told him that he could breathe.

The millionaire looked at his surroundings. He thought he knew New York like the back of his hand, but he had no idea where he was. Classical in their architecture, the skyscrapers did not rise up very high, nothing compared to those downtown. The streets were deserted.

"We're in Harlem," said Kristin, anticipating his question. "We're going to walk a little while we chat."

"Suits me," said Michael, stretching himself.

She took his hand.

"You're not afraid that we might be spotted?" asked Michel, having lost the initiative.

"Friends are watching the place, and will warn me if anyone arrives."

She opened her jacket and Michael perceived a revolver. She closed the flaps again immediately.

"Tell me about your encounter with Agent Dyers."

The millionaire did as he was asked and told her the whole story. He did not hide anything, including the part where he had revealed their previous meeting, under constraint. When he evoked the fashion in which the agents had threatened his brother, Kristin reflexively tightened her grip on his hand. She did not say anything, and let his story run on until his arrival in the park.

"Perhaps your brother's right, you know—there's still time to get out."

Michael did not reply, but by the glance that he darted at Kristin, the latter understood that he would not give up. She raised her arm, in a sign of surrender.

"Okay, okay—I just said it."

They walked in silence. Michael realized that he had never walked in Harlem. For him, it was almost a foreign land, or at least, a zone to be avoided. They passed several young men who looked at them suspiciously before going on their way.

"Kristin," he said, regretting breaking the silence, because he felt comfortable with her, "I know why Nathan was killed."

The young woman stopped. She released his hand and looked at him. Her lips stretched into a slight smile.

He went on: "It's completely crazy, utterly insane, but you have to believe me."

"I'm listening."

Michael searched for his words momentarily, petrified by the amplitude of Tyler's discovery. He would have like to have a copy of the incriminating photograph in his possession, but he had not dared bring it with him in case the situation went bad.

"Among the photographs you entrusted to me there's one of Marilyn posing in the subway." His interlocutor nodded, and he went on: "Well, the most important thing about it isn't the actress herself but the man in the background. He was reading a magazine, remember?"

"Yes, I remember. The magazine hid part of his face."

"Exactly," he said, in the same passionate tone as in their first encounter. "The man's identity doesn't matter. The secret's hidden in the cover of the magazine he's reading"

The millionaire took a malign pleasure in beating around the bush and making his audience salivate. The young woman raised her eyes skywards.

"For pity's sake, get to the point—quickly."

"It's an issue of *Life* magazine dated July 1969."

Kristin took several seconds to comprehend the implications of the revelation.

"That means that Marilyn didn't die in 1962, as everyone thought," he concluded, with a broad smile.

The revelation did not have the expected result.

"You're putting me on. That's just…ridiculous."

Michael sighed.

"Believe me, I understand how you feel. When the cover was shown to me I thought it was a hoax. It goes against everything I believed. But we've eliminated all the hypotheses: a double, a montage, nothing holds up. My friend, an expert in computer science, assures me a hundred per cent that the photo is real."

The former soldier did not reply immediately.

"It's insane." She raised her arm to cut Michael off as he made as if to reply. "But this whole story is. It's obvious that that photo hides a big secret, even if I can't swallow your conclusion. There must be another explanation."

"All right, you don't believe me. But let's admit the hypothesis for a moment, and consider that Nathan reached the same conclusion. Marilyn might be alive. Very well—where my reasoning vacillates, I grant you, is the reason why anyone would want to kill you. It'll soon be fifty years since Marilyn disappeared. She was an icon—the greatest of all, in my opinion—but nothing we know about her can explain what's happening."

Next to him, Kristin reflected in silence. The golden boy would have paid a great deal to know what she was thinking. However, he let the former activist digest the new information.

A corpulent black woman went past them, taking four children for a walk, whom she was holding in tether. Kristin could not help smiling on seeing them.

"There are some things you don't know. After confiding the USB key and dropping you at home, we set out in search of the men who tried to kill me…"

"What!" exclaimed Michel, "But you're…"

He stopped before saying something very stupid. He still recalled the last time he had let his tongue speak instead of his brain.

"...mad," she finished for him. "Yes, perhaps. But we were missing pieces of the puzzle. According to the man we interrogated, it's the Carneglia family who are behind all this, Just now I told you that two groups were watching you—the F.B.I. and another, unknown. That's not entirely true. I'm almost certain that they're also from the New York Mafia family."

The millionaire had noticed that the young woman had remained vague regarding the fashion in which she had obtained that information, but he did not seek to know more."

"Did that informer tell you the reason why he tried to kill you?"

"Yes...no. Well, not in any precise fashion. He said that the Carneglia family was honoring an old debt to a woman. He didn't know her identity, but I have reason to believe that it's a matter of..."

"Marilyn!" he cut in.

Michael stopped. A completely crazy idea had just crossed his mind. He turned to her. "My God!" he exclaimed. "Now that I think about it, a legend ran around concerning Marilyn's penultimate night. Rumor had it that she spent it in the company of a local godfather with whom she'd fallen in love. If that's true...it explains the presence of the Mafia."

"But not that of the F.B.I.," the young woman temporized,

"But not that of the F.B.I.," he agreed.

Visibly slightly embarrassed at having cut the ground from under him, the young woman went on: "Let's sum up. Aided by the Mafia, Marilyn staged her death and succeeded in deceiving everyone. One question remains for us to answer: what reason did she have for doing that? And apart from the F.B.I. and the Carneglia family, I can't see anyone who can tell us..."

Chapter 36

Long Island, 24 November.

Kristin told the driver to head for the beaches of Long Island, and saw that they would arrive rapidly, given the density of the traffic. The car pulled up near Sunken Meadow State Park.

It was not far from three o'clock in the afternoon, and Michel proposed that they have something to eat. Kristin acquiesced. They went into a deserted fast foot outlet, where they ordered and then installed themselves at a table. There, to their surprise, they did not talk about the affair, but confided in one another. She told him about her military past and the reasons for which she had resigned. He talked about his career before going further back and talking about his childhood. The break did them good.

Kristin and Michael left the restaurant with full stomachs and went down toward the ocean. The beach was not crowded, the fault of the bad weather. The only exceptions were a young man walking his dog and a retired couple walking on the sand a short distance from the waves.

The millionaire and the former soldier advanced along the wooden walkway, between two rose-bush hedges, meager protection against the wind blowing from the ocean.

"Let's go back to the beginning," said Kristin. "In your view, what reason could Marilyn have had for faking her death?"

"I can only formulate hypotheses. She was going through a difficult period from every viewpoint: her private life, her public life and her career as an actress were all at a low ebb. She'd set up her production company in New York, but it had been a failure financially and artistically,"

"All that adds more credit to the suicide thesis."

Michael acquiesced. What could push an icon to stage her own death? "Marilyn might have wanted a quieter life. But given her stature, that would have been impossible. She decided to have a memorable death? Yes, I know…it's a bit far-fetched."

They continued to exchange ideas while strolling like an amorous couple.

"Some people," said Kristin, "think she was murdered by the Mafia or the Kennedys."

"The famous conspiracy theories. Even so, it's true that there are several shadowy zones around her death."

"What?"

"Firstly, we have the declaration of Eunice Murray, Marilyn's housekeeper, who admitted in 1983 that Bobby Kennedy had visited Marilyn on the day of her death. Moreover, according to her, Marilyn was still alive when the doctors arrived."

"What did she mean by *still alive*?"

Michael shrugged. "Simply that she wasn't dead."

Kristin laughed aloud. "That doesn't get us any further forward. I suppose the worthy lady is no longer alive?"

"She died in the early nineties. On the other hand, the presence of Bobby Kennedy is interesting. If there's anyone who could have helped her disappear, it's him."

"What was their relationship?"

"They'd been lovers, but the adventure didn't last long. A few days at the most. It was a love triangle such as one normally sees in the cinema. Bobby loved Marilyn, but it wasn't reciprocal. Marilyn was madly in love with John, who according to her, considered her a new trophy in his collection. John slept with the most beautiful women in the world. When he left her, Marilyn didn't take it very well. According to those near to her, she never forgot him completely. Difficult to disentangle the true from the false in that story, the Kennedy family always having taken care to cover their tracks. Once, they even succeeded in stopping a documentary on the relationship between Marilyn and John that was made for TV.

We at the Foundation haven't been able to obtain a copy. Nevertheless a few fragments have filtered out recently."

"And?"

"Nothing. At any rate, nothing very interesting. To tell the truth, many fans were disappointed. According to rumor, the reportage was going to present tapes on which John and Marilyn could be heard making love..."

Michael smiled.

"What if it were the Kennedy family who are pulling the F.B.I.'s strings?"

"Improbable, in my opinion. There isn't much of the Kennedy family left, and after having failed to keep the Nazi ideas of John's father secret, I don't see that a new scandal could do them any more harm..."

"I don't know. Perhaps there's an element that we don't know yet—a piece of the puzzle we lack. I have difficulty believing that the Kennedys aren't implicated in this. From what you've told me about Marilyn's life, they constitute the only force in presence capable of explaining her disappearance. When someone wants to disappear, it's rarely by choice."

"I agree," the millionaire replied. "Which brings us back to the original question: why disappear? I've given you my theory. What's yours?"

"She loved John. He dropped her. To get her revenge, she might have tried to blackmail him."

"I don't think so; it wasn't in her character. She loved him, truly; she would never have sought to harm him."

"Even to get her own back?"

Michael shrugged his shoulders

"Her death was staged, planned in advance," the young woman continued. "Did anything notable happen in the preceding months?"

"I can't see what? Except, perhaps, for her performance in Madison Square Garden, virtually her swan song, on the occasion of J.F.K.'s birthday."

"Kennedy—always him. I'd really like to go back in time to find out what happened on that day."

Michel took her hand, He smiled. "I think, in fact, that I do know someone who can help us. A Monroe 6." He paused, his brows furrowed. "I have an idea. Lend me your phone."

Chapter 37

"We've arrived," said Tom, who had reverted to being a taxi-driver for several days.

The young woman gave him a payment for his services. The former soldier was not greedy with respect to the remuneration; to resume the service, even for a personal affair, amused him greatly.

"Can you take a turn around the block?" asked Kristin. "I'd like to take a look at the place."

The driver obeyed. Sitting beside her, Michael darted an interrogative glance at her, to which she made no response. Perhaps she was manifesting an excessive prudence, but events of recent days had rendered her suspicious. The future would prove her right or wrong.

During the journey the millionaire had told her what the Monroe 6s were and their function. Behind that mysterious name, in fact, a group of unfailing worshipers was concealed, the ultimate fans, who followed the actress wherever she went, to film sets or charity galas. To thank them for their devotion, the actress granted them favorable treatment and sometimes received them in her home. Among them, old Peter Gallardo was one of the most eminent members of the group.

"If my memory serves me right," Michael affirmed, "he was in Hollywood when Marilyn died. He was the one who organized her funeral."

"And we're going to see his son?"

"Yes, Andrew. He lives at 18 Walker Street. As you can imagine, with such a father, he was steeped in the cult of Marilyn from a young age. Having worked as a professor of mathematics, he retired and did some work at one time for the

164

Foundation, where I crossed his path. It's him we're going to see. He might be able to help us."

Michael had phoned him using Kristin's mobile. Andrew's wife had told him that her husband was working, but that he would be at the apartment at six o'clock.

Between the tall buildings, the street was swarming with passers-by, residents for the most part, who were coming home after their day's work. The former soldier examined certain side-streets, blind alleys and parked vehicles with particular care—anything that could potentially hide killers. The proximity of a police station, doubtless designed to reassure the rich inhabitants of the neighborhood, two blocks away, made up her mind.

"We'll go," she said. "You stay here, Tom. If anyone shows up, warn us."

Tom nodded his head. Kristin got out, followed by Michael, and put her hand inside her jacket. The cold contact of her weapon reassured her. They both headed for the entrance door, sheltered by a flowery porch. She pressed the button of the intercom. Ten seconds later a female voice replied: "Yes?"

"Hello, Ma'am. It's Michael Pear. I called your husband just now to arrange a meeting."

"My husband told me, He should be here in ten minutes. Can you wait for a little while?"

The proprietress did not give them time to insist. A disagreeable crackle old them that the conversation was over.

Kristin and Michael looked at one another, surprised.

"Not very welcoming, Mrs. Gallardo," she said.

Michael did not have time to reply. A screech of tires made them turn round. At the corner of the street, a black saloon plunged toward them. Launched at top speed, the car slammed into their own vehicle. The impact, metal against metal, resounded throughout the neighborhood.

Tom!

At the same moment, the doors of the vehicle opened simultaneously and spat out four men clad in black, their faces hidden by superhero masks, with automatic rifles pointed in their direction.

Without thinking, Kristin dived behind the low wall of the porch, dragging Michael with her. A second later, the first shots rang out. A multitude of projectiles dug into the entrance door, just behind them. The young woman hoped that Mrs. Gallardo was standing well back.

Kristin brought out her weapon and darted a prudent glance over the wall. The street emptied at top speed, the pedestrians taking to their heels while the four assailants sprayed their position. In spite of the surrounding chaos, one question imposed itself on her mind. How had they known where to find them?

She did not have time to think about it for long.

Suddenly, silence fell in the street.

With a gesture of the arm, one of the men in black gave the signal to attack. She had to react or they would be shot down like rabbits; the low wall, more decorative than anything else, would not hold for long.

While she was reflecting as to the best solution, Tom threw himself on one of the killers, whose throat he cut violently with the switchblade from which he was never separated. The riposte was only to be expected.

"No!" howled Kristin, standing up.

Too late. An avalanche of bullets traversed the chest of the former soldier, who collapsed to the ground, dead,

Taking advantage of the diversion, Kristin took aim at one of the aggressors and pressed her trigger twice—successfully; the target's head exploded like an overripe fruit.

Only two left.

She did not have time to line up another. The two remaining men turned their firepower on her. She threw herself behind the wall again, while bullets flew all around her. She felt a pain in her leg which she suppressed immediately. She had to protect Michael.

Lying beside her, the millionaire looked at her. In his eyes she read his distress at being unable to act, unable to come to her aid. She made him a sign to remain under cover.

Her mind was working at top speed to find a solution, in order not to die in that street in Tribeca. She could not count on another diversion. At that thought, her heart constricted. Tom had given his life for them.

She strove to empty her mind, as she had learned to do in the army. She held her breath and tensed her muscles, in order no longer to be anything but one with her weapon, and peppered the area where the survivors were standing. Without standing up, she fired three times, by guesswork. She might have missed; she had no idea. At any rate, at the same moment, police sirens resounded in the distance. The concert of bullets ceased.

Kristin raised her head slightly. The two men in black were heading for their vehicle, one supporting the other. Evidently, he had been hit. The temptation to shoot them in the back sprang to mind, but after a few seconds of hesitation, she did not yield to it. In any case, it was too late. The vehicle backed up in order to turn in the direction of the road, and pulled away.

Kristin turned to Michael.

He was breathing, which was one good point. She could not see any trace of blood on him, which was another good point. The young woman tried to stand up, but pain prevented her from doing so. Her right leg gave way beneath her and she fell to the ground.

Michael took her gently by the arm, and helped her to stand up. Thus sustained, she limped as far as Tom's body, face down on the ground. Gritting her teeth, she turned him over. The former soldier's eyes were staring, but all trace of life had deserted them. She could do nothing more for him.

"We have to get out of here as quickly as possible," she hissed in the ear of the millionaire, to whom she was still hanging on. "The cops will be here soon."

The howl of police sirens was getting closer.

"You're wounded. We ought to go to the hospital."

"We can't. If we're ever caught, the police will pin Nathan's murder on me."

"For once, Kristin, trust me. Be realistic. You're wounded, and we have no chance of getting away." He looked her in the eyes. "I can't do anything against the F.B.I. or mafiosi armed to the teeth, but the police are subject to the law, and that's a terrain on which I can maneuver."

The young woman tried to respond, but a cough prevented her.

"I'll take care of everything, that's a promise. Above all, don't say anything—nothing at all. I know a very good lawyer, who'll get you out of this in no time."

Two police cars pulled up at the adjacent pavement. Four policemen sprang out of the vehicles, weapons in hand.

"Drop your weapons and put your hand on your heads! Lie down!"

"Do as they say," Michael murmured to her, kneeling down. "It will all be all right."

Chapter 38

Manhattan, Little Italy, 24 November.

Vito Carneglia thumped the table violently. Facing him, on the other side of the desk, Joseph did not flinch, and contented himself with staring at him, waiting for the calm after the storm.

"You're an incompetent!" howled the mafioso. "Not even capable of getting rid of one woman. I wasn't asking for the impossible, though, Joe..."

As he son did not reply, he went on: "What have you done with the vehicle?"

"Burned it and sent it to the bottom of the Hudson, with the weapons. Nothing left to link us to the gun-battle."

"Incompetent," repeated the old man, in a whisper. "In my time, it would all have been settled in less than a minute. You're nothing but a dishrag, good at best for beating up your whores."

This time, Joseph did not let the insult pass. "It's your fault too!" he roared. "From the start, you've hidden information from me. You don't trust me!"

"You don't have any excuse," howled Vito. "None!"

His son's words wounded him more than he would have thought. Fundamentally, Joe was not wrong; he had divulged as little as possible to him about the affair—just the necessary, perhaps even a little less. Where he was mistaken, on the other hand, was on the question of trust. He would have liked to tell him everything...but he could not. He had promised, and that promise could not be broken. All that, all that shit, surpassed them to a point that Joe could not imagine.

And now, he was going to have to cut all the threads, before they led back to them...back to *her*.

He came back to the present when Joe placed a hand on his shoulder, desirous of being forgiven.

"It's not too late, Papa. I'll put them under surveillance. I'll take care of them personally, that's a promise. When they leave the hospital. Our men will keep us fully informed."

"You aren't going to do anything more," he cut in.

Vito Carneglia got up from his desk, advanced toward his son and looked him straight in the eyes. What he was about to do was unqualifiable.

He slid his hand into his right-hand jacket pocket and brought out a pistol. He pointed it at his son's face.

Joseph's eyes widened; he scarcely had time to comprehend. The shot resounded throughout the office, and Joe's body collapsed on his armchair.

Two bodyguards immediately hurtled into the room, weapons in hand—his two lieutenants. The mafioso rummaged in a drawer rapidly and brought out a wad of bills, which he held out to them.

"We're abandoning everything; it's finished. You two, take a vacation. Spend a few days in Miami, or somewhere else, I don't care, but leave me alone. No one is to disturb me!"

The two men darted a glance around before daring to seize the wad of cash. The old man might have lost his mind, but he was still their boss and the head of the family. What was more, such a windfall was not to be refused.

As they were about to leave, Vito Carneglia said: "And get rid of that idiot for me. Make sure no one finds his body before judgment day."

Without a word, the two men did as they were told, seizing the cadaver and leaving the room.

Alone, Vito let himself fall into the armchair that he had occupied for years before confiding it to his son. He wiped away a tear; it was no time for sentiment. Killing his son was the worst thing he had ever done, but he had no choice. He could not escape that debt.

When he had abandoned the reins of the Family to his only son, he thought he could end his life tranquilly. But the past had caught up with him, a past that he had thought lost for decades.

He remembered that evening with Marilyn. He was the one who had provided the body—a perfect double of the actress, whom he had killed by forcing her to swallow drugs. The memories flooded back. He had always been a fan of Marilyn Monroe, he had met her several times in New York. With other people, he had created the Monroe 6, a club of unconditionally devoted admirers.

At the end of July, Marilyn had wanted to bring them together, because she needed them urgently. She had simply told them that she had to disappear, that the whole world must believe that she was dead. They had agreed to help her without asking why; their admiration was faultless.

After setting the scene, the Monroe 6 had taken care of the rest of the operation. They had smuggled the actress away and had prepared a new life for her. He had never seen her again—the woman he loved most in all the world. More, even, than his son.

And then there had been the meeting ten days before. One of the sons of the Monroe 6 had warned him about the exhibition. He had read an article in a paper that mentioned unpublished photographs. Marilyn was in danger again. Vito had to act.

Now, it was all over. Lost.

An hour earlier, he had received a telephone call. It was her. She had ordered him to stop everything; the woman's death was no longer on the agenda. She had thanked him and asked him not to intervene any further—ever. And she had hung up. He had perceived reproach in her voice, disappointment.

As for the sequel, he had made the decision alone. The members of the Triangle were not imbeciles, and possessed unlimited means. Today or tomorrow, if they did not know already, they would know. In this ultra-securitized world, eve-

171

rything was always discovered. Cameras and satellites were there to make sure of it. Joe might have got rid of the car and the weapons, but they would follow the trail back to them from the two dead men.

That was why he had not hesitated to kill his only son. For a promise. For love of a woman.

The old man stood up, closed and locked the door and came back to sit in the armchair. He seized the pistol, which was still warm, and put the barrel into his mouth. He had rubbed shoulders with violence and death throughout his life, but he trembled at the moment when he was about to press the trigger.

At least he would rejoin his son.

With him dead, there was no longer anyone who could lead back to her. He had kept his word, and that was what counted.

Reassured, he pulled the trigger.

PART FIVE

Chapter 39

Manhattan, Battery Park, 25 November.

Clyde Kaplan threw a morsel of bread to the squirrel, which seized it with its forepaws before fleeing without asking for the rest. Clyde picked up the cup placed on the bench and finished his coffee.

Like numerous New Yorkers, he liked to eat facing the Atlantic, on the promenade bordering Battery Park. In front of him extended Ellis Island, the Promised Land on to which the entire world's migrants had disembarked for decades. Behind his back was the Wall Street district, and then Ground Zero, where the second tower was rising ever higher into the sky. A few cables away, the Statue of Liberty, the symbol of America, watched over the city and its inhabitants.

"May I sit down?"

The voice of Norman Dyers pulled him out of his thoughts. Kaplan indicated the bench, and he F.B.I. agent sat down next to him.

"Progress in your investigation?"

"An unexpected development. I don't know whether you read this morning's papers, but there was a gun battle yesterday in Tribeca. Our two friends were attacked by four masked men. Balance-sheet: three dead, two of whom were attackers, in the process of being identified. The third victim, a former soldier named Tom Yates, seems to have acted on Arroyo's behalf. At this stage, of course, we're not sure of anything, but things ought to become clear in the next few hours.

"And our two fugitives?"

"The man's unhurt. Arroyo, for her part, took a bullet in the leg—not serious. She ought to be on her feet soon."

"The police?"

"I don't know much more than has been revealed in the press. The police are still searching for the survivors. As for the fate reserved for Arroyo, difficult to say. I assume that in the first place, they're going to interrogate her.

"That's all?"

Dyers sniggered. "I can't go see the police and ask them to take account of an affair on which I'm not even supposed to be working. Don't forget that I'm walking on eggshells. The other day, when you told me to put pressure on Pear, I did it, I took a risk for you, but if a man like him ever makes a complaint against me to my superiors, my career would go down the toilet."

Kaplan did not reply. Dyers was right; by attacking Michael Pear—on his insistence—a few days earlier, he had taken unconsidered risks that might have unfortunate repercussions if the millionaire decided to talk. The F.B.I. wouldn't tolerate knowing that its ranks had been infiltrated by moles, even if they were working for the Triangle. Agent Dyers was a competent element, even promising; the Triangle couldn't risk losing him.

"I beg your pardon."

Dyers waved way his apologies with a gesture of the hand. "That's not all. I've kept you the best for last." He took an envelope from his jacket, which he held out to him.

"As we suspected, it's the photographs that are the origin of this whole story. Those you have before your eyes are poor quality copies. Look at the man in the background and the magazine he's reading."

Kaplan understood immediately.

"Where did you get these photos?"

"From an acquaintance of Michael Pear. The satellite surveillance of the millionaire has borne fruit. A few days ago our friend went to an apartment in Brooklyn, twice, the first time for ten minutes, the second time for a full half-hour. The place is registered in the name of Tyler Hoffman, a computer degenerate who works for himself. After Pear's departure I paid him a visit, alone. A good move—he was destroying all the documents on his hard disk.

A malevolent gleam traversed the agent's eyes. After a brief discussion with him, Hoffman had proved to be very chatty. "The photos belong to Peat. He had asked him to work on them, which he did right away. He discovered the secret."

Kaplan nodded his head, his mind already elsewhere.

"These photos were taken from the negatives stolen from the photographer's place? Those the Foundation were to recover after the exhibition?"

"I think so."

After their first visit, Pear had kept his word, constrained and forced. The millionaire had sent them the photographs that the Foundation had just acquired at a high priced. As for the negatives, it was Nathan who had them. Going through the material, Dyers had succeeded in retracing the history of the session, and after a long and fastidious inventory he had come to the conclusion that a few items were missing, doubtless in Stewart's possession on the evening of his death. The killers had taken everything away.

"The man who informed you, I suppose he won't talk to the police?"

Dyers smiled. "The man felt lonely. He's hanged himself."

"Good."

Kaplan reflected.

So, the whore really hadn't committed suicide in 1962, as everyone thought. Nevertheless the photo wasn't recent, and there was nothing to say that she hadn't died since, taking her secret to the grave.

"What's my mission now?"

"First, find out who these mysterious killers are who are popping up all over the city. Afterwards, concerning Pear and Arroyo, it's best to keep our distance from them as long as they're under police surveillance. Let them breathe, let them think we've abandoned them, but keep a permanent watch on them. I want to know their slightest moves."

Chapter 40

Manhattan, Bellevue Hospital Center, 26 November.

"My client won't tell you anything," proclaimed the stentorian voice of John Wingfield. "The operation she's just undergone has left her exhausted. She needs rest."

The man was one of the most highly-reputed lawyers in New York. Michael had called him immediately after their arrest. He had arrived ten minutes later, while the paramedics were carrying Kristin into the hospital. In the vehicle, a policeman had tried to get her to talk, but the young woman had remained mute, as the millionaire had advised.

The doctors had operated during the night to extract the bullet lodged in her thigh. The following day went by in the fog of anesthesia. She remembered, however, the lightning passage of the lawyer, who had repeated that she should keep her mouth shot. First he had to take care of Michael, apparently being grilled.

Gradually, the young woman had recovered her senses. In the morning a police lieutenant had appeared to inform her that a uniformed officer would be standing guard at her door. Although she had suspected at first that the forces of order wanted to make sure that she did not try to escape, she understood in the afternoon that she was quite mistaken. The policeman was protecting her.

At the threshold of the room, Wingfield found himself at odds with another policeman. After having whispered for a few minutes in order not to wake her, the two men were now arguing loudly. Still a little confused, Kristin attempted nevertheless to read between the lines. From what she could pick up, Michael had not stood by with folded arms during her operation.

"I'd simply like to know what connection there is between Miss Arroyo and the Carneglia family."

As you doubtless know, Miss Arroyo has been exonerated this morning in consequence of other testimony," the advocate continued. "You can't force her to answer your questions if she doesn't want to."

The policeman uttered a slight sigh. He didn't have the stature to stand up to the lawyer. "I know," he said. "I just want to know her version of the affair." He looked in Kristin's direction. "Miss Arroyo, I'm not trying to trap you. I want..."

"Officer, if you continue to question my client without her consent, I shall find myself obliged to bring a complaint of harassment."

Kristin felt a pang of sympathy for the policeman, who was only doing his job. She was about to open her mouth when a black look from Wingfield dissuaded her.

The policeman beat a retreat.

"You win, for the moment...but I haven't said my last word. Make sure that your client doesn't leave the city; we need to hear her testimony for the continuation of the investigation. She's also killed two men, when bearing arms in New York is prohibited."

The lawyer looked at her, with a smile on his lips. "Legitimate self-defense. As for the continuation of the investigation, no problem; my client will maintain herself entirely at your disposal."

Without a farewell, the policeman turned his back and went away, leaving her alone with the lawyer.

"I've been...exonerated?" Kristin asked. "Would you care to explain that?"

Wingfield pulled up a chair and sat down beside the bed. "The two men you killed belonged to the Mafia. But I don't think that's news to you...."

"The Carneglia family."

The lawyer nodded his head. "During his interrogation, Mr. Pear pointed them in that direction. His testimony, combined with the identity of the Italian-American gunmen sent the police to Carneglia's headquarters. They reaped a considerable reward; when they arrived, they intercepted two men loading the corpse of a certain Joseph Carneglia to a truck, presumably with a view to disposing if it."

Still slightly dazed, Kristin was not sure that she had heard correctly.

"Joseph Carneglia is dead?"

"Killed by his own father, according to the testimony of the two mafiosi surprised by the police. They hastened to explain the whole affair when they understood that they were at risk of being charged with homicide. In exchange for a reduction in their sentence they confessed that their boss had killed Mr. Stewart, exonerating you."

Kristin felt the beginning of a headache. Too much information in too little time...

"But that's not all," the lawyer went on. "In the Mafia HQ the police also found he corpse of Vito Carneglia, known to be the family's godfather. According to the initial analysis, he committed suicide."

Worse and worse...the young woman would reflect on the implications of those revelations, but later. She massaged her temples.

"If I understand correctly, I'm in the clear regarding Nathan's murder. I've still killed two men."

"Don't worry about that; I'll take care of it. You'll be acquitted without any problem. The witness statements from passers-by and inhabitants all agree that the mafiosi opened fire first. In addition, they were better-armed and more numerous. With those arguments in your favor, I could plead legitimate self-defense with my eyes shut."

"Then why did the policeman demand that I remain at his disposal?"

The lawyer laughed briefly before replying. "Don't take any notice of that. The lieutenant had just got a mighty kick up the backside. He just wanted to leave with his head held high."

Kristin did not reply; she needed time to assimilate all that.

Respectfully, Wingfield stood up. "If you have no more questions, I'll leave you in Mr. Pear's company. He's waiting in the corridor."

Chapter 41

"Hello, Kristin," said Michael, as he came into the room, with a bouquet of flowers in his hand. How are you?"

"Still a little foggy, but I feel better. To think that after spending ten years in the army, I had to come back to New York in order to get wounded."

Michael slid his gift into a vase placed next to the window, in the light, and then sat down in the chair left free by the lawyer beside the bed. He took her hand.

"Thanks for the flowers...and the lawyer," Kristin went on. "Without him, I think I'd have panicked. You've handled the situation in masterly fashion—thanks again."

"John Wingfield is a top man in his field. He knows the procedures and is used to dealing with the police. With him you're in good hands."

"I suppose he doesn't offer his services for free..."

Michael dismissed the implication with a wave of the hand. "Trivia. You saved my life during the gun battle yesterday, it's perfectly normal to return the compliment." He adopted a serious expression that she had not seen before. "I've had enough of lying down before the F.B.I. and the police and hiding. I've decided to seize the bull by the horns. I've engaged Wingfield, but also a personal protection company. Although the Mafia is, as it seems, out of the game, the F.B.I. surely hasn't said its last word."

She nodded her head. His decision didn't surprise her. She still remembered the impotence in his gaze when he watched the gun battle that could have cost both of them their lives, as a spectator."

"Wingfield told me what you've done for me."

"That's quite natural. It's me who led you into that trap."

"What do you mean?"

"I'm not certain yet, but it's probable that it was Andrew Gallardo who sold us out to the mafiosi. The police tried to find him the day after the gun battle, but he's disappeared, along with his wife. The neighbors heard their car leaving shortly after the shooting. They've bolted.

"If that's not a confession, I don't know what is," Kristin murmured. "If that's the case, the Monroe 6 are still protecting Marilyn."

The millionaire shrugged his shoulders. The treason of his former collaborator was visibly still stuck in his throat. Kristin realized that he had unconsciously drawn closer to her. She looked at him for a few seconds, and then put her head against his chest. In spite of the perfusion drip, Michael drew her to him gently.

The kiss was intense, exquisite. An immense disturbance took possession of her. A warmth spread through all the fibers of her being. The young woman let herself go, and the kiss became more torrid. She felt her heart hammering. Michael excited her; she wanted him to make love to her, there, right away…but she remembered where they were.

She pulled away, regretfully.

"Did I hurt you?" Michael asked.

"Not at all," Kristin replied, smiling. "If we weren't in a hospital, I think I'd have torn your clothes off."

She could not help laughing on seeing the millionaire's discomfited face.

"It's only a postponement," she added. By means of a simple pressure, Kristin raised the bed beneath her back in order to make herself more comfortable.

"I hope so," Michael murmured, recovering his composure. "Now that you're in the clear, what are your plans?"

The young woman's gaze became clouded. "Taking care of Tom's funeral, to begin with. Rendering him a final tribute. He sacrificed his life for us…."

Michel squeezed her hand gently. "I'm taking care of that. I've notified his sister. The funeral will be held tomorrow in Brooklyn."

"I hope I can get out."

"According to the doctor, yes. We'll borrow a wheelchair, if necessary."

Kristin acquiesced. She smiled mischievously. "Are you going to push me?"

"I thought you'd never ask. But you haven't answered my question. What are your plans?" He leaned forward. "Reassure me that you're not going to continue living in the tunnels underneath the city."

"How do you know that?"

"I haven't been sitting around sugaring pills for two days." His smile vanished. "Ian came to see you, shortly after the operation. He wanted to talk to you but the doctors refused. There was an argument. He told me where you'd been hiding, where he lives in the company of former soldiers. I..."

He did not finish the sentence.

"You couldn't know," said Kristin, in a soft voice. For former soldiers, the hardest thing is often coming back. Finding a job and a roof. Society prefers to ignore them..."

Only silence replied to her. Desirous of changing the subject, she went on in a lighter tone: "As for your question...for the moment, I'm just in a hurry to go home, to sort out my apartment." She looked the millionaire in the eyes. "But I have no intention of abandoning the affair. The mafiosi were acting on someone's behalf. I want to know who and why."

Chapter 42

Brooklyn. First Presbyterian Church, 27 November.

Outside the church, Michael supported Kristin, who was still experiencing difficulty walking as far as the limousine unaided. The young woman had abandoned the wheelchair as soon as she was out of the hospital. The doctor had given her permission to leave for the morning.

The millionaire had come to find her in her room, and then they had headed for the First Presbyterian Church in order to attend the funeral. The former soldier's family had been surprised to see fifty homeless people invade the place, anxious to render their former comrade a final tribute. The army had sent a simple wreath.

After having bid everyone farewell, they went back to the millionaire's long vehicle. On the way, the couple exchanged their impressions of the service. The conversation had turned to a subject recently neglected—Marilyn—when Kristin asked the millionaire why he was incessantly yawning.

"Sorry. I was working late last night. As it appears that Andrew Gallardo isn't going to surface any time soon, I went to the Foundation's archives to cast an eye over Marilyn's autopsy. I don't notice the time passing..."

"Did you find anything interesting?"

The millionaire smiled. "I succeeded in establishing a precise chronology of events. Do you want me to tell you?"

"Gladly."

"It all began with Dr. Hyman Engelberg, who certified Marilyn's death at four-twenty-five in the morning before calling the police. It was Sergeant Clemmons who responded; it was his report that I read. Clemmons was received by the housekeeper. In the room, apart from Dr. Engelberg, was Dr. Ralph Greenson. Marilyn's psychiatrist. The report mentions that the body was already covered by a sheet. For all those present there was no doubt: Marilyn had committed suicide."

Michael paused before continuing. "The two men told the policeman that they hadn't tried to resuscitate her, because they'd arrived too late. The housekeeper's testimony is more astonishing. At the time of the interrogation, she was folding linen in the laundry. According to Clemmons she seemed agitated."

"A curious manner of occupying herself when her employer had just committed suicide."

"She was the one who found the body. She'd just finished work for the day when she noticed the light under the actress's bedroom door. She knocked but got no reply. She called Marilyn's psychiatrist, who lived nearby. He arrived at about half past midnight. He knocked on the door too, with no more success, and then tried to open it; it was locked. Greenson then looked through the bedroom window, from the balcony and saw Marilyn lying on the bed, motionless. He called Dr. Engelberg immediately. The two men forced the door and found the body lying on the bed—dead."

"One detail strikes me," said Kristin. "If I've understood correctly, the body was discovered at about half past midnight, but the police weren't informed until half past four, four hours later."

"Yes. According to the witnesses, the two doctors hesitated over what to do. They called the studio in order to receive directions—it's necessary not to forget that they were both employed by the studio. It was only afterwards that they informed the legal authorities."

"And they stayed there for four hours, doing nothing. Were they playing cards, or what?" sniggered Kristin.

The millionaire shrugged his shoulders.

"The ensuing events don't enlighten us on that subject. At about six-thirty the medical examiner arrived, a certain Thomas Noguchi. In a subsequent interview, Noguchi confessed to having been surprised that the autopsy was confided to him."

"Why?"

"According to him, the autopsy ought to have been confided to a more experienced physician—he had just completed his studies. A little anecdote: consequently Noguchi made a specialty of carrying out the autopsies of the biggest stars. He carved up, among others, Sharon Tate, Janis Joplin. Natalie Wood and even John Belushi."

"Quite a cast list."

"Quite a cast list, indeed. But let's get back to Marilyn. On arriving at the morgue the day after the death—which was Monday morning—Noguchi found no trace of the actress's body. It hadn't been transferred—or rather, not to the right place. The corpse had been sent to a funeral parlor in Westwood Village. By whom? Why? No one knows. Let's pass on. When Noguchi was finally able to begin the autopsy, he determined that death was caused by a massive ingestion of barbiturates. Nothing abnormal, the existence of such medicaments in the bedroom having been confirmed by the police. Marilyn had bought them the day before her suicide, with a doctor's prescription. I'll pass over a few details to get to the two points that offered most sustenance to various conspiracy theories. Pont one: the cadaveric lividity. I don't know whether you know, but that's due to the post-mortem displacement of blood into the lower parts of the body. In concrete terms, the lividity is manifested by the presence of dark patches on the skin. During the autopsy, Noguchi noted two zones of lividity: one situated on the face, the neck and the chest; the other on the posterior surface of the arms and legs. For some people, that would prove that the body had been moved."

"As if the person hadn't died in the house?"

"That's what some people think. Others assert that the two doctors had moved the body."

"And the second point?"

"According to Noguchi, the actress's stomach was empty. Completely empty. No medicament, no sedative. An observation by microscope confirmed the absence of refringent crystals. I won't explain what they are for the simple reason that I don't understand myself. The fact is that the absence of those crystals is incompatible with the ingurgitation of a large quantity of barbiturates."

"And people say that the conspiracy theories concerning Marilyn are far-fetched?" she said. "It's rather the official version that is."

"The majority of the theories point more in the direction of murder than disappearance, but I think we'll have to wait until your final discharge from the hospital, tomorrow, to reflect on it," Michael said. "We've arrived."

Chapter 43

Manhattan, Grant Memorial, 27 November.

Clyde Kaplan stopped in front of the memorial dedicated to General Grant. Standing to attention, he saluted the hero of the War of Secession who had become President of the United States; then he went up the steps and went inside the mausoleum, where James Powell, one of the seven members of the Iron Triangle, was waiting for him.

"I don't have much time to give you," snapped the old man, after shaking his hand limply.

Nor had Kaplan, but he refrained carefully from letting him know it.

"An affair requires me to plunge my nose into the Triangle's archives," Kaplan commenced. "An important affair..."

Powell made an irritated hand gesture to tell him to get to the point.

"Unpublished photographs of Marilyn Monroe have recently surfaced." He handed him the two copies that the F.B.I. agent had provided. "They've both been authenticated."

The other seized them and examined them, moving forward.

"Let's walk a little, murmured Powell, in a slightly tremulous voice. "You're sure of yourself?"

Kaplan had sharpened his arguments in the last few hours. He had to destabilize his mentor, back him up against the wall, facing his greatest failure. He wanted not only to obtain unlimited means to put an end to this affair once and for all, but also to weaken Powell's position in the hierarchy of the Triangle, with a view to his future ambitions.

"Marilyn's alive?" asked Powell.

"Alive, I don't know. These prints are beginning to get old, and Marilyn might well have passed over in the interim.

Nevertheless, a series of recent murders leads us to believe that she's still in this world."

The other's face fell. Nothing remained but to administer the death-blow. He waited for the next question.

"You think that she might talk, after all this time?"

Kaplan suppressed a smile. He had him. However, it was necessary not to act precipitately. Powell was an old man, but a powerful one, of whom it was necessary to be wary. He therefore chose to tell the truth.

"I don't know. For the moment, we lack certainty."

He summarized the whole story: the death of the New York photographer who was devoting an exhibition to the star, the various shootings in the city, and finally, the climax of the drama, the tragic fate of the Carneglia family. Then he evoked the difficulties encountered in the course of the investigation, and the lack of means at his disposal.

Powell did not reply immediately, doubtless lost in the mists of the past.

"You're right," the old man replied, finally. "It's our duty to get to the bottom of this affair."

Kaplan nodded his head. It was necessary to play the game with finesse.

"Ought we to inform the other members of the Triangle?"

Powell turned round abruptly and put a hand on his shoulder. He pressed hard. "Kaplan, need I remind you who you're working for? Who supported your candidature for the position you presently occupy?"

Kaplan gritted his teeth. *The old bear still has claws*, he thought.

"You, of course. I didn't want..."

"The other members," Powell cut in, "will be brought up to date with this disagreeable development at the right time. As for you, put a final period to this affair, which has gone on too long. You have carte blanche to get there."

Kaplan had to recognize his defeat.

"I won't disappoint you."

Chapter 44

Manhattan, Chelsea Market, 28 November.

The couple went through the glazed doors of Chelsea Market and then frayed a passage through the crowd of customers. After having recuperated at the bottom of the hospital steps, the millionaire had proposed to the young woman that they eat at his home, but she had refused. After an obligatory stay in hospital, she needed to breathe. They strolled between the shops for a while before their stomachs recalled themselves to their memory.

"Seafood, does that appeal to you?" asked Michael, as they came to a halt outside the aquatic window-display of a restaurant.

"Anything suits me—I'm dying of hunger."

Kristin limped toward the first free table. She seized the menu and decided on the day's special, lobster. Michael preferred a steak. Having ordered, Kristin considered the room.

"Do you think the F.B.I. is watching us?"

"There's every chance. Nevertheless, I don't think they can overhear our conversation."

"With them, one never knows." She darted a glance at the two bodyguards hired by Michael, who were standing in front of the window of the restaurant. "But we're going to ruin the day looking over our shoulder. Yesterday, I didn't think we'd finished out discussion about Marilyn."

"The autopsy? Yes that's true. I'd like to continue, if it doesn't disturb you to talk while we eat."

"Nothing could ruin my appetite more than hospital food."

"Very well. Where was I?"

"A matter of refrigerant crystals."

Michal smiled indulgently. "Nearly...refringent. But you're right, I'll return to that point. I told you that traces of those crystals ought to have been found in the body, but that wasn't the case. Nevertheless, that anomaly, like all the others, was consigned to the report, then forgotten...and buried."

"No one ever asked for complementary analyses?"

"In that era, no. The family wanted to recover the body for the funeral. It was Peter Gallardo, Andrew's father, who took charge of organizing the funeral—a small ceremony to which no Hollywood star was invited."

Kristin nodded. "And what about the will? She must have had a lot of money?"

"Not especially; Marilyn was a spendthrift. Her fortune was estimated at four hundred thousand dollars in today's money. Royalties derived from her films, of course, but most of all the utilization of her image: calendars, mugs, plates...the props are infinite."

The waiter interrupted them and set the dishes before them. They attacked them without delay, and ate in silence for a few minutes. Michael cracked first.

"One last interesting point that I haven't mentioned is the existence of a secret notebook."

Kristin looked at him in surprise, but he said nothing immediately, his mouth full.

"Well, officially, the notebook doesn't exist. For many connoisseurs it's an urban legend, no one having had the notebook in their hands. Among the actress's intimate circle however, several mentioned it in their testimony: a red notebook that she called her book of secrets. I'd completely forgotten its existence until I plunged back into the Foundation's archives the other evening."

"Is it known what she wrote in it?"

"There's very little information about that. According to some, it was an intimate journal. The actress recorded her conversations with her lovers in it. Hence the thought that she might have done that with John Kennedy..."

"A kind of protective guarantee?"

"Not even that, Once, a friend asked her why she was making notes, Marilyn retorted that she wanted to seek information about the subjects mentioned by her lovers in order not to seem like an idiot."

Kristin, who was dismembering the carcass of the lobster, replied: "That fits with what's known about her personality."

Michael smiled. "You're becoming a veritable specialist. Having said that, I agree with you. The greatest fear Marilyn had was of being considered an imbecile."

The waiter interposed himself again, an envelope in hand.

"A gentleman asked me to give you this."

Kristin seized the envelope and studied it from every angle. At first glance, nothing permitted the identification of the sender—no name, no address, nothing. Was the F.B.I. reminding them that they had not been forgotten?

"Have you finished?" the waiter asked, as she prepared to opened it.

The couple acquiesced, and he cleared the table before offering them the dessert menu. The young woman thanked them, and then opened the envelope under the curious eye of the millionaire. On the letter that she took out, a few lines were handwritten:

I would like to talk to you. I shall wait for you tomorrow on a bench on Brooklyn Bridge. Come alone. Marilyn Monroe.

Chapter 45

Manhattan, Chelsea Market, 28 November.

"You're sure that that really is Marilyn's handwriting?" she asked him, for the second time.

"Certain. I've spent years reading her correspondence. I'd recognize her handwriting in a thousand. I can assure you that Marilyn has really written that note." He looked her straight in the eyes. "I can't get over it. She's alive..."

Marilyn, or a gifted imitator. Kristin did not share the millionaire's enthusiasm; her natural mistrust led her to suspect another trap. The F.B.I.?

On a sudden impulse she took the note from the millionaire's hand and turned to the waiter, who was a few tables away. She summoned him with a hand gesture.

"Have you chosen a dessert?" he asked them, a few seconds later.

Kristin indicated the envelope to him. "Not yet, no...I want to know whether the person who gave you this envelope is still here."

"No. They left immediately after giving it to me, ten minutes ago."

Kristin could not mask her surprise. "They?"

"Yes, there were two. The man was accompanied by an old lady. In the beginning, I thought she must be his mother, but in view of the fashion in which he occupied himself with her, I think he probably works for her...a nurse, or something of that sort.'"

"Can you describe the old lady?" asked Michael.

The waiter frowned. "I remember thinking that she was very elegant for an old lady, but I can't tell you the color of her hair or any other physical detail—I'm sorry. She was rather small, that's all I remember."

Kristin thanked him and ordered a coffee. Michael did not have anything. While the waiter drew away, the millionaire looked at her, all smiles.

"*She* was here."

The young woman raised her eyes to the heavens; her companion had the expression a child on Christmas morning. But his good humor was contagious and she smiled in her turn.

"Apparently."

"Are you going to meet her?"

"Difficult to refuse. If it really is her, there are two or three things I'd like to hear from her mouth. In the contrary case...we'll, we'll face up to it."

Michael became serious again.

"In either case, it's risky."

The waiter deposited a cup in front of her and went away.

"That's true, but we don't have much choice. Our investigation is treading water. We need answers. As for the danger, between the guys you've recruited and the mole-men, we're not defenseless."

Michael acquiesced.

"If it really is Marilyn, there's still the risk of leading the F.B.I. to her."

Kristin blew over her coffee.

"It's up to us to make sure that doesn't happen."

PART SIX

Chapter 46

Manhattan, Brooklyn Bridge, 29 November.

As he passed close by, the man in the dark suit addressed a nod of the head to her. With four of his colleagues, the bodyguard moved off. They distributed themselves around the bridge in order to secure the area. Invisible, a few mole-men were also on watching, sitting on the sidewalk or on benches. Tom's death had stimulated them, and they were eager to come to blows.

For the moment, all was going well.

Kristin did not feel at ease for all that. There was no doubt that Dyers and his men were lurking there, somewhere before her eyes or above her head, guided by a satellite.

With a mechanical gesture, she checked the earpiece that the private security company hired by Michael had provided. At the slightest problem, the watchers would be alerted. She felt the metallic contact of a revolver against her belly—a risk, in New York, where carrying weapons is forbidden, but she would have no choice if the situation deteriorated.

She looked at her watch. Fifty-three minutes to the meeting.

The day before, after their escapade at Chelsea Market, Kristin and Michael had returned to the millionaire's apartment, where they had literally thrown themselves into one another's arms. They had retired to the bedroom, leaving a trail of scattered garments in their wake. There they had made love several times, passionately

Much later, their hunger sated, they had drawn up a plan of action, with a map of the city before their eyes. The location of the rendezvous Brooklyn Bridge, only had two exit points. In the case of a complication, the trap could close on them rapidly, blocking them in.

The young woman believed that they could succeed, however, firstly, because for the first time, she was leading the game. Since her relaxation and the fall of the Carneglia family, she had recovered her rhythm and no longer had more than one declared enemy: the F.B.I. agents. They, in addition, had always maneuvered in the shadows, manipulating, and looking for answers themselves. Unlike the Mafiosi, they would not take the risk of jumping in with both feet, especially in an area as busy as the bridge.

In fact, Kristin had placed the bodyguards at the strategic points, at the two entrances—Brooklyn and Manhattan—and between the two arches. Two homeless men were going back and forth along the cycle-track, others were sitting on benches are regular intervals, and other were watching the entrances situated beneath on the vehicular causeway. In all, a good twenty men where quartering the area.

Michael had abandoned her early in the morning to go to see his brother, who was about to fly to Spain, but he ought to return to the bridge at any moment; she knew she keep him up to date via her earpiece.

The young woman's gaze shifted skywards, toward the starry flag that was floating over one of the two pillars. She sketched a slight smile as she recalled the mnemonic means that her father had given her for remembering the order of the island's three bridges: BMW, Brooklyn, Manhattan, Williamsburg. The most recognizable of them, Brooklyn's, was mythical, rising majestically over the East River. Every day it attracted thousands of tourists with its impressive structure: the two enormous pillars linked by cable supporting two stages, a double six-lane roadway underneath for vehicles, and a promenade above reserved for pedestrians and bicycles, covered in wooden laths. The bridge possessed a unique style, to the point of becoming one of the symbols of the city, concurrent with the Statue of Liberty and the Empire State Building. It was by that route that the great majority of the wounded had been evacuated after the nine-eleven attacks.

Lost in her thoughts, Kristin was nearly knocked over by a bicycle. The cyclist called her to order, because she was on the cycle track.

In spite of the cold and the wind, the tourists walking across the bridge in both directions were numerous, young and not so young, of all nationalities, taking advantage of the magnificent view of the skyline of south-eastern Manhattan. Some waxed ecstatic on perceiving the State of Liberty in the distance, while others put a padlock on the bridge cables as a souvenir of their visit.

Kristin walked at random for a while, rehearsing their plan. It was simple. Under the vigilant eyes of their protectors, bodyguards and mole-men, they would bring Marilyn as far as one of two motor-cycles stationed at either end of the bridge— one for each scenario. With Marilyn behind her, Kristin would race to a taxi that was waiting for them in a side-street in Brooklyn. There, sheltered from surveillance cameras and satellites, two women hired for the occasion would take their place on the two-wheeler. Afterwards, they would go in the taxi to a hiding-place designated in advance.

Having validated the scenario, she had called Ian on the prepaid phone that he had also bought on her advice. For his part, Michael had informed the team of mercenaries that he had hired of their intentions. Both of them, of course, remained uncertain regarding the identity of the person they were going to meet.

Thinking about her lover, Kristin examined both sides of the promenade reserved for pedestrians, trying in vain to spot him. He had not arrived yet.

She looked at her watch: ten forty-seven. Another thirteen minutes.

The young woman took a step forward and put her hands on the rampart. The breathtaking panorama expelled Michael from her mind. She breathed in deeply—she needed to smell the city, to draw in strength for the battle to come—and then breathed out at length. She repeated the exercise several times.

Ten fifty-two.

Time seemed to have slowed. In eight minutes she would have the report of her men. Every quarter of an hour.

She resumed her surveillance of the passers-by.

An elegant woman, the waiter had declared. Around her, a few aged women corresponded well enough to the description, but none resembled the image—old and doubtless falsified—that she had of the actress. In her mind, the Marilyn of today was smiling as in the photographs of her grandfather, with only a few white hairs.

A heady perfume reached her nostrils and brought her out of her reverie: a mixture of jasmine and vanilla that she recognized. Chanel no. 5.

Kristin turned round and tracked the perfume to its source.

A few yards away, sitting on a bench, an old lady with snow-white hair was staring at her, with a broad smile. She addressed a hand gesture to her.

Kristin realized, after a few seconds, that it was Marilyn. Clad in a blue coat, she passed unnoticed in the crowd, resembling all the little old ladies of New York.

"Thank you for coming," Marilyn said.

Chapter 47

Manhattan, Brooklyn Bridge, 29 November.

Marilyn had the same voice as in the films, warm and sensual. In addition, her perfume seemed to act on her like a charm. It confused her mind and gave her the false impression of being secure.

Kristin shook herself. It was not a time for mundanities.

"You're in danger," she began without preamble. "The F.B.I. is on your heels. We don't have much time; we have to go."

"It's not the F.B.I.," Marilyn retorted, with an enigmatic smile. "Those people are far above that. They've been pursuing me or fifty years, and won't stop until I'm dead."

Dozens of questions were jostling in Kristin's head. She would have liked to have a few minutes to spare to interrogate the former actress, but even if no warning had yet resounded in her earpiece, she knew that time was against her."

"I owe you an apology," Marilyn went on, in a soft voice, without giving her time to respond. "The situation hasn't been easy for you recently. People who are dear to you have died because of me. When I learned…my supporters wanted to protect me, to continue to preserve the secret of my existence. They killed innocent people, including the photographer. They also tried to eliminate you."

As if unconscious of the danger, the former actress had delivered her monologue, not without difficulty. Her voice charged with emotion, she had sought for words, stumbling over them several times, as if offering apologies constituted a first for her.

Suddenly a crackle resounded in Kristin's earpiece. Her stomach knotted.

She looked around, her hand on her pistol, while a voice said. "Position One. Nothing to report."

The young woman breathed out, relieved. In the heat of the moment, she had forgotten the report that she had ordered every quarter of an hour. Thus, the first voice soon gave way to a second, and then a third. One after another, mercenaries and mole-men checked in, testifying that the F.B.I. had not yet shown the tip of its nose.

The false alarm acted on her like a shot of adrenalin.

"We'll talk about all that later, Ma'am. Come on—we need to get out of this place, and quickly."

Kristin extended her hand to help the old lady to stand up. Marilyn seized it, and pressed her fingers, tenderly, for a few seconds, before looking at her. Her gaze had not lost its intensity with age—quite the opposite.

"If I'm here today, it's to tell you that I'm sorry, for the harm I've caused you, for your friend's death. Offer my apologies, too, to Mr. Pear, who has gone to so much trouble to make sure that I'm not forgotten."

Newly disconcerted by the strange behavior of her interlocutor, Kristin had the impression of talking to a wall. The former mannequin seemed to be living in a different space-time.

"I'll tell him. Now we have to go. The F.B.I. won't take long to spot us; we need to get off the bridge. My men are waiting for us not far away with a vehicle."

Marilyn kept her hands in her own.

"That's kind of you," she said, "but I'll stay here. For me, the comedy ends today. It's gone on too long..."

The young woman swore silently. Now the former actress was experiencing suicidal desires! At the same time, she thought: *Difficult to find a better setting for a tragic conclusion than Brooklyn Bridge*.

"You know," the old lady went on, imperturbably, "I have the impression that I know you. A good friend of mine went to the opening of the exhibition the other day. What an idea of genius Stewart had of exhibiting us together!"

Kristin could not get her to quit the bench of her own will.

Suddenly, she heard shouting at the other end of the bridge, in the direction of Manhattan. A second later, there was chaos in her earpiece. Everyone was communicating at the same time. From what she could comprehend, armed men had just put in an appearance: members of the special forces.

Evidently she was mistaken; the F.B.I. did seem disposed to intervene in broad daylight. Marilyn's warning came back to mind.

It's not the F.B.I. Those people are far above that. What if she were right?

The surrounding clamor brought her back to reality.

For the moment, no one was shooting—none of the camps seemed disposed to strike first, but already, the panicked crowd were flooding off the bridge, in a concert of screams.

The young woman did not seek to know any more. She got up and obliged Marilyn to do likewise. Behind her, two mole-men placed themselves to either side of them to protect them.

"We have to go; they're here." She paused. "I'm sorry for what I'm about to do, but I can't let you fall into enemy hands. I need to understand."

Without asking for her permission, Kristin took the old woman in her arms and lifted her up; she was as light as a feather. Thus encumbered, she could not make use of her revolver. Her legs were her only weapon.

Over her shoulder she saw a troop forming twenty meters away. In the center, Ian Fountain was shouting like a maniac to organize the resistance. Soon, the men under his orders formed a blockade.

Armed men were arriving from Manhattan.

She began running in the other direction, toward Brooklyn.

She hoped that she was not throwing herself into the wolf's jaws.

Chapter 48

Manhattan, Brooklyn Bridge, 29 November
Five minutes earlier.

Comfortably installed in the rear set of an immense white saloon with tinted windows, Kaplan was watching Arroyo, thanks to two high-definition screens placed in front of him. Through the surveillance cameras deployed all along the bridge, he could follow events from his personal vehicle without difficulty.

That morning, when Arroyo had left Pear's apartment in company with a veritable private army, he had understood that something important was happening.

On the pretext of arresting a dangerous terrorist, he had used all Powell's influence to persuade the F.B.I. to mount an emergency operation, and confide its reins to Dyers. A few telephone calls had convinced the head of the Bureau to accept without asking too many questions.

At an early hour he had fixed himself at the two screens, sponging his forehead regularly, He was sweating copiously. What if he were being played? What if he had mobilized everybody for no good reason? On asking Powell to give him a free hand, he knew that he did not have the right to make any errors. At the slightest hitch, if anyone died, he would blow up, along with his chief.

A prudent politician, he had put out other lines, just in case.

On the screen, Arroyo turned round. Until then, she had been content to admire the view, like a tourist. The former lieutenant approached a bench. Someone was already occupying it. Unfortunately, his—or her—back was to the camera. Doubtless one of the homeless who were working for the young woman. She exchanged a few words with the newcomer.

In the F.B.I. post, a technician switched cameras. He took several seconds to regulate the zoom correctly.

When he saw the face of the mysterious stroller, Kaplan shuddered as if he had received an electric shock. It was an old lady.

"Dyers it's *her!*" she shouted into the mike. "Get hold of those two women!"

Michael got his breath back. He had just been running like a lunatic in order to get the meeting-place where, as promised, one of the bodyguards he had hired was waiting with a bicycle. He thanked his guardian angel and got astride the machine.

Earlier that morning, he had gone to J.F.K. International to say goodbye to his brother before the latter took off for Europe. He owed him that, after all that he had put him through. The airport was on the far side of Brooklyn, thirty minutes by car, not enough to prevent him from being on time to see Marilyn. Unfortunately, his brother's plane had been delayed, and he had not been able to stay until the end.

Later, on the return journey, an official visit had immobilized the great avenues and disrupted his schedule. Angry with himself for not having kept up with the news, he had phoned the director the private security firm to ask him to bring a bicycle toward his position at top speed. Then he had quit the security of his limousine, caught in the gridlock.

Kristin's idea of using motor-cycles to weave through the traffic had only become more brilliant. In case of hot pursuit, she would possess an advantage that was not negligible. He merely hoped that Marilyn would agree to climb on behind her.

With regard to his own situation, he had not informed Kristin for fear of worrying her.

The millionaire leaned harder on the pedals. His heart was hammering—because of the effort he had just made, obviously, but also from excitement. He was about to meet Marilyn Monroe!

Out of breath, he had just arrived at the bridge when he heard a distant clamor at the other end of the construction.

Dyers ran in the direction of the first arch of the bridge, not truly delighted to have got involved in this business. Furthermore, he had not been able to have his partner by his side, who was ill in bed.

The day had begun badly. Scarcely had he arrived at work after a conjugal dispute—divorce was approaching rapidly—than his boss had summoned him to his office. Furious, the latter had wanted to know why someone high up had charged him with a top secret operation whose broad outlines he was not allowed to know.

Dyers had played the idiot, pretending to know nothing, but his boss was not an imbecile; sooner or later he would get wind of his extra-curricular activities, and then…he preferred not to think about that.

His days in the bosom of the Bureau were counted.

As usual, Kaplan had acted with the heavy boots of an old military man, and he would pay for the broken pots. What a mistake it had been to agree to work for that nut job and his shitty secret society! Crazy ambition!

Kaplan would lose nothing by waiting.

An hour before, he had disembarked a few steps away from Brooklyn Bridge with a special forces squadron. The hardest part had begun: to explain to twenty goons that their mission consisted of arresting two women suspected on terrorism, one of whom had blown out her eightieth candle long ago, without seeming to be stupid. The presence of armed guards had attenuated the ridiculousness of the pitch.

And that wasn't all; they had orders to intervene, armed with nothing but tranquilizing darts. No deaths, those were the orders! Dyers had had the impression of reading his men the scenario of a Michael Bay film. A great moment.

Fortunately, those fellows were as thick as broom-handles. They had swallowed it all and were now awaiting orders.

A black spot in the setting; although the first crew were in position on the Manhattan side, the other was caught up in the gridlock. Prepared in haste, the operation found itself compromised by the visit to the U.N. of the Russian president Vladimir Putin. All the main arteries were immobilized. It was impossible, of course, to pass over Brooklyn Bridge without alerting Arroyo and her people.

And now, two minutes earlier, Kaplan had identified the target. All it had needed was for Marilyn Monroe to emerge from her tomb on this accursed day!

Conscious that he could not wait indefinitely for the second crew, Dyers had launched the assault. But with half a special forces squadron, it was difficult to pass unnoticed. Once in the open, the first screams had soon been heard.

After that, they frayed a course through the panicked crowd, with the impression of trying to swim upriver against the current.

His mind seething, Dyers switched on his radio.

"Where's the second crew?"

"Still caught in the gridlock."

"Fuck! Fuck! Fuck" repeated Dyers, continuing to run. He shoved aside a frightened tourist with a wave of his arm and continued his forward march. With the second jaw of the intended vice absent, he could only count on speed.

He finally arrived within sight of the first arch, where the members of the special forces ran into the blockade set up by Arroyo and Pear. The couple had a veritable private army at their disposal.

A general brawl was engaged, as in the days of the gangs of New York, in which the two camps rendered blow for blow.

Better equipped, with tasers and tranquilizing darts, his men rapidly succeeded in piercing a breach in the opposing wall. Taking advantage of the fact that no one was paying any heed to him, Dyers immediately plunged into it. Focused on his objective, he did not lend a hand to his troop. Almost all the tourists had reached one or other of the exits. The bridge was empty, the way clear. Three hundred meters away he recognized a silhouette drawing away rapidly in the direction of Brooklyn. Arroyo?

The F.B.I. agent launched himself in pursuit.

Chapter 49

Manhattan. Brooklyn Bridge, 29 November.

In her arms, Marilyn weighed no more than a sparrow. Nevertheless, thus encumbered, Kristin could not run as rapidly as she would have wished. She even had the impression of lagging seriously. In front of her, the bridge seemed to extend infinitely.

She had no idea of how the situation was evolving. In her haste she had lost her earpiece and all contact with her allies. The F.B.I. had struck rapidly and forcefully—and above all, in broad daylight—throwing all her plans out of kilter.

The young woman looked ahead. She still had at least five hundred yards to run to reach the place where the motorbike was parked. She hoped that her men were holding firm.

"Someone's running after us," Marilyn murmured in her ear.

"Michael?" she asked, in a breath,

The response made her wait. She felt the former actress twist in her arms.

"I don't know. He's too far away."

Kristin did not have time to check for herself. If it was the millionaire, his aid would be welcome. If not, she would waste precious seconds. She could not take the risk.

On the contrary, she accelerated.

The millionaire was trying to weave his bicycle through the mass of frightened tourists arriving in the opposite direction when one of them knocked him down.

On the ground, jostled and trampled, Michael could not succeed in getting up again immediately. After several attempts, he succeeded in getting to his knees, then leaned on a passer-by and finally stood up.

His bicycle lay two yards away. He would never get through the flood with it. He forsook the two wheels and chose to go around the crowd by running along the safety rail.

The excitement of encountering his idol had faded away; all his thoughts were directed toward a single objective: to find Kristin.

As quickly as possible.

Dyers was almost there.

It really was Arroyo in front of him. She was holding an old woman in her arms. doubtless Marilyn Monroe. At this distance, it was impossible to be certain. They were still twenty meters away.

A few seconds more, and he would be able to hurl himself upon them. His pistol would be no help then; Kaplan had been very precise in saying that he wanted them both alive.

Ten meters.

Almost out of breath, the F.B.I. agent felt a smile extending his lips

It was not Michael. Marilyn had confirmed that,

But whoever it was, he was getting closer. Marilyn had repeated that to her few seconds ago, as if it might change the situation.

Kristin reviewed her options—too limited for her liking.

The exit was very close, scarcely fifty metes, but before being able to reach the motor-bike it would be necessary to get through a veritable human barrier of frightened tourists with Marilyn in her arms and an adversary at her back. Impossible.

There remained the other alternative: to confront her pursuer. That way, at least she would not be waiting passively for the *coup-de-grâce*.

She was about to turn round when a familiar voice ordered: "Go on! I'll take care of it!"

Michael ran into the F.B.I. agent full tilt.

In the collision, Dyers' weapon spun away, several meters, and landed near the rampart. Shocked, the two men took a moment or two to get up.

Then they challenged one another with their gaze for a few seconds, neither daring to take the initiative.

Michael ignored the anger that urged him to attack first. Every second gained permitted the two women to get closer to the motor-cycle.

Dyers hurled himself upon him and knocked him to the ground.

The two men rolled over the wooden lining of the bridge.

This time, the millionaire gave free rein to his wrath and hammered his adversary with his fists. Surprised by that rush of violence, the F.B.I. agent protected himself with his arms, drunk with rage. Michael continued to molest him, without trying to take aim, just to land as many blows as possible.

Nevertheless, he had never been a brawler. He was fighting for the first time in his life. That was not the case for Dyers.

The latter only struck once—an uppercut to the chin— but it was sufficient. Michael fell backwards, stunned. A second blow to the temple knocked him out completely.

"Quickly! The motor-bike's here!" a voice called to her.

On the other side of the river of panicked tourists, the bodyguard who had remained by the motor-cycle was coming to meet her. He offered to carry the old woman and Kristin accepted. In spite of the former actress's light weight, her arms were beginning to go stiff.

The man steered toward the parking-lot. She followed him at an automatic pace,

A battle was raging around her. The temptation to go to Michael's aid was enormous—after all, what did the identity of the pilot of the bike matter, provided that it reached the taxi?

At the same time, the former soldier in her drove her to continue her mission no matter what. Even if it meant sacrificing the man she loved.

The bodyguard had put Marilyn down, and was now helping her to climb aboard.

"Do you know how it's going?" she asked him.

The man looked at her. "Not very well. They're more numerous and better armed."

She made her decision and climbed on to the bike in her turn. Alone, she had no chance of turning the tables. At the worst, she would be captured too. And who would command the ship then?

Her heart splitting, she turned the key to start the motor and, without waiting to discover whether the former actress was ready, joined the traffic. Behind her, she felt Marilyn clinging to her hips.

She looked in the rear-view mirror. The last thing she saw of Brooklyn Bridge was the American flag floating above the arches.

Pinned to the ground by two members of the special forces, the one-legged man looked them straight in the eyes, proudly. In spite of his handicap he had fought like a demon, only yielding after an electric discharge had forced him to do so. Even if Dyers would never have admitted it in a loud voice, the organized resistance he had encountered had impressed him to the highest degree, Arroyo had been very lucky to be able to count on such men in her ranks, ready to do anything for her.

Two minutes earlier, his men had embarked the millionaire in the truck. He had stayed in place in order to interrogate the amputee. As the F.B.I. agent had expected, the latter had not said anything. Worse than that, lying on the ground, the fellow continued to stare at him, as if he were a fucking hero.

"I can see that you'll be a hero at Rikers."

This time, the former soldier could not mask a slight tremor. He doubtless knew that a white ex-soldier like him would not live to grow old in the famous New York prison.

Dyers smiled.

"You have no desire to go to Rikers, if I'm not mistaken. That can be arranged..."

Chapter 50

Brooklyn, 29 November.

Kaplan asked the driver to take him to his apartment.

The operation had been a veritable fiasco. Arroyo and Marilyn had succeeded in escaping and taking off on a motorcycle. In the beginning, following their progress had been rendered possible thanks to the cameras disseminated throughout the city. The technician stationed in the F.B.I. post had worked wonders while Arroyo multiplied subterfuges in order to lose them. Unfortunately, the most recent had reckoned with him.

When a patrol had succeeded, on his orders, in immobilizing the vehicle, Kaplan had been jubilant. But cruel disillusionment had followed when they had discovered the identity of the two women: two unknowns paid to ride around the city; bait.

The cunning of which Arroyo had given proof almost compelled admiration.

The evening to come promised to be stormy. It would be necessary for him to extinguish the fire caused by the attack and the panic that had followed. Journalists and politicians were demanding explanations, not to mention the head of the F.B.I., who was only waiting for that disappointment to come at him.

He had to give them a bone to gnaw: Dyers. The Bureau agent had shown his incompetence in this affair. Everything was his fault. Whatever came down on top of him, he had deserved it.

On the seat, his mobile vibrated. Powell. Kaplan switched it over to voicemail. He had no desire to speak to his superior. Not now. He had to regain the upper hand.

It wasn't all over. Michael Pear was in their possession, and he counted on making use of that card.

He tapped out a number. His contact answered at the first ring.

"I believe it's time to reunite the two brothers."

Chapter 51

Manhattan, 29 November.

After having dropped them at the requested address, the taxi did not waste time and disappeared rapidly into the traffic. Baseball caps on their heads, the two women were standing in front of a three-story building of classic architecture, a carbon copy of the others in the vicinity.

"This is where I live."

Half an hour earlier, when they had exchanged the motor-cycle for a place in a taxi booked the precious evening, Kristin had been obliged to revise her plans. With no news of Michael and the others, she could not take the risk of going to the hiding-place decided in advance, doubtless already revealed, or about to be. She knew that from experience; sooner or later, someone would sit down at table, and the best option she had was to get ahead of her enemy.

When the driver had asked her for a destination she had not reacted immediately. Sick at having abandoned her lover in the hands of the F.B.I., she could no longer succeed in thinking and making a decision with discernment. They could not take refuge in her apartment—that was the first place the F.B.I. agents would go—nor in the subway tunnel.

Marilyn had put a hand on her shoulder then. Why not go to her house? After all, she had been hidden there for several years under the noses of the Iron Triangle. Resistant to the proposal at first—the idea of taking shelter with the person she was trying to protect seemed grotesque—Kristin had finally allowed herself to be convinced. At any rate, she was not in any condition to concentrate.

The journey in the taxi had passed without a word. With a knot in her stomach, Kristin was going back over the episode on the bridge repeatedly, convinced that she had made the wrong decision. Because of her mistake, because she had not imagined a frontal assault, Michael was now in the hands of the F.B.I., doubtless in the process of responding to a forceful interrogation. Marilyn had respected the young woman's ill humor and silence, contenting herself with looking out of the widow. It was only once they were out of the taxi that the former actress spoke.

"Pay no attention to the disorder," she warned her, as she inserted the key in the lock. "I wasn't expecting a visitor. To tell you the truth, I didn't expect to be coming back."

She had scarcely begun to turn the key when the door opened abruptly, revealing a masculine silhouette.

Still lost in her regrets, Kristin did not react instantly, as was her habit. When she became conscious that they might have just walked into a trap, the stranger uttered an enormous sigh.

"Oof! You've succeeded in getting out of it!" he said, in a mannered tone

Marilyn looked at him.

"Kristin, may I introduce Matthew Zimmer. Matthew lends me a hand with the everyday housework in return for a room on the first floor. It was him who took me to Brooklyn Bridge."

Visibly angry and upset, the man named Matthew went on: "I saw the attack, you know. I told you not to go, and of course, you didn't listen to me. As usual, once you get an idea in your head…!"

Marilyn took the man in her arms. The latter had tears in his eyes.

"I'm all right, Matthew I'm all right," she repeated, patting the butler on the back. "Kristin here saved my life. But for her I'd be dead now. Or worse... She's my guest, at least for this evening."

The man acquiesced, broke the embrace and then stood aside to let them enter."

The interior contrasted with the building's sober façade. Dozens of posters and paintings, all of Marilyn, ornamented the walls from floor to ceiling. One might have thought it a temple dedicated to the former actress. An odor of wax-polish, of cleanliness, floated in the air. Contrary to what the old woman had suggested earlier, everything was perfectly tidy, in its place. The man took off their coats. Kristin understood that here did more than help Marilyn with the daily housework; he behaved like a veritable butler. Doubtless he was the one who had accompanied the former actress when she had sent the letter in the restaurant; she would ask her for confirmation later.

"Are you sure that no one followed you here?" asked the servant.

Marilyn took her aside. "Reassure him, Kristin, or he'll pester us all day long."

"No one followed us, Matthew, you can trust me on that. I'm a former soldier."

Appeased, the servant invited them to go into the drawing room. Unsurprisingly, the new room was also crammed with posters, portraits and photographs with the effigy of the actress. *Not sure that the Foundation could do better*, the young woman thought. With its old waxed furniture and its dust-free fitted carpet, however, the room also gave an impression of comfort.

"Make yourself at home, I beg you. Would you like anything: coffee, tea?" the owner asked her. "Or something stronger? I have an excellent bourbon."

"A bourbon, please."

"For me it will be tea. Would you like to join us, Matthew; I believe you could do with a pick-me-up as well."

The butler did not succeed in masking a smile before leaving the room to fetch the drinks. Kristin let herself fall on to a sofa, which extended its comforting arms to her.

Chapter 52

Manhattan, Financial district, 29 November.

Michael raised his head.

Lost in his thoughts, he had not heard the door open. His wrists handcuffed to the back of a chair and his feet bound by a cord, he attempted to reconstitute the thread of his memories, since he had been knocked out on the bridge to his reawakening in this room ten minutes earlier. In vain.

Total blackness. And a headache, like a block of wood. He had been drugged, in order to move him more easily, no doubt, perhaps to make him talk. He did not have time to think about it much longer.

A man of about sixty came into the room—a former military man to judge by his bearing. The newcomer placed himself directly in front of his and gave him a terrible slap.

Michael bit his tongue. His headache intensified.

"I don't believe we've been introduced, Mr. Pear. My name is Clyde Kaplan. I work for an organization whose members prefer to remain in the shadows. A common acquaintance, Agent Dyers, has told me a great deal about you. From what I know, you don't like him very much. It might perhaps supply some balm to your heart to know that Agent Dyers is confronting the worst difficulties at present. He's certain to lose his job, and I don't believe he'll survive the day."

The millionaire did not reply.

"Agent Dyers had qualities," the man name Kaplan continued. "For example, he knew how to judge men. In his report, he presented you—forgive my language—as a bloody nuisance, a rich man short of sensations. Dyers also said that you were loyal, ready to do anything to protect your entourage. Believe me, that's a virtue I respect. Unfortunately, even with the information you've given us three hours ago, it transpires that I now have to put that loyalty to the test."

So, he had talked. Under the influence of a drug, but he had talked. Fortunately, from what he understood, the information he had furnished under constraint had not permitted Kristin's capture.

His interlocutor did not give him time to meditate for long. He knocked on the door and a man appeared, also a former soldier.

"But Agent Dyers' greatest quality, Mr. Pear, is that he knew how to discover a man's weak point." He turned to the man. "Send him in."

Michael uttered a howl on seeing his brother, also attached to a chair, almost naked, covered in bruises, burns and wounds of every sort. The millionaire's heart skipped a beat as he realized what his brother hand endured because of his fault.

In his gaze, however, Michael could not perceive any accusation. On the contrary, Daniel, seemed to be experiencing a certain serenity.

Michael turned his eyes away.

Kaplan stood beside him, in such a fashion as not to interpose himself between the two brothers.

"I must say that your brother is a rare fellow. My men have been working him over all day and he's never uttered the slightest whimper. A man of honor, of whom one would like to have more in the army. A pity that his allegiance lies elsewhere." He paused. "Just now I confided to you that I was about to put your fidelity to the proof, Mr. Pear, and I think you'll agree in saying that those weren't empty words. Today, your brother has been through a veritable Hell."

Michael was only following the discussion with one ear. He did not understand. At this moment his brother ought to be in Europe, far from this nightmare.

"How?"

Kaplan looked at him with a condescending expression.

"How was I able to put my hand on your brother? This morning, following a telephone call, his plane was delayed.

But I'm not telling you anything—you were there to bid him farewell at the airport. What you don't know, on the other hand, is that after your departure, customs officers invited your brother to go to their offices, because of a problem with the baggage. Your brother Daniel never caught the plane.

The millionaire looked at his torturer.

"What do you want?"

"A means of contacting Arroyo. So far, you've already told us all the places where she might have gone to ground. She wasn't in any of them. It's obvious that you have no idea where she is now. On the other hand, I believe that you have a means of contacting her. Give it to me, and we'll organize an exchange. Both your lives in exchange for Marilyn's."

Michael darted a final glance at his brother.

"Perhaps I have an idea."

Chapter 53

Manhattan, Tribeca, 29 November.

Kristin finished her glass of bourbon. For a few minutes, no one had dared to break the silence, taking advantage of the simple fact of appreciating a warm drink after a day rich in emotions. Then, although Michel was still and incessantly coming back to her mind, the young woman had launched the hostilities.

"A little while ago, you said that it wasn't the F.B.I. on the bridge."

"Indeed; it's a matter of the Iron Triangle."

"The Iron Triangle? Another top secret intelligence agency?"

"More of a private agency belonging to the military-industrial lobby," Marilyn replied. "American millionaires, for the most part."

"Are you serious?"

"Does it astonish you as much as that? The world has always belonged to the big fortunes. They're above frontiers and laws. They buy the media, pay for presidential campaigns and diffuse stupefying entertainment." Marilyn turned to her servant. "Matthew, can you prepare the blue room for our guest?"

By the expression on his face Kristin understood that the man was leaving the room regretfully.

"He'll hold it against me for a few days, but it's safer for him if he doesn't know anything. The Iron Triangle has existed since the end of the Second World War—I don't know the exact date. It remained in the shadows of history until January 17, 1961. That day, former President Dwight Eisenhower made a speech on television known as the 'military-industrial complex speech.' To summarize, he warned American con-

220

sciousness against the increasing and illegitimate influence of the military-industrial lobby. No one took any notice, of course, with the exception of John. The two men didn't like one another much, but they were nevertheless in agreement on that point. I know that they met in order to discuss the case of the Triangle, to put an end to their activities."

"And I suppose you're going to tell me that it was these lobbyists who killed Kennedy," sighed Kristin, with a disillusioned expression.

Marilyn set her cup down on the table.

"Is that difficult to believe? Today, historians are rare who take Oswald's motives seriously. Although he pulled the trigger, what seems certain is that someone else had put the idea..."

She did not finish the sentence. Kristin did not reply; she had thought herself that the assassination of the former President benefited too many people for it to be solely the work of a madman. She reorientated the discussion.

"It's the Iron Triangle who was after you?"

No, it's more complicated than that. The Triangle had nothing to do with my disappearance."

Kristin shook her head. "I don't understand. If the Iron Triangle had nothing to do with it, who wanted you dead?"

"The Prez. John himself."

Once again, the young woman could not mask her surprise. "Because you were his mistress?"

Marilyn uttered a loud burst of laughter. "No, if John had had to eliminate all his mistresses, the garden of the White House wouldn't have been sufficient to bury them."

"Why, then?"

"John confided a secret to me. A secret that he should never have repeated to anyone. It happened after the evening of his birthday at Madison Square Garden. We spent the night together—our last night—and he revealed the secret to me. You know how men are after making love? They're fatigued, they say what's passing through their head—it's also the only

221

moment when one can be sure that they're telling the truth," she added, with a wink.

Kristin smiled, but made no reply, allowing the actress to continue telling her story.

"He went to sleep immediately after having told me. Not me. I was terrified. I knew that she should never have confided that to me. I looked ahead, I understood that when he remembered, the next morning, he wouldn't have a choice."

"He would have to kill you."

"Exactly. Oh, for sure, he wouldn't have acted himself; John wasn't a coward, but he had a horror of getting his hands dirty. He would have confided the mission to his brother Bobby, who would then have handed it over to Hoover. He would have eliminated me without the slightest hesitation."

Kristin did not relaunch the conversation. Marilyn was beating around the bush, without daring to approach it frankly. Conscious of the silence extending, the former actress looked at her, as if to gauge her. Finally a broad smile appeared on her face.

"It's time, I think, that you asked me the question that's burning your lips."

"So what was the secret that he revealed to you?"

Marilyn swallowed her saliva before replying.

"It all began with Nikola Tesla."

Chapter 54

Manhattan, Tribeca, 29 November.

"Nikola Tesla?" murmured Kristin. "Never heard of him."

Marilyn smiled. "One of the greatest geniuses of the end of the nineteenth century and the beginning of the twentieth. Undoubtedly one of the most little known, as well."

"I'm the living proof of it. Who was he?"

"I don't know all the details of his life. I remember that he was born mid-way through the nineteenth century somewhere in the Austro-Hungarian Empire and died here in New York shortly before the end of the Second World War. He was one of the pioneers of electrical energy. He registered more than three hundred patents and collaborated with Thomas Edison. If I remember correctly, he gave his name, Tesla, to a magnetic unit, but I couldn't tell you which one."

"And it's because of him that you've been in hiding all these years?"

Marilyn took a deep breath before going on.

"Because of his genius, yes. I'm not a scientist but I've read up on him over the years in order to try to understand. To summarize, he focused on electricity and developed the concept of free energy. For him, terrestrial forces could produce an infinite supply of gratuitous energy. Just before his death he constructed a vortex turbine with a power of 3.15 megawatts, capable of transmitting energy without wires."

"Without wires?"

"That what John told me."

"And why has that discovery never seen the light of day?"

"He was working on that discovery on his own account, at home, and never spoke to anyone about it while he was alive. That's not so astonishing, in regard to his habits. He was a man of the shadows. For example, he was the true inventor of radio, as the Supreme Court recognized a year after his death. Some think he was the originator of the first X-rays, the fluorescent lamp, and even the laser."

The former actress had evidently taken advantage of her new life to inform herself on the subject.

"In what fashion did Kennedy learn of the existence of this machine?" said Kristin.

"On the night of the seventh and eighth of January 1943, Tesla was found dead in his room at the New Yorker Hotel here in Manhattan. He was eighty-six. Immediately, on the orders of Hoover, who always kept talented scientists under surveillance, F.B.I. agents searched his room and seized all the documents."

"So it was at that moment that Tesla's great idea fell into Hoover's hands and then Kennedy's?"

"No. As I told you, Tesla has always been underestimated. The two F.B.I. agents who seized the records of his research didn't understand their importance. They relegated them to the Bureau archives before forgetting them. It's necessary to say that in that era, the whole profession was concentrated on the Manhattan Project. Then, at the beginning of 1962, with the Cold War as at its height, an F.B.I. agent—John never told me his name—fell upon the documents. He would normally have been obliged to refer them to his superior, Hoover, as it happened, who was still in place, but the agent didn't trust him and his anticommunist obsession. So he made direct contact with John."

Marilyn sipped her tea, which must have been cold by now, before continuing.

"What I haven't told you is that Tesla had imagined several applications of that energy. One of them was a weapon. The peace ray, or the death ray—he hadn't decided on the name."

Kristin smiled. The story was beginning to veer toward science fiction. Marilyn misinterpreted the significance of her smile.

"Yes, I agree with you—Tesla might have been brilliant, but he didn't have the genus of names. According to John, the weapon would utilize an accelerator that would transmit particle beams through the air. The energy deployed could have destroyed more than ten thousand aircraft at a range of five hundred kilometers."

"I imagine that Kennedy saw a means of putting an end to the Cold War?"

"Not at all. For many people—the members of the Iron Triangle first and foremost—John was a coward, a weak president. In truth, John didn't like war—that was one of the things I appreciated about him. He was a pacifist. Without him, the Cold War would have degenerated, and if you look closely, it was only after his death that the Vietnam War gained amplitude. In brief, when he discovered the existence of the weapon, John immediately burned the plans. As I told you, he detested the Iron Triangle like the plague. In that era, the lobby wanted to lead the country into a war against the Soviet Union and China."

"You never saw the plans for the weapon?"

"Never. He didn't show them to anyone, not even his brother. He hinted to me that he had the F.B.I. agent who had brought them to him killed."

Marilyn stopped, lost in the mists of the past.

"The other research, on the other hand, he certainly had the intention of utilizing, especially the machine for generating energy freely and gratuitously. The Iron Triangle is an industrial complex, and John wanted to hit them where it would do the most harm—not in the heart, it has none, but in the wallet. According to him, part of their wealth came from oil and commerce in nuclear energy, which was beginning to become more important. If he succeeded in utilizing the alternative energy discovered by Tesla, he said, he would ruin them all. But one lone man, even the President of the United States, can do nothing against the Triangle. It owns everything: media, banks, the law, etc. He had to find allies. He began to talk about it to people around him, people he trusted. I don't know how the Triangle got wind of it, but obviously, John talked about it the wrong person. The consequence, you know. John was assassinated. Five years later, it was his brother's turn."

"John talked to you about this machine that night?"

"Yes. I understood the importance of the secret immediately. I told myself that my life was only hanging by a thread. Then I decided to disappear."

Chapter 55

"Allowing people to believe that it was a murder committed by the Kennedys?" Kristin exclaimed.

"Yes. An idea of genius, but it wasn't my doing, I must confess. It was Peter Gallardo who had the idea first."

"Andrew's father?"

"Yes. Peter was my greatest fan. He was ready to do anything for me. As for Andrew, he's always been in on the secret. When Mr. Pear telephoned him asking to talk to me about the night of my death, he was scared and called Vito. Don't judge him too severely, he's a good man, and devoted to me body and soul."

"You aren't afraid that the Triangle will find him?"

"No, with his wife, he's fled to England. They have sufficient liquid money to spend happy days there."

Kristin chose to return to the evening of Marilyn's presumed death.

"Why did Bobby Kennedy come to see you that evening?"

"Bobby always wanted to protect me, even after his brother told him to shut me up. I think that, although John desired me, he really loved me. That evening he advised me to get as far away as possible. He was the one who postponed my execution for two months. He told me that Hoover had now been given full powers in the matter, that he would act within a fortnight. He also gave me a copy of the plans for the Tesla machine—a precious gift from John—in case the Triangle moved against me. I've never made use of them."

She savored a gulp of tea before continuing.

"I didn't tell him but his visit came at a bad time. I was getting ready for the final scene."

She was interrupted by Matthew, who told her that he had prepared the room. The domestic withdrew without another word, and Marilyn was able to resume her story.

"We had anticipated everything. I knew the journalists. I knew that once the announcement of my death as made, some of them wouldn't be able to help looking further and going through my dustbin. They'd done it all my life. Why wouldn't they do it after my death?"

"How did you find the body?"

"People searched for one capable of deceiving the world for several weeks. It was then that I brought Vito in, the only one who could find that for me."

"How did you know him?"

"I met him through Sam Giancana, one of the bosses of the Mafia. So, I asked Vito to find me a body. Today, our mission would seem impossible but then, several elements were in our favor. It's necessary to recall that in that era, a lot of women were trying to look like me. I was at the height of my popularity. Nevertheless, finding the right body wasn't as easy as we thought. To tell the truth, we were beginning to despair...Vito even suggested accelerating the search, choosing a living woman. I refused, as you can imagine."

She stopped for a few seconds.

"By pure coincidence, it was the morning when Bobby came to see me that the rare pearl was unearthed. After Bobby's visit I telephoned Vito, and the operation was launched immediately."

"Where did you go, after the staging?"

"To Los Angeles first, but I didn't like the city. So, as soon as I could, I returned here, to New York."

"It wasn't difficult to change your life? To pass from the status of world-wide celebrity to that of anonymity?"

Marilyn took a cushion from the sofa, which she slid behind her back.

"I never missed my work...on the contrary. The celebrity, on the other hand...that's like a drug. In the beginning, it was all right...but several times, I had crises of a sort. I wanted to let my fans know that I was still alive. It was on one of those occasions that I ran into your grandfather."

"How did you meet him?"

"He was one of the most eminent members of the Monroe 6. He was also in on the secret. He was a marvelous man and a faithful friend. And as for the question that's burning your lips, no, I was never his mistress."

Kristin smiled, surprised by the old lady's sagacity.

"After my fake death, I lost sight of him, but when I returned to New York, he was the one who held me install myself here, in this apartment."

"He also continued to photograph you—like the photo in the subway?"

"Yes, that wasn't our most brilliant idea. As I told you, several times in the course of my second life, I fell prey to crises. At times, they were almost painful. I wanted to pose in front of a lens. To feel that I was desired again. Once, I cracked. It didn't take long to convince your grandfather. He was burning with desire to photograph me, too. We did several shoots in little-known places. I felt alive then—you can't imagine! I was happy, I was unconscious... Afterwards, we realized our error, the risk that the existence of those photos suspended over us. We were frightened, and chose to destroy them all..."

"But my grandfather wasn't able to resolve to destroy them," she finished, yawning.

"I should have suspected it. Edward would have died rather than destroy photos. But I'm being a very poor hostess. You've had a hard day, you must be exhausted. Come with me—I'll show you to your room."

As Kristin got up, her prepaid mobile buzzed. She looked at the number: unknown.

A presentiment urged her to answer it.

PART SEVEN

Chapter 56

Manhattan September 11 Museum, 30 November.

Kaplan allowed his gaze to wander over the names of the victims of nine-eleven engraved on the bronze plaques. Powell was waiting on the other side of the commemorative monument, but for once, he was in no hurry to cross swords with him. Unfortunately, the old man spotted him, and the old soldier was obliged to march in his direction, in order not to lose face.

Kaplan sighed. It was only a matter of hours before Marilyn fell into his hands, but the former military man was apprehensive of the encounter in spite of everything. In asking Powell three days before to put the power of the Iron Triangle at his disposal he had known that he was signing a pact with the Devil, in which the right to make mistakes was not tolerated. Since the fiasco of the operation mounted on Brooklyn Bridge and the media and political fall-out that had followed it, his position in the bosom of the Triangle had become fragile. In consequence, Powell had tried to reach him several times; he had not responded, delaying the inevitable. If the Triangle decided to dispense with his services, as he had done himself with Dyers, his days were numbered. Kaplan examined the surroundings, in search of an invisible sniper. No one. The Triangle member seemed to have come alone when he planted himself in front of him.

"Your phone isn't working any longer?" Powell commenced, without any polite formula. The old man was taking a malign pleasure in mocking him, but Kaplan kept his tongue tied.

"Your call this morning surprised me," his interlocutor continued. "I hope that you've come to tell me that you've finally captured her."

"Not yet, but she'll be ours this evening; I have the situation in hand again," he relied, although the confession cost him. "I've succeeded in contacting Arroyo. She's confirmed that identity of the woman on the bridge. It really is Marilyn."

"Go on."

"In a little more than two hours, I'm going to meet her in a parking lot to make an exchange—Pear and his brother for Marilyn."

"I hope your men will perform better than yesterday."

"They will. I've recruited a crew of mercenaries with my own funds—former soldiers who served under my orders, for the most part. We'll no longer have the F.B.I. treading on our toes."

The old man remained marble. He stared at a group of tourists who were taking selfies and laughing. People no longer had any respect.

"And Arroyo?"

"I took advantage of the night to make a few calls. It's time to cut the ground from under her feet. She doesn't know it yet, but one of her trump cards has just changed hands."

Powel nodded. "Who?"

"A man named Ian Fountain. A former soldier who served under Arroyo in Iraq. I've convinced him to work for us, in exchange for which no charges will be brought against him and his men regarding the episode on the bridge."

He was lying. It was Dyers who had persuaded Fountain to change sides by offering him immunity. He had only to take over, not without having removed Dyers from the equation beforehand. Through intermediaries, he had informed anyone who cared to listen—politicians, the media—that the F.B.I. agent had mistaken homeless men for terrorists during a special operation. The TV had rapidly taken up the affair, especially when an anonymous source had added the further information that the homeless men were, in fact, former soldiers, heroes of the fatherland.

Dyers was presently hospitalized after two hooded men—in reality, his own men—had attacked him outside the offices of the F.B.I.

Kaplan smiled, thinking about how easy it was nowadays to stitch people up, with a few means.

One point remained to broach. "There's just one problem," he went on, grimacing. "Arroyo knows about Tesla."

"She told you that?"

"Yes. Marilyn told her the whole story. If the exchange doesn't happen as arranged, Arroyo has threatened to reveal the secret to the whole world. She claims to have the plans."

Powell clenched his fists.

"So that infernal Kennedy also gave her the plans." He fell silent for a few seconds. "I've decided that I need to regulate this myself. We'll go to the rendezvous together. My limousine is parked over there."

"But…what about my car?"

"You can call your driver on the way. Then you can explain to me exactly what you intend to do. Those plans must never resurface, you hear me!"

Chapter 57

Michael did a few exercises in order to revive his painful muscles. He had spent the night on an old camp bed, unable to sleep, his mind tortured by bloody and mortal scenarios in which his brother perished every time, by his fault.

The millionaire sat down on the ground in order to stretch his legs more easily.

The previous evening, Michael had succeeded in contacting Kristin via the intermediary of Ian; he did not want to contact her directly in case the enemy attempted to locate the young woman's phone. He had given the homeless man's telephone number to Kaplan, who had then left the room in order to speak to him alone. The exchange had lasted several minutes, and for a moment Michael had been afraid that the one-legged man would refuse to relay the message to the young woman—an unfounded fear, however, since Kaplan had come back ten minutes later, all smiles, holding the phone out to him. It was Kristin. He had told her almost nothing—just that he and his brother were still alive. His captor had not given him time before snatching the phone back.

When he had ended the call, Kaplan had explained to him the broad outlines of their liberation. The rendezvous would take place in the parking lot of Pier 81, a place that Michael knew well because he had taken several of his conquests there for a cruise around Manhattan. According to Kaplan, if Kristin respected the terms of the exchange, everything would work out well for his brother and him. Michael did not know whether to believe the old military man or not, but he had obtained a promise from him that his brother would received medical care. That had already been done.

The millionaire stood up. Then he gnawed his bit in the empty, windowless room, not knowing whether the sun had risen—his watch had been removed—waiting for one of his guards to come to liberate him from his prison.

His nerves on edge, he let himself fall on to the camp bed. He did not even have a book or magazine to hand in order to kill time or chase away the black ideas that were bottled up in his skull. Finally, he closed his eyes and tried to go to steep.

"On your feet!"

The voice extracted him from a dream, the memory of which immediately vanished. Michael opened his eyes and stood up, grimacing. One of his guards was standing before him, features fixed.

"It's time."

"Is my brother coming with us?"

"No, he's taking another vehicle."

"I want to see him first."

The guard uttered a brief ironic laugh. "You'll see him later. Get a move on!"

He could not win the argument. Michael obeyed. Framed by two security men, he left his "room" without regret, went along a long corridor and then went into an elevator. The descent was made in quasi-religious silence. The metallic door opened, grating, on a subterranean parking garage.

A fourth man was waiting for them at the entrance—a driver, to judge by his attire. When they drew level with him he pressed a plastic key. In the distance, the lights of a vehicle responded: an immense white German saloon with tinted windows.

"You're lucky—the boss is lending you his car," said one of the armed men.

He obviously did not know with whom he was dealing; he had two of them himself, one of which was at least twice the price.

The millionaire was shoved into the back seat, in the middle, while the two guards sat beside him. They obliged him to put on his seat-belt, more to avoid eventual attempts at escape that in concern for his safety, of course. The other two men sat in front. An armored security window separated the two compartments.

No trace of Kaplan. The former military man must be going to the exchange location by another means, doubtless to divide the chances of a trap. The military man distrusted Kristin like the plague, he had told him.

Michael smiled as he thought about the young woman, so dangerous beneath her apparent fragility.

The vehicle pulled away immediately. They left the parking garage and plunged into the traffic. To cap the irony, Michael could see the building that lodged his company in the distance. The building that had served as his prison was in the heart of Manhattan.

Through the tinted windows the millionaire watched the streets file past as if in a film. The seconds appeared to flow slowly, stretching out infinitely. In spite of the cold weather, sweat was already dampening his short.

In the car, the three agents were as mute as the grave—as if they were taking him to the abattoir.

At that moment, Michael knew for sure that Kaplan intended to eliminate both of them, his brother and himself—and doubtless Kristin too. He could not leave witnesses alive.

The spell that had weighed upon him since he had been drugged in order to interrogate him suddenly broke. For the first time in forty-eight hours he could see clearly.

He had to find a way to escape.

Pretending to be relieving his neck muscles, he looked around, in search of a weapon, or an exit—anything that might permit him to get away.

To either side of him, the two guards were amusing themselves with their phones—video games or texts, it hardly mattered. Michael turned his head both ways. A bump at chest height betrayed the presence of a pistol.

If he could manage to get hold of it...

He could not wait any longer. He was about to play his last card. To hell with the consequences!

As the vehicle reached an intersection, Michael took a deep breath in order to give himself courage.

At the same time, an ambulance appeared to the right, sirens howling, without paying any heed to the red light. The driver did not have time to brake, and could not avoid the brutal impact.

The saloon flipped over, colliding with two other vehicles before crashing into the display window of a Five Guys restaurant, coming to rest, by a fortunate chance, on its wheels.

Chapter 58

Manhattan, 30 November.

A fit of coughing woke him up. Stunned, Michael looked around. The two guards lay on the back seat, still unconscious. The one on his left had broken his nose, probably the fault of the airbag placed behind the driver's seat, which had inflated at the moment of impact.

An accident—a simple traffic accident! A few moments before, he had been ready to go into action to get rid of his captors, but now found himself in a favorable position. If his ribs had not been hurting so much, he might almost have laughed.

The millionaire pricked up his ear. In the front compartment, on the other side of the security glass, someone was recovering contact with reality—doubtless the man who had coughed a few seconds earlier.

No time to hang about! He had to get out of the saloon as fast as possible.

Michael succeeded in unbuckling the seat-belt easily enough. He was leaning forward to open the door when it opened of its own accord.

Rapidly, he perceived an armed silhouette, but the exterior luminosity dazzled him, obliging him to close his eyes.

His last moment had arrived.

He heard two muffled gunshots. The aggressor was using a silencer.

What an idiot! Of course the accident hadn't happened by chance!

For a moment, he hoped that it was Kristin who was at the wheel of the ambulance, but he renounced that idea rapidly. The young woman would never have made the decision to crash into a vehicle at that speed and risk killing him.

The millionaire clenched his teeth, ready to pay the ultimate price for his stupidity.

He waited for what seemed to him to be an eternity.

"It's not worth the trouble of paying dead—I know you're alive."

He knew the voice but did not succeed in identifying it immediately. He was dragged out of the vehicle unceremoniously, by the arm.

Outside, Michael blinked several times in order to adapt to the daylight. Standing facing him was Agent Dyers. The latter looked exceedingly nervous—far more than usual, in fact. What was more, he seemed to have had a bad time; his face was covered with numerous bruises.

"Where's Kaplan?" he demanded, peevishly.

"In another car, I think," Michael stammered, his mouth thick.

"Fuck!"

The F.B.I. agent opened the front door of the saloon and pressed the trigger twice.

"Fuck! Fuck! Fuck!"

The millionaire, caught between Scylla and Charybdis, tried to make himself very small in order not to be the fifth victim of the murderous folly that had taken possession of Dyers.

Then, in a flash, he remembered what Kaplan had said to him the day before about the Dyers situation. "Agent Dyers is confronting the worst difficulties at this moment. He's sure to lose his job and I don't believe he'll survive the day."

If he was not mistaken, the Triangle had, for some unknown reason, let Agent Dyers go—and the latter was visible seeking revenge. An idea that would have been completely unthinkable a few days earlier commenced to germinate in the millionaire's mind: an alliance with the man who had beaten him up twice. Perhaps the accident had seriously softened his brain.

But he had no choice. The lives of Kristin and Daniel were at stake.

Michel took his courage in both hands in order to negotiate with a madman—worse, an armed madman.

"I know where Kaplan is."

Immediately, the barrel of Dyers' pistol was pointed at him. It might have been better to keep quiet...

"I know where he is," he continued, scorning all reason, "but I won't tell you unless you take me with you."

Dyers did not reply.

"Kaplan's going to set a trap for the woman I love and kill my brother. I no longer have anything to lose."

The former F.B.I. agent smiled. Without a word, he turned around and headed for the ambulance. The bastard was hooked.

Dyers opened the door of the vehicle, and started the engine before shouting: "Get in!"

Chapter 59

Pier 81, 30 November.

"Start spreading the news. I'm leaving today. I want to be part of it—New York, New York."

With Sinatra's voice in her ears and the setting sun before her eyes, Kristin sensed the adrenalin surging through her entire body.

The urban lighting came on in relays to illuminate the vast parking lot that welcomed several hundred vehicles every day. For the moment, it was almost empty, the busy season having ended a month and a half earlier. A few courageous walkers were strolling along the waterfront, scarves around their necks. The entire length of the Hudson had been adapted for tourists or sportsmen: sports stadia, cruise boats, tours on foot or bicycle, little parks, naval museums, etc.

In the center of the tarmac two vehicles with tinted windows, hired for the occasion, were parked. Four homeless men were on watch, divided between the two vehicles—armed. Marilyn was waiting elsewhere, but her enemies were not supposed to know that.

The young woman knew the place vaguely. For her eighteenth birthday her parents had given her a cruise on the Hudson, during which she had eaten an incredible gastronomic repast: three hours of pleasure. In her memories, they had taken the boat at the very place where she was now.

In a few minutes, the moment of truth would come: the exchange.

For now, the young woman was taking advantage of the present moment, the calm before the storm. She switched off her MP3 player and took off the earphones. Since Kaplan's phone call the previous evening she had assembled her forces and imagined a means of cheating death one last time.

An hour earlier she had handed Matthew an envelope containing a copy of the plans of the Tesla machine: a guarantee in case things turned sour. In tears, the domestic had promised to do what was necessary, if the two women did not come back. He understood that it was time finally to put an end to the affair, which had gone on too long. Too many people had lost their lives—Nathan, Tom, but also, more distantly, the Kennedys—and others were once again in danger of death: Michael and his brother Daniel, not to mention the victims making the exchange.

Kristin could not help thinking that the Triangle would not tolerate witnesses, once the plans were in their possession. If the lobby hoped to cheat her, it would be at their expense. She would not let go. She was a New Yorker, suckled since childhood on one of the city's slogans: to "make it."

She headed toward Ian's location. After the episode on the bridge, the one-legged man and all his men had been released, to general surprise, and her own too. In the media scandal that had followed the brawl and the panic, numerous heads had fallen in high places. The press had not cited any names, but on reading the morning paper. Kristin had been surprised to see the support given to former combatants who had become homeless, by internet users or journalists.

The evening before, when she had phoned Ian immediately after the call from the man named Kaplan, the amputee had immediately given his consent to the operation to come. The young woman had thanked him several times and promised to return the favor one day. The mole-man had not replied, doubtless more touched than he had wanted to say.

Kristin quit the docks to go to the exit from Pier 81, where Ian had set down his blanket and cup. The rare strollers only saw a beggar, but the young woman knew that his blanket was hiding weapons, and his worn pullover a bulletproof vest.

"The zone's secured," he murmured. "No vehicles, no suspicious individuals. Everything permits the belief that they aren't preparing an ambush and have every intention of proceeding with the exchange."

"Thanks. For this…and everything else."

The homeless man's face contracted imperceptibly. "You know that I can't refuse you anything," he said, lightly.

That at least had the merit of making her smile.

"Everything's ready. Now, the hardest thing is waiting.. Don't bring Marilyn until I have confirmation of the presence of Michael and his brother.

The old woman was waiting in the ticket-booth, in the company of two mole-men. Kristin thought about the discussion they had had when they left her domicile. Marilyn had seemed astonishingly serene.

"Everything all right?" Kristin had asked.

"Yes. I'm a little nervous," the star confessed, with a wry smile. "I feel as if I'm going on set for one last time."

The young woman shook her head in order to return to the present. She was about to look at her watch when a limousine escorted by two four-by-fours came into the parking lot by the main entrance.

Finally!

She made a sign of encouragement to Ian—more for herself than for him—before returning to the center of the arena where five vehicles were now waiting, disposed in a parody of a circle fifty meters in diameter.

After the media racket of the last few days, the Triangle was moving discreetly—to prove its good intentions, of course, but also to avoid a new scandal.

The car doors opened simultaneously. It was her move.

Chapter 60

Pier 81, 30 November.

Framed by a close guard—ex-soldiers, Kristin would have bet her shirt—a man of about fifty, his temples graying, came forward. He stopped two meters away and looked her up and down suspiciously

An old member of the family, the young woman thought. *High-ranking, even.*

"Monroe isn't here," he snapped, in a voice accustomed to command, confirming her intuition.

"Not are my friends as far as I can see. Mr. Kaplan. I presume?"

The man had introduced himself the previous evening when he had phoned her to reveal the terms of the exchange.

"That's me. The Pear brothers are in another vehicle, some distance away. It won't budge until I have proof that Marilyn is really with you."

"We're in an impasse, then. I've asked Marilyn not to show herself until I have proof that Michael and Daniel are here, and alive."

Her interlocutor darted a glance at the two vehicles parked behind her, ten meters away, but the tinted windows were doing their job and prevented him from obtaining the desired conformation. On the other hand, Kaplan had no difficulty observing the homeless men placed around the vehicles.

"You've brought the cavalry."

"The Iron Triangle hasn't really given me the impression of being trustworthy. I'm made my arrangements in consequence. I don't think they like negotiation; they're more inclined to elimination, according to what I've been told."

A heavy silence fell over the assembly: electric.

In both camps, everyone was tense, hands on weapons. A single order on either side, and everything would immediately kick off.

"In the name of God, Kaplan," cut in a voice from the limousine, "tell the car in which the Pears are being held to get into gear and let's finish this as quickly as possible!"

Kristin could not mask her surprise.

"To whom do I have the honor...?"

For a few seconds, no one replied. Then a silhouette was detached from the shadow of the limousine and an old man emerged. Kristin examined him. He must have been in his eighties. He stood about a five-four, and held himself upright. His keen gaze posed on Kristin. She saw in the eyes that were studying her that he was a man who did not accept contradiction, a powerful man who did not recoil before anything.

Hus gaze went back to Kaplan, but the latter drew away, holding a phone to his ear.

"James Powell."

Kristin reflected at top speed. "So Mr. Kaplan isn't at the top of the pyramid—although I suspected as much. I suppose you're part of the mysterious Iron Triangle."

The old man smiled.

"You suppose correctly. If I understand correctly, Marilyn has told you the whole story—Tesla, the Kennedys, etc."

Kristin did not reply, not knowing what attitude to adopt.

"That means yes. It won't take as long if I don't have to explain everything. Yesterday, you confided to Mr. Kaplan on the phone that you have documents in your possession—plans."

The young woman acquiesced.

"Go, very good. Excellent. You don't want to reveal where Miss Monroe is, I understand. You have every reason to be suspicious...."

"Get to the point."

Kristin was beginning to get angry. The man was as chatty as a politician. He probably was one.

"Straight to the point! You're a former soldier, no doubt about that. What I propose to you, Miss Arroyo, is a bargain. I'll ask for the vehicle in which your friends are being held to join us, and in the meantime, you show me the plans that interest us."

The young woman hesitated. She had the impression that the man was setting a trap, without being able to distinguish its nature. Perhaps she was becoming paranoid... That he was asking to verify the plans seemed quite acceptable. Better, it would permit her to make sure that Michael and his brother were still alive. Then the exchange could take place.

She made her decision.

"All right. But no dirty tricks, of course. At the first sign of trouble, I'll ask my men to evacuate Marilyn and you'll never find her. I've made copies of the plans, which will be sent to several national and international media."

"There'll be no dirty tricks, I give you my word. As for your threat of sending the plans to the national media," the old man went on, laughing, "know that it would do no good. They all belong to us."

Kristin felt her anger mounting, but she could no longer retreat.

"Your arrogance will doom you," she said, dryly.

But the old man was no longer listening. He gave the order to have the fourth vehicle come forward, as he had promised.

Irritated, Kristin took a copy of the plans out of her pocket, which she held out to Kaplan. The old soldier seized them and took them to his superior, who studied them at length.

Visibly satisfied, the two men came closer.

"I'm not an expert," said the old man, "but these documents seem perfectly authentic. Yes, they really are the Tesla plans."

"I told you so. I've keep my word. Your turn. Where's the car?"

"What car?" asked Powell, in a reedy tone. "Of, of course…the car with Mr. Pear."

Then he addressed one of his men. "Have Mr. Pear brought out of the vehicle. He must be stifling."

The man obeyed, He headed for one of the four-by-fours and opened the trunk.

Kristin could not believe her ears. Powell was laughing in her face. Michael had been in the trunk from the start.

Angrily, she brought out her weapon, and behind her. She heard her men doing likewise. But she did not press the trigger. A nasty presentiment told her to follow the scene to the end.

As if unconscious of the tension that had just gone up a notch, Powell was still smiling. He watched his man pulling a corpse out of the vehicle.

Kristin's heart missed a beat.

Chapter 61

Pier 81, 30 November.

Although the man had numerous features in common with him, it was not Michael.

The relief only lasted a few seconds. Kristin gasped when the horror of the situation struck her like a whiplash. She understood who it was.

It was Daniel, Michael's brother.

Dead.

For a moment, prostrate under the weight of the revelation, the young woman remained devoid of sensation, incapable of reaction. Soon, horror gave way to anger, and she threatened Powell with her weapon again.

"Where's Michael?"

The old man raised his hands.

"I haven't the slightest idea! A car was supposed to join us with your friend aboard. It never arrived. We tried to call it, but no one replied. I believe your millionaire has packed his bags and run."

"You're going to regret what you've done."

Powell smiled again.

"No, I don't think so. Look behind you."

Her pistol; still aimed at the Triangle member, Kristin did as she was told. She sensed events escaping her.

A nightmare vision. The mole-men were not pointing their weapons at the agents of the Triangle, as she had thought earlier, but at her. Worse, behind the two parked vehicles, Ian was pushing Marilyn toward the group, straight into the wolf's jaws.

Treason.

She was trapped. Gradually, in her mind, certain pieces of the puzzle—certain questions, certain answers—took on a new significance.

Why had Ian and the others been released so quickly after the incident on the bridge?

Why had Kaplan arrived with so few reinforcements?

And finally, why had Powell wanted to study the plans and not make sure of Marilyn's presence?

Powell knew that Marilyn was already there; perhaps he even knew where she was hiding. On the other hand, with regard to the plans, he had not been certain. On reflection, Kristin had never raised that issue with Ian—not for lack of confidence; she simply hadn't thought of it—and the homeless man had not been able to inform Powell on that point.

Alone against everyone, she could not win. The enemy was too strong, too numerous.

Nevertheless, before laying down her weapon, there was one last thing she needed to understand—futile, given the situation, but necessary for her peace of mind.

How had the Triangle turned her own men against her? She asked the question aloud.

"Everything can be bought," said Powell, with the arrogant smile that was characteristic of him, "Even soldiers."

"I don't believe you," she whispered, raking Ian, who had joined them, with her eyes. He turned his head away in order not to meet her gaze.

Powell was about to reply, but Kaplan got in ahead of him. "We spared him ten years at Rikers in exchange for his services." The former military man did not seem to have appreciated Powell's speech with regard to the saleability of soldiers overmuch.

Kristin nodded her head. At least Ian and the others had not abandoned her for money.

"Lieutenant Arroyo," said Kaplan, "I'm going to ask you to put down your weapon. You have no chance of escaping."

As if that were at the back of her mind... Before obeying, Kristin sought Marilyn with her gaze, to apologize. She had trusted the wrong people, and now the former actress was at grips with those she had fled forty years earlier.

The old woman detached herself from the grasp of the one-legged man and crossed the few yards that separated her from Kristin. She hugged her for a few seconds, without saying a word.

When the embrace was concluded, Kristin dropped her weapon.

"Mr. Powell," said Marilyn, turning round. "I didn't think I'd see you again."

"I wasn't certain that you'd remember me," the Iron Triangle man replied.

"I have an excellent visual memory. I remember our meeting as if it were yesterday. That day, John had invited me to the White House. There had been a rift between Jackie and him. She suspected something. It wasn't the first time he'd cheated on her, of course, but it was doubtless the first time that one of his extramarital affairs had lasted so long..."

Marilyn's voice became distant. "We were having lunch with a few intimate friends of the Prez when you irrupted into the room. I'd never seen John like that. He was beside himself. John repeated to you that he'd never make a deal with you. Never. After your departure, I asked John for an explanation. He didn't tell me anything that night. It was only later that he confessed everything to me..."

"A President confiding in a whore! The Kennedys were only good for running after starlets!" Powell spat.

Marilyn smiled at the insult.

"John had his faults, that's certain. He liked women too much, and sex for its own sake. But John also loved his country profoundly. He didn't seek to enrich himself on the backs of his compatriots, or plunge the country into an unnecessary war under false patriotic pretexts..."

Powell raised his hand to strike her, but he held back at the last moment. The howl of a siren in the distance restored his calm.

"Enough games! We'll have plenty of time to talk politics later. Put everyone in the cars. We've had enough play-acting for one day." He turned toward Kristin, his smile returning. "Kaplan tells me that you participated in several interrogations in Iraq. I'm eager to know how you react when the roles are reversed. You have a great deal..."

He did not finish his sentence. The siren was getting closer.

An ambulance drove into the parking lot and headed toward them at top speed.

Chapter 62

Pier 81, 30 November.
Two minutes earlier.

"Do you at least have a plan?"

It was the first thing he had said since he had brought Dyers to the location of the rendezvous fifteen minutes earlier. To begin with, he had been afraid that the former F.B.I. agent might throw him out of the ambulance at the first opportunity once he had provided the information, but the latter had contented himself with driving to the place at top speed. Twice he had narrowly avoided an accident, God alone knew how.

In the compartment, silence reigned. Michael had sought hard for a means of breaking it, in vain. It is difficult to find a topic of conversation with a man who has beaten you up twice. Then he had thought of what was going to happen next. What did Dyers intend to do when they got there? And he had asked the question.

The latter took his time answering.

"Simple. You free Arroyo. I kill Kaplan."

"Is that a joke?"

The F.B.I. agent shrugged his shoulders.

A scenario passed through the millionaire's mind.

"You don't intend to land us in the shit, though? They'll see us coming..."

Dyers smiled, and switched on the siren

Immediately before the collision, time seemed suspended.

The two homeless men taking Marilyn to one of the four-by-fours had released her in order to grab their weapons.

Strange as it might seem, however, no one opened fire. Everyone thinks twice before firing at an ambulance.

In spite of the distance, Kristin perceived the faces of two men in the cabin. She thought she recognized Michael.

The young woman blinked.

The driver bore a striking resemblance to the man who had pursued Marilyn and her on Brooklyn Bridge. Absurd.

"It's Dyers!" howled Kaplan.

Suddenly, time reclaimed its rights. The ambulance slammed into the limousine, with a screech of metal and shattering glass.

All around, there was chaos.

Then a deluge of fire commenced.

Crouched behind a four-by-four, Kaplan darted a glance over the roof of the vehicle.

Dyers was spraying their position with automatic fire— large caliber, which prevented them from replying. The former F.B.I. agent had already scored two hits.

Dyers had come for him.

Kaplan was about to take shelter behind the limousine when he met the gaze of another man. Plastered behind the ambulance, Pear was staring at him.

That was the reason the millionaire had never arrived. Dyers had intercepted his vehicle, hoping to find him inside it, but had missed. By changing his plans at the last minute, Powell had probably saved his life.

But Pear had brought Dyers here.

Pear and Dyers. An unexpected collaboration, which he would never have imagined.

A bullet whistled over him, closer than the others, and obliged him to regain his former shelter. Kaplan backed up against the wheel of the four-by-four and contemplated the disorder that reigned in his camp.

Powell had lost his calmness definitively. Used to pulling the strings from the wings, the Triangle member was hurling abuse at everybody, the mercenaries and the homeless men. His fury only seemed to be equaled by his terror. A little old man who ruled the planet but had never experienced the reality of a battlefield.

Two guards were supporting Marilyn and dragging her toward the two vehicles parked further way, those in which Arroyo and her men had arrived. In his haste, or perhaps because he considered her less important, the old man had not taken Kristin with him. Still in play, she was observing events intently. Kaplan would have bet that she was seeking the best way of taking advantage of it. He hoped that her two guards were paying attention.

A roar forced him to turn his head.

Having reached the car door, Powell shouted something in his direction, but a few feet away, the windscreen of the four-by-four behind which he had taken refuge exploded into a thousand fragments and prevented him from hearing it.

Kaplan shrugged his shoulders,.

Too bad for Powell!

Dyers had come for him; he would not disappoint him.

In the parking lot it had become every man for himself.

On the one hand, Kaplan had recovered his spirits and was now organizing a counter-attack aimed at eliminating Dyers. Ian had recognized the F.B.I. agent.

On the other hand, Powell was about to take off in a car.

Now was the moment to act, or never, and to change a situation badly engaged.

Agent Dyers, and then Kaplan after him, had obliged him to turn his coat and betray Kristin, the only person who had ever extended a hand to him when his life had collapsed; the only person who had preoccupied herself with him when his family had abandoned him. At the time, he had had no choice; a former soldier did not make old bones at Rikers. He had accepted the deal proposed to him and his men, with the firm intention of finding a solution in days to come. Now, Dyers' arrival with a fanfare had procured him a golden opportunity.

Taking advantage of the fact that no one was paying any attention to him, the homeless man approached the two men holding Kristin. Ian took the right hand of the first and pulled him toward him in order to unbalance him, before striking him violently on the head. The mercenary collapsed, stunned.

The amputee turned to oppose the second, but his handicap caused him to lose precious seconds. The second enemy already had his gun aimed at him...

But he did not press the trigger. Kristin did not give him the chance. She seized him from behind and, with her knuckles folded, gave him a mighty punch in the ribs. The fellow howled in pan and dropped his weapon. The young woman did not stop there; she forced her adversary to face her, leaned on his shoulders to oblige him to bend over, and delivered a terrible blow to his face with her knee. The knockout that followed was not in doubt.

Ian still liked to watch the young woman fight. Implacable, and yet careful not to kill.

She rearranged her hair with her right hand before looking at him with a grave expression. They exchanged a long glance. Gratitude. Forgiveness, Loyalty. Friendship.

"Go save Marilyn. I'll take care of Kaplan."

Then he rallied his men with a hand gesture, and headed in the direction of the gun-battle.

Chapter 63

Pier 81, 30 November.

Kristin bent down to pick up the gun that had fallen at her feet. She checked that it was still loaded before heading in the direction of the car whose headlights had just lit up fifteen yards away.

Like all the politicians in the world, Powell had decided to set sail as soon as the situation had begun to go bad. Kristin imagined him returning to the scene of the battle the next day or the day after, once events had concluded. Then he would make a speech looking straight into the camera. Merely thinking about it, the young woman felt nauseated.

Kristin did not launch herself n pursuit of the vehicle; that was a race lost in advance. On the contrary, she put one knee on the ground and put herself in a firing position. She took meticulous aim at the tires and fired three shots.

The vehicle slowed down but did not stop for so little.

Twenty yards.

The young woman held her breath, and took aim at the engine.

Thirty yards.

She pressed the trigger twice.

The result of the shot was scarcely what she desired. Two interminable seconds later, the driver lost control of the vehicle, which concluded into course against an advertising hoarding. In view of the reduced speed at which it was traveling, diminished by two tires, the impact was not violent.

Kristin ran toward the immobilized vehicle, her weapon directed forward.

Is she had counted correctly, she still had one bullet let.

The rear door opened.

The firing had ceased a few seconds earlier, and the two camps were now looking at each other like china dogs, waiting for...Ian did not know what yet.

A few seconds earlier, his initiative had taken Kaplan by surprise. The latter was ready to launch his assault on the ambulance when the one-legged man had called to him, his men arranged in a line, ready to fire.

At the same moment, he had heard three gunshots behind him.

Kristin.

The temptation to turn round was strong, but he pushed it to the back of his mind. The lieutenant was big enough to look after herself. Then two other shots had run out. He had ignored them in the same fashion, in order to concentrate on his own situation.

Kaplan had looked at him, surprised—furious, even, to have been cut off in his stride. For some unknown reason, he seemed to be burning to get to grips with his former hireling.

In the direction of the ambulance, Dyers' machine-pistol had also fallen silent. Behind the vehicle, riddled with bullet-holes, two silhouettes were designed. Dyers...and Pear. Ian did not recognize the millionaire immediately. His face bore the stigmata of the last few days: fatigue, violence and pain.

As for Dyers, he still had in weapon in hand, but he was pointing it at the ground, waiting to see what would happen.

"Surrender, Kaplan!" the one-legged man repeated. "You're surrounded!"

The former officer had not responded immediately, doubtless evaluating the exits that there available to him. Caught between the hammer and the anvil, however, between the homeless men and Dyers, his options were limited. In addition, he had suffered several losses in his ranks: two dead and at least two more wounded, not to mention the two who had gone with Powell. In the judgment of the one-legged man, he had lost in every calculable case.

Kaplan reached the same conclusion. He ordered his men to surrender. The latter did so without delay, and rid themselves of all their military apparatus with a metallic clatter.

A warning suddenly rang out....

"Look out!" shouted Pear.

...Immediately followed by a gunshot whose echo reverberated several times in the nascent darkness.

For one brief moment Ian thought that one of his men had lost control of his nerves, but he was mistaken.

A few yards away, Kaplan collapsed in the restored silence. Behind him stood Dyers, who had approached his superior silently, without anyone noticing, except for the millionaire, who had tried to warn him, but too late.

The former F.B.I. agent had swapped the machine-pistol with which he had raked them earlier for a more traditional pistol.

"Agent Dyers, drop your weapon. I won't repeat myself."

The man darted a demented glance at him before obeying.

He was smiling.

Marilyn came out of the vehicle first, with Powell on her heels, a gun in his hand.

"It's over," said Kristin. "You have no chance of getting away."

Powell tightened his grip on the former actress, and clung to her, in order not to offer an easy target.

At the same time, the front door opened in its turn, revealing the presence of a mercenary.

The young woman did not know how to react. With only one bullet left, she could not confront two enemies at the same time, or permit herself to waste it.

The former soldier darted a rapid glance at her before taking to his heels. Evidently, he thought that the conflict was not his concern. A stroke of luck for her.

No news on the other hand, of the driver. Perhaps the impact of the collision had affected him more severely than she had supposed, but there was no means to be certain.

Powell spoke.

"You're going to let us go," said the Iron Triangle man, "or I'll kill her."

Kristin was about to reply in order to calm herself, but Marilyn got in ahead of her.

"You failed to kill me forty years ago," she said. "I'm sure you're capable of missing me again even with a gun to my head."

"Shut up!" snapped Powell.

He stepped sideways, keeping Marilyn between them.

"John told me you were a coward. The members of the Triangle wanted to make the war, he said, but they'd have wet their pants at the thought of getting into it. Yes, that's it, you're nothing but a coward!"

The former actress seemed possessed, as if she were playing a role.

"Shut up!" howled Powell. "Shut up, or I swear I'll kill you!"

"Kill me, you! You make me laugh, you members of the Iron Triangle. You think you run the country, but you're not even capable of shutting up a *whore!*" She spat the word out. "John might have had his faults, but he knew what do with women. I bet yours is very tiny!"

Marilyn turned toward her and winked. Kristin understood that she was ready to go into action. The old woman grabbed her captor's testicles with her right hand and squeezed with all her strength.

His face contracted, Powell grimaced, but did not let go of his weapon.

Marilyn pressed her advantage and stuck a heel into his foot.

This time, Powell could not repress a screech of pain.

"Slut! You'll pay for that!"

He moved sideways in order to shoot. Furious, he did not think of taking his human shield with him, authorizing Kristin to open fire.

The young woman did not hesitate to press the trigger.

The two weapons rendered their verdict at the same time.

Powell fell to the ground, a bullet in his head.

A second later, Marilyn collapsed in her turn.

Chapter 64

The millionaire let himself fall to his knees, deaf to the exterior world.

Daniel was lying on his back in the midst of broken glass, his eyes open.

Michael had seen numerous films in which dead people merely seemed to be asleep, as if they were waiting for a friend to come and wake them up. That was not the case with his brother.

Daniel bore new stigmata inflicted since the last time he had seen him, during his detention: bruises, cuts, burns, fingernails torn out. "Your brother has been though a veritable hell," Kaplan had said. "My men have been working him over all day, and he's never uttered the slightest whimper." Evidently, his torturers had not stopped there, and had taken a malign pleasure in humiliating him.

And now his brother was dead.

Daniel was dead.

And it was his fault.

He was the one who had dragged him into this business.

Disgusted with himself, his stomach contracted, and the millionaire vomited up a food of bile. Then he uttered a howl in which rage disputed with pain.

And finally, he wept.

"An ambulance! Quickly!" Kristin shouted. "Someone call an ambulance!"

A voice in the distance shouted that it would take charge of it.

"It'll be all right," she continued, taking Marilyn in her arms. "Help will come and you'll get out of this."

The young woman did not believe a word of it. During her military career she had seen too many bad wounds not to know that the one she had before her eyes would be fatal.

She tried to hold back the tears that came, without success.

With her finger, the former actress wiped away her chagrin. A smile lit up her face.

"No, it's not true, it won't be all right—you know that as well as I do. But it's not serious...I've had a good life. I've even had the right to two lives, one more than most people. I..."

A fit of coughing prevent her from going on.

"I've always had the sentiment of being apart from my life, of being a usurper, misunderstood, and even of having lived someone else's life. Everyone feels that, I suppose, at times in their life...bad moments, doubtless. But in my case, it goes further. In recent years, I've come to think that I'm nothing but a manufactured monster, an incarnation of masculine desire, a mere plaything in the hands of men. Sometimes, I've had the impression that John knew perfectly well what he was doing in confiding his secret to me..."

Kristin tried to interrupt, but the former actress took her hand. A distant siren pierced the silence of the night.

"You're someone good, Kristin. A woman must stronger than I've been, Have no regrets concerning me—I have none. I'm glad to have known you. If only it could have lasted a little longer..."

A trickle of blood oozed from the corner of her lips. Marilyn smiled at her one last time before expiring.

"An ambulance has arrived," said a voice behind her.

"Too late," Kristin replied, closing the old woman's eyes.

Epilogue

Brooklyn, 6 December.

The first snowflakes of December whitened the grass in the park at the foot of Brooklyn Bridge. Michael placed the funerary urn on the wooden table near the floral wreath. A dozen people accompanied them: Marilyn's last admirers, those who had protected her all these years; Andrew Gallardo, his wife, and a few others they did not know. All of them were there to render a final tribute to the former actress.

Kristin sat down on a bench and thought about the events of the last few days.

After the arrival of the New York police, Kristin and Michael had spent the night in the cells without being able to telephone Wingfield, their lawyer. Early in the morning, however, they had been released without explanation. At the time, exhausted by the ordeals they had just undergone, they had not even tried to find out why.

Later, they had read in the newspapers about a gun-battle, the work of a lone madman who had killed several people before shooting himself.

Faithful to its habit, the Iron Triangle had buried the affair under a mountain of lies. James Powell was dead, but the military-industrial lobby had survived him and was continuing to pull the strings from the shadows.

Although it still seemed premature to envisage the baton being handed on, the couple knew that one day, the Triangle would remember their existence, especially given that the millionaire, who had difficulty forgiving himself for the death of his brother and that of his friend Tyler Hoffman, had decided, in spite of the young woman's warnings, to launch an enterprise aimed at developing Tesla's free energy: the best means of attracting the Triangle's wrath. It was impossible to make him see reason, though. To ward off eventual reprisals, Kristin had nevertheless succeeded in convincing him to hire a private security company. There again, Michael has surprised her by proposing to hire the homeless men on a permanent basis, their aptitudes and their fidelity no longer needing proof. They had not had to be begged to accept.

Michael sat down on the bench next to her. There were still rings around his eyes.

The previous day, Kristin had accompanied him to Daniel's funeral. The ceremony had been held in St. Patrick's Cathedral, in the company of numerous churchmen and all of Wall Street: a surprising mix for such a beautiful service.

At the end of the ceremony, the members of the Foundation had come to announce that they had the firm intention of buying Nathan's premises in order to put it at the disposal of young photographers—with her consent, of course. Although the young woman had sensed Michael's hand behind the project, she had hastened to give her approval. Nathan would have loved the idea that his gallery would survive him. She could not see herself getting involved in the business; without Nathan, there was no longer any reason...

Michael had rejoined her in the car. He had thanked her for her presence at that difficult moment, before taking her to dinner at one of the best restaurants in the city. Then they had gone back to his apartment, where they had made love tenderly.

Today they were accompanying Marilyn on her ultimate voyage, even if the name on the urn was not hers. When help had arrived, Kristin had given her false identity, the one under which she had been living for forty years. Afterwards, she had called Mathew Zimmer, who had immediately taken things in hand, in spite of his immense grief. According to him, Marilyn had not wanted a second grave; her body would be cremated and her ashes thrown in the East River, in order to disappear forever, carried out into the ocean.

On the table next to the urn there was a floral wreath on which a sonnet was written. It began:

How do I love thee? Let me count the ways...

And ended:

...I love the with the breath
Smiles, tears, of all my life; and if God choose,
I shall but love thee better after death.

A few minutes earlier, when she has asked him about it, Matthew had replied that it was a text by Elizabeth Barrett Browning—the same one that the Monroe 6 had deposited anonymously on August 8, 1962 in the chapel of Westwood Memorial Park during her first burial. As for the meaning of the poem, he had not dwelt on that.

Lost in her thoughts, Kristin had not heard Michael get up. The millionaire had seized the urn, which he was now holding out to her. He left the task of dispersing the ashes to her.

Having gone to the edge she opened the jar, which she inverted cautiously. The ashes scattered at the whim of the wind, mingling with the snowflakes in the winter morning.

"Goodbye, Marilyn. I hope you're happy where you are."

When it was over, Kristin came back to the little group that was waiting in silence. The Gallardos thanked her with a nod of the head. She handed the urn to Matthew, who was inconsolable.

She could not hold back her own tears. The millionaire, who had rejoined her, held her tightly against him. They remained like that for a minute, without moving. Finally, Michael pulled away.

"I'm going to need you."

Kristin looked at him, slightly surprised.

Michael seemed to be searching for his words before launching forth.

"No, it's not that. I...Daniel was going to go to Spain to recover some important documents linked to Ignatius Loyola.

I'd like to go in his place, to finish his work. I don't speak Spanish. And above all, I'd very much like to have you beside me. Will you go with me?"

Without hesitation, the young woman replied: "Yes, of course."

www.ingramcontent.com/pod-product-compliance
Lightning Source LLC
Chambersburg PA
CBHW060345030726
47497CB00003B/602